Waves of Hope

Judith Keim

BOOKS BY JUDITH KEIM

THE HARTWELL WOMEN SERIES:

The Talking Tree – 1
Sweet Talk – 2
Straight Talk – 3
Baby Talk – 4
The Hartwell Women – Boxed Set

THE BEACH HOUSE HOTEL SERIES:

Breakfast at The Beach House Hotel – 1
Lunch at The Beach House Hotel – 2
Dinner at The Beach House Hotel – 3
Christmas at The Beach House Hotel – 4
Margaritas at The Beach House Hotel – 5
Dessert at The Beach House Hotel – 6

THE FAT FRIDAYS GROUP:

Fat Fridays – 1
Sassy Saturdays – 2
Secret Sundays – 3

THE SALTY KEY INN SERIES:

Finding Me – 1
Finding My Way – 2
Finding Love – 3
Finding Family – 4
The Salty Key Inn Series . Boxed Set

THE CHANDLER HILL INN SERIES:

Going Home – 1
Coming Home – 2
Home at Last – 3
The Chandler Hill Inn Series – Boxed Set

SEASHELL COTTAGE BOOKS:

A Christmas Star
Change of Heart
A Summer of Surprises
A Road Trip to Remember
The Beach Babes

THE DESERT SAGE INN SERIES:

The Desert Flowers – Rose – 1
The Desert Flowers – Lily – 2
The Desert Flowers – Willow – 3
The Desert Flowers – Mistletoe & Holly – 4

SOUL SISTERS AT CEDAR MOUNTAIN LODGE:

Christmas Sisters – Anthology
Christmas Kisses
Christmas Castles
Christmas Stories – Soul Sisters Anthology
Christmas Joy – (2022)

THE SANDERLING COVE INN SERIES:

Waves of Hope – (2022)
Sandy Wishes – (2023)
Salty Kisses – (2023)

OTHER BOOKS:

The ABC's of Living With a Dachshund
Once Upon a Friendship – Anthology
Winning BIG – a little love story for all ages
Holiday Hopes
The Winning Tickets (2023)

For more information: **www.judithkeim.com**

PRAISE FOR JUDITH KEIM'S NOVELS

THE BEACH HOUSE HOTEL SERIES

"Love the characters in this series. This series was my first introduction to Judith Keim. She is now one of my favorites. Looking forward to reading more of her books."

BREAKFAST AT THE BEACH HOUSE HOTEL is an easy, delightful read that offers romance, family relationships, and strong women learning to be stronger. Real life situations filter through the pages. Enjoy!"

LUNCH AT THE BEACH HOUSE HOTEL – "This series is such a joy to read. You feel you are actually living with them. Can't wait to read the latest one."

DINNER AT THE BEACH HOUSE HOTEL – "A Terrific Read! As usual, Judith Keim did it again. Enjoyed immensely. Continue writing such pleasantly reading books for all of us readers."

CHRISTMAS AT THE BEACH HOUSE HOTEL – "Not Just Another Christmas Novel. This is book number four in the series and my introduction to Judith Keim's writing. I wasn't disappointed. The characters are dimensional and engaging. The plot is well crafted and advances at a pleasing pace. The Florida location is interesting and warming. It was a delight to read a romance novel with mature female protagonists. Ann and Rhoda have life experiences that enrich the story. It's a clever book about friends and extended family. Buy copies for your book group pals and enjoy this seasonal read."

MARGARITAS AT THE BEACH HOUSE HOTEL – "What a wonderful series. I absolutely loved this book and can't wait for the next book to come out. There was even suspense in it. Thanks Judith for the great stories."

"Overall, Margaritas at the Beach House Hotel is another wonderful addition to the series. Judith Keim takes the reader on a journey told through the voices of these amazing characters we have all come to love through the years! I truly cannot stress enough how good this book is, and I hope you enjoy it as much as I have!"

THE HARTWELL WOMEN SERIES:

"This was an EXCELLENT series. When I discovered Judith Keim, I read all of her books back to back. I thoroughly enjoyed the women Keim has written about. They are believable and you want to just jump into their lives and be their friends! I can't wait for any upcoming books!"

"I fell into Judith Keim's Hartwell Women series and have read & enjoyed all of her books in every series. Each centers around a strong & interesting woman character and their family interaction. Good reads that leave you wanting more."

THE FAT FRIDAYS GROUP :

"Excellent story line for each character, and an insightful representation of situations which deal with some of the contemporary issues women are faced with today."

"I love this author's books. Her characters and their lives are realistic. The power of women's friendships is a common and beautiful theme that is threaded throughout this story."

THE SALTY KEY INN SERIES

<u>FINDING ME</u> – "I thoroughly enjoyed the first book in this series and cannot wait for the others! The characters are endearing with the same struggles we all encounter. The setting makes me feel like I am a guest at The Salty Key Inn...relaxed, happy & light-hearted! The men are yummy

and the women strong. You can't get better than that! Happy Reading!"

FINDING MY WAY- "Loved the family dynamics as well as uncertain emotions of dating and falling in love. Appreciated the morals and strength of parenting throughout. Just couldn't put this book down."

FINDING LOVE – "I waited for this book because the first two was such good reads. This one didn't disappoint.... Judith Keim always puts substance into her books. This book was no different, I learned about PTSD, accepting oneself, there is always going to be problems but stick it out and make it work. Just the way life is. In some ways a lot like my life. Judith is right, it needs another book and I will definitely be reading it. Hope you choose to read this series, you will get so much out of it."

FINDING FAMILY – "Completing this series is like eating the last chip. Love Judith's writing, and her female characters are always smart, strong, vulnerable to life and love experiences."

"This was a refreshing book. Bringing the heart and soul of the family to us."

THE CHANDLER HILL INN SERIES

GOING HOME – "I absolutely could not put this book down. Started at night and read late into the middle of the night. As a child of the '60s, the Vietnam war was front and center so this resonated with me. All the characters in the book were so well developed that the reader felt like they were friends of the family."

"I was completely immersed in this book, with the beautiful descriptive writing, and the authors' way of bringing her characters to life. I felt like I was right inside

her story."

COMING HOME – *"Coming Home is a winner. The characters are well-developed, nuanced and likable. Enjoyed the vineyard setting, learning about wine growing and seeing the challenges Cami faces in running and growing a business. I look forward to the next book in this series!"*

"Coming Home was such a wonderful story. The author has a gift for getting the reader right to the heart of things."

HOME AT LAST – *"In this wonderful conclusion, to a heartfelt and emotional trilogy set in Oregon's stunning wine country, Judith Keim has tied up the Chandler Hill series with the perfect bow."*

"Overall, this is truly a wonderful addition to the Chandler Hill Inn series. Judith Keim definitely knows how to perfectly weave together a beautiful and heartfelt story."

"The storyline has some beautiful scenes along with family drama. Judith Keim has created characters with interactions that are believable and some of the subjects the story deals with are poignant."

SEASHELL COTTAGE BOOKS

A CHRISTMAS STAR – *"Love, laughter, sadness, great food, and hope for the future, all in one book. It doesn't get any better than this stunning read."*

"A Christmas Star is a heartwarming Christmas story featuring endearing characters. So many Christmas books are set in snowbound places...it was a nice change to read a Christmas story that takes place on a warm sandy beach!" Susan Peterson

CHANGE OF HEART – *"CHANGE OF HEART is the summer read we've all been waiting for. Judith Keim is a*

master at creating fascinating characters that are simply irresistible. Her stories leave you with a big smile on your face and a heart bursting with love."

Kellie Coates Gilbert, author of the popular Sun Valley Series

<u>A SUMMER OF SURPRISES</u> – "The story is filled with a roller coaster of emotions and self-discovery. Finding love again and rebuilding family relationships."

"Ms. Keim uses this book as an amazing platform to show that with hard emotional work, belief in yourself and love, the scars of abuse can be conquered. It in no way preaches, it's a lovely story with a happy ending."

"The character development was excellent. I felt I knew these people my whole life. The story development was very well thought out I was drawn [in] from the beginning."

THE DESERT SAGE INN SERIES:

<u>THE DESERT FLOWERS – ROSE –</u> "The Desert Flowers - Rose, is the first book in the new series by Judith Keim. I always look forward to new books by Judith Keim, and this one is definitely a wonderful way to begin The Desert Sage Inn Series!"

"In this first of a series, we see each woman come into her own and view new beginnings even as they must take this tearful journey as they slowly lose a dear friend. This is a very well written book with well-developed and likable main characters. It was interesting and enlightening as the first portion of this saga unfolded. I very much enjoyed this book and I do recommend it"

"Judith Keim is one of those authors that you can always depend on to give you a great story with fantastic characters. I'm excited to know that she is writing a new series and after reading book 1 in the series, I can't wait to

read the rest of the books."!

<u>*THE DESERT FLOWERS – LILY*</u> – *"The second book in the Desert Flowers series is just as wonderful as the first. Judith Keim is a brilliant storyteller. Her characters are truly lovely and people that you want to be friends with as soon as you start reading. Judith Keim is not afraid to weave real life conflict and loss into her stories. I loved reading Lily's story and can't wait for Willow's!*

"The Desert Flowers Lily is the second book in The Desert Sage Inn Series by author Judith Keim. When I read the first book in the series, The Desert Flowers-Rose, I knew this series would exceed all of my expectations and then some. Judith Keim is an amazing author, and this series is a testament to her writing skills and her ability to completely draw a reader into the world of her characters."

Waves of Hope

The Sanderling Cove Inn Series – Book 1

Judith Keim

Wild Quail Publishing

wildquail.pub@gmail.com
www.judithkeim.com

Published in the United States of America by:

Wild Quail Publishing
PO Box 171332
Boise, ID 83717-1332

ISBN# 978-1-954325-40-1

Dedication

For grandmothers everywhere who wish only the best for their grandchildren.

The Five Families of Sanderling Cove

Gran **– Eleanor "Ellie" Weatherby** – husband deceased – dating John Rizzo

3 daughters – Vanessa, JoAnn, Leigh

Granddaughter – ***Charlotte*** "Charlie" Bradford (Vanessa's child)

Granddaughter - ***Brooke*** Weatherby (Jo's child)

Granddaughter - ***Olivia*** "Livy" Winters (Leigh's daughter)

Granny Liz – Elizabeth "Liz" Ensley – husband Sam

2 sons, Henry, m. Diana, then m. Savannah, and 1 other son

Grandson – ***Shane*** – lawyer in Miami

Grandson – ***Austin*** – IT guru who sold business and is looking for next opportunity

Mimi- **Karen Atkins** – husband deceased

1 daughter – KK, m. Gordon Hendrix, and 1 son, Arthur

Grandson -***Dylan Hendrix*** – artist

Granddaughter -***Grace Hendrix*** m. Belinda – owns restaurant called Gills in Clearwater

Grandson – ***Adam Atkins*** m. Summer; has daughter Skye

Grandson – ***Brendan Atkins*** – in construction business with Adam

G-Ma – Sarah Simon – husband deceased

1 son – Benjamin

Grandson – ***Eric*** - plastic surgeon in Tampa, specializes in cleft palates

Granddaughter – ***Shelby*** m. Douglas Sheehan baby due

Grandma – Pat Dunlap – husband Ed
1 daughter – Katherine m. William Worthington
Grandson – ***Kyle*** - talent agent in Hollywood
Granddaughter – ***Melissa*** – engaged to Texas oilman
Granddaughter – ***Morgan*** – spoiled baby of family

PROLOGUE

Eleanor "Ellie" Weatherby sat on the front porch of the home she and her deceased husband, William, had built in the 1970s at Sanderling Cove on the Gulf Coast of Florida. Since its original construction, the house had been renovated several times, buildings had been added to the oversized property, and Ellie was now co-owner of an upscale operation called The Sanderling Cove Inn.

She'd invited her three granddaughters to visit her. At the thought, waves of hope swept through her. She loved her granddaughters with all her heart and hoped to settle a family issue with them. Born within eighteen months of one another, they were a remarkable trio. But which one of them would be willing to do as she asked? They were each unique. But then her three daughters were very different and, to her disappointment, not close.

At fifty-nine, Vanessa, her oldest, was overly involved in New York society, a woman focused on appearance. Vanessa herself was a stunning, auburn-haired, gray-eyed woman who was used to being noticed. She'd had a tragic first marriage that fell apart after her three-year-old son drowned in the surf not far from Sanderling Cove. Charlotte, Vanessa's twenty-nine-year-old daughter, was still trying to find her place in the world. It was no wonder. Neither of her parents was the warm, cuddly type. Ellie sighed.

Ellie thought of JoAnne, her middle daughter. Two years younger than Vanessa, Jo was a single mother. Of all her daughters, Jo was the sweetest and the one who'd suffered most in life. She'd struggled with depression for years and now fought every day with numerous symptoms of fibromyalgia and the problems associated with it. Jo's daughter, Brooke, just turned twenty-eight and was a strong supporter of her mother, but, in Ellie's opinion, her granddaughter should be out on her own. Both Brooke and Jo needed to add sparkle to their lives, brighten their appearance, buy some new clothes, enjoy what fun they could. Jo made a good living working from home doing IT work for an understanding company, and Brooke worked in an accounting office. They lived in upstate New York, where Jo had been her happiest before her fiancé was killed in Iraq.

Last but certainly not least, Leigh, her youngest and her father's favorite, entered her thoughts. She was a beauty with caramel-colored hair and green eyes that sparkled. At 49, Leigh still attracted attention and favors from others, but it hadn't always been easy. She'd had her daughter out-of-wedlock at 20, and after going back to work when Olivia was less than a year old, she'd ended up marrying her boss a few years later. Her husband, Jack, pampered her, which seemed appropriate after she gave him two sons, whom they both adored. But it was Olivia, with strawberry-blond hair, blue eyes, and a short figure, who was Ellie's favorite.

Ellie kept in touch with her daughters frequently, but she didn't often see them. Vanessa hated Florida after losing her son there, Jo didn't like to travel, and Leigh was a social butterfly, a southern belle who was usually too busy. However, all three daughters encouraged their girls to visit her in Sanderling Cove. Ellie loved their times together, loved them in a way that was easier than being a parent to them. Grandmothers could get away with saying quite a lot, and Ellie was known for not holding back. She tried to be a supportive, loving figure in the family and did her best to hold them all together.

Ellie stared out at the waves that filled her with hope. They rushed into shore to embrace the sand and quickly pulled away again, like a shy teenager after her first kiss. Seagulls and terns floated in the sky, riding the wind, their white wings like the sails of a boat against the blue background. The air on this May day caressed her skin. She lifted her face to the breeze, enjoying the tangy taste of salt.

She glanced around. Sanderling Cove held only five houses and the Inn and hadn't changed that much from all those years ago when she and William first bought land there. She loved it and never wanted to leave her home.

If only things would work out the way she wanted.

CHAPTER ONE

CHARLOTTE

Charlotte Bradford told herself not to stomp back to her office at the North Public Relations company in New York City, but it took every bit of will power to keep from doing it. Rand Michaels, her co-worker, had once again attempted to take credit for work she had done for a client. Rather than be called out for it, their boss had praised Rand for adding to Charlotte's campaign, though neither couldn't deny that the idea had been Charlotte's to begin with.

She went into her office and closed the door before taking a seat at her desk and staring out at the scenery below. Charlotte knew she was excellent at her job. Clients loved her and her work, but she was tired of constantly fighting for the recognition she deserved. She knew damn well that Rand Michaels would be made partner before her. That wasn't fair.

The six o'clock traffic below had created a scene that reminded her of the movement in an ant farm she'd owned as a child. Cars moved as best they could in the streets and the sidewalks filled with people moving faster than they. Was she like an ant working hard but going nowhere?

She sighed. It was time for a change but she didn't know how, when, or where.

"I'll be there as soon as I can, Gran. Thanks." Charlotte ended the call with her grandmother and impulsively danced around her room. An extended visit with Gran was just what she needed. She hated her job, knew she didn't want to stay in New York, and needed to do something that resonated with her. Not something that pleased her mother.

Charlotte felt she'd been a disappointment to her mother from a young age, that she could never measure up to her brother, David, who'd died in a drowning accident when he was just three years old. Two years younger, she'd never really known him though her mother talked about him frequently. By the time Charlotte came to understand what had happened to him and why she'd never have another sibling, he was already on a pedestal she could never climb.

Her parents divorced a year or so after David died. Her father kept his commitment to Charlotte with financial support and the occasional visit, but he'd moved to California and had a busy, happy life with his new family, one she wasn't a part of. Shortly after her divorce, her mother married Walter Van Pelt and he provided her with an upscale lifestyle that was more suited to her.

Charlotte had plenty of friends, but in her restlessness, she was ready to move on and away from their expectations of what life should be like in their high-society circle. She especially wanted to get away from Jeremy Probst, the man her mother wanted her to marry. Her mother and Jeremy's mother had planned this romance for years, but it was never going to work. There was no physical attraction, and though she'd never discussed it in depth with anyone else, she was pretty sure Jeremy was gay. She knew he'd be much happier after he had the courage to come out. And if she ever were to meet a man whom she'd consider marrying, Charlotte had to feel she couldn't live without him. He had to be someone she could trust to love her for herself.

The next day, Charlotte went into work and gleefully gave her resignation letter to her boss. In the competitive marketing company where she constantly had to fight for recognition, Charlotte had no real regret about leaving.

Later, at home, Charlotte was busy sorting through her things at the apartment she shared with a roommate when her mother called. "I understand you're moving to Florida for the summer. When did this happen, and why wasn't I told? I had to hear it from Marjorie Probst, of all people. She said Jeremy is devastated that you broke it off with him."

Taking a deep breath and letting it out slowly, Charlotte sank onto her bed. "I was going to tell you when we met for lunch this weekend. And, I don't believe Jeremy is the least bit upset. We both know it wasn't going to work. My stay with Gran is for an unspecified amount of time. I'm just trying to figure things out. You know I didn't like my job."

"You shouldn't have to be worried about a job. There are opportunities for you to get involved in various volunteer positions and plenty of other suitable young men for you to consider. You're a beautiful woman, Charlotte. And being Walter's step-daughter is a big plus."

"Mother! Do you realize how archaic you sound?"

"The reality is that you could have a nice life going forward, Charlotte. Don't waste the opportunity to meet new people."

"You mean here in New York," Charlotte said. "I need to get away, and being with Gran for a while is the perfect solution. She's always been honest with me."

"She's never appreciated all I've done for you, my charity work, or the life I've made," said her mother with an edge to her voice.

"I'm not sure that's true," said Charlotte. "But she knows I want something different."

"Well, try not to burn too many bridges. Life has a lot of surprising twists and turns. Some of them are heartbreaking."

Charlotte knew her mother was talking about David and

said softly, "I know."

"Well, I hope you know what you're doing. I suppose there's no way I can get you to change your mind."

"No, Mother," said Charlotte. Thinking of the future she'd have if she'd decided to turn Gran down. Her spirits lifted at the thought of leaving that life behind.

Several days later, Charlotte drove her BMW convertible down Interstate 95, intent on getting to Sanderling Cove as quickly as she could. She had stuffed the trunk of her car and the backseat with suitcases and bags full of shoes and things she wanted in her new life. She'd left most of her dressy clothes behind at her mother's house. She knew from earlier visits she wouldn't need them. A pleasant thought.

When at last, after a couple of days of hard driving, she saw the sign for The Sanderling Cove Inn off to the side of Gulf Drive, she filled with excitement. She'd always felt Gran's love and acceptance. Her unwavering devotion meant the world to her.

She turned into the driveway and pulled up to the main building. The white clapboard siding of the building was trimmed in turquoise, a nod to some of the colorful homes and buildings in this area of the Gulf Coast of Florida.

A man wearing a New York Yankees baseball cap came out to the front entrance to greet her.

"Hey, Charlie, I'm glad you made it," he said, giving her a wide smile. "I've already called your grandmother to let her know you've arrived."

Charlotte smiled with pleasure. Here in Florida, Charlie seemed a much more suitable name than Charlotte. Far less formal, especially when spoken by John Rizzo, Gran's long-time business partner and special friend. Charlotte hadn't been very old when she realized Gran and John were more than two people who owned a business together. But no formal announcements were made about their relationship. It was simply a fact. And now, they lived together in Gran's house.

Tall, in great shape for his age, and with a shock of gray hair that couldn't be totally covered by the cap, John was a handsome, jovial man whom all the guests loved.

John gave her a peck on the cheek. "Better go see Ellie now. She's been waiting to see you."

Charlotte gave him a little wave and headed over to Gran's house sitting in a corner of the property. Gran and her husband had purchased the two oversized lots that provided enough space for the main building and its wing, along with the owner's house, all with beach access and Gulf water views. In today's market, the land itself was worth a small fortune.

She parked in the back of Gran's house, got out of the car, and let out a soft groan as she stretched. The trip took longer than she thought it would.

"You're here!" cried Gran, rushing out of the house to greet her.

Charlotte flew into her grandmother's open arms. "Thought I'd never make it." She stepped back and studied her grandmother. "How are you?"

Gran's blue eyes sparkled as she returned Charlotte's smile. "I'm fine. A little older and not much wiser. And definitely not thinner."

Charlotte laughed. At barely five-foot-three, her grandmother had gray curly hair that she kept short, forming a halo of sorts around her head, and didn't seem to realize how adorable she was. At the moment, Gran was wearing a T-Shirt that said, "*Love Happens*," a pair of khaki shorts, and pink flip-flops with sparkly pink bows.

"It's starting to feel like home already." Charlotte hugged her. All the constraints of living a lifestyle she didn't like fell away from her. Gran was all about being yourself without judgment from her. The T-shirt she wore would have made Charlotte's mother shudder.

Charlotte turned as a young man approached. He saluted Gran with a bob of his head. "John sent me over to help with the luggage."

"I'm glad you came," said Gran. "It looks like we're going to need your help. Jake McDonnell, meet my granddaughter, Charlotte Bradford."

Charlotte gazed into his chocolate brown eyes that seemed to reach inside her. Jake had straight dark hair and a buff body.

"Jake is a financial consultant and our accountant. He's looking over the numbers for the business," explained Gran.

Charlotte stared at his horned-rimmed glasses, wondering how such a nerdy guy could be that sexy.

"It's an interesting operation that your grandmother runs," Jake said.

"I told him he could take as long as he wants to complete the work," Gran said, smiling at both of them in a way that Charlotte thought was a blatant attempt at matchmaking. But Jake didn't seem to mind.

"Well, guess I'd better help you unload," said Jake, winking at her as if he knew what she was thinking.

Charlotte opened the trunk of her car and began lifting boxes from the back seat, hoping he hadn't noticed how she'd reacted to him.

"Okay, Charlie, I've got your old room ready," said Gran.

Jake turned to her with a grin. "Charlie, huh? I like it."

Charlotte followed Jake up the stairs to the second story, where four bedrooms and three bathrooms were situated. The master suite was on the first floor. Gran told her she planned it so when her granddaughters got together, they'd each have a room of her own upstairs. The last room was reserved as a formal guest room with an ensuite bathroom.

Charlotte stood at the threshold to her room and took a moment to survey it. She'd chosen sunny yellow paint for the walls, white trim, white plantation shutters at the windows, and white wicker furniture. The king-size bed was covered with a blue and yellow patchwork quilted spread that she loved.

Jake set down the suitcases. "Guess I'd better get back to work." He smiled at Charlotte. "Hope to see you around."

"Oh, you will," said Gran. "Charlie's here to help me."

Charlotte hid her surprise. She'd come for a visit and to get a better idea of her future. And if that included a way to help Gran, it was even better.

CHAPTER TWO

BROOKE

Brooke Weatherby looked up from the column of figures on the report she'd just printed out and sighed. She'd worked hard, studied hard to become a CPA, but thinking of her life now, dealing with numbers every day was depressing. Numbers and dealing with her mother.

She stood and went into the small kitchen of the accounting firm in Ellenton, New York, that claimed most of her life and wondered if that was what she wanted for the foreseeable future. Her stomach twisted at the thought. Really, there had to be something better. But what?

"Are you sure you're going to be okay?" Brooke asked her mother. "Gran said for me to keep the time open. I've told my boss I'm taking an extended vacation, using up all the vacation days I never took off, days that I had coming to me. So, he's okay with it."

"I'll be fine," her mother said, giving her a bright smile that eventually wavered.

Brooke loved that her mother tried to be pleasant, but she knew what dark days her mother sometimes suffered both mentally and physically. Gran, bless her heart, understood and surprised them with gifts and treats. This invitation to visit her was another example of it. Brooke didn't often let life get her down, but since breaking up with a man she'd thought loved her, she found it hard to keep her spirits up. The worst part? Her mother was to blame for unknowingly contributing to the breakup when Brooke constantly had to change plans to accommodate her mother's requests.

It was time to move on. Brooke was more than ready to make some changes in her life. Gran agreed with her. That meant more than anything to Brooke. Conversations with Gran always filled her with hope.

Brooke hugged her mother. "The practical nurse I've hired to check in on you should be a big help. She comes highly recommended."

"Go, don't worry about me. It'll do us both good to be on our own," said her mother. "I know how unhappy you've been these past few months."

"Thanks, Mom." Brooke hugged and kissed her, then left the house with a determined stride, and headed to her reliable Honda. She'd probably overpacked, but she didn't care. There was plenty of room in the car to hold the things she thought she might need. All in all, there wasn't that much. She'd been raised to be frugal.

Once Brooke was on I-95 heading south, she truly felt as if she were escaping. Each mile brought a deeper feeling of contentment.

By the time she saw the sign for The Sanderling Cove Inn, Brooke was ready to kick up her heels. Being here with Gran was just what she needed. She pulled up to the main building.

Before she could get out of the car, John came out of the Inn smiling as he headed right to her. "Well, if it isn't Brookey. How are you?" He kissed her cheek. "I put in a call to your grandmother when I saw you enter the driveway. She'll be right here to greet you."

Gran appeared around the corner of the building. She was

wearing a pink T-shirt that read, "*I Need to Speak to the Manager,*" a pair of tan shorts, and her favorite flip-flops with a sparkly pink bow. The smile that crossed Gran's face filled Brooke with love. Gran might be the only grandparent she had, but she was the best she could imagine for anyone.

Brooke jumped out of her car and into Gran's welcoming arms.

"I'm so glad you're here," said Gran, squeezing her hard. "Charlie arrived yesterday and has put some fresh flowers and a bottle of water in your room. Let's go down to the house and get you settled."

"Charlie's here? How wonderful! I haven't seen her in months," said Brooke, surprised but pleased by the idea.

Gran climbed into Brooke's car, and they drove to the far corner of the land Gran owned. There, behind the house, Brooke parked the car.

She'd no sooner stepped outside the car than Charlie appeared, beaming at her before hugging her tight. "Haven't seen you in forever."

"I know," said Brooke, delighted by Charlie's welcome. Older than she by one year, Charlie seemed sophisticated in comparison. Charlie always looked put together, beautiful in an unstudied way that Brooke could never achieve.

As they were standing there, a young man approached. "John sent me here to help you with the luggage."

Brooke's breath caught as his gaze settled on her. Those brown eyes, outlined by horn-rimmed glasses, seem to reach inside her, making her wish she'd bothered to wash her hair that morning. In a hurry to get here, she hadn't thought it worth the time. But, then, she didn't fuss with her appearance that much. Indeed, her life at home hadn't called for it.

"Thanks, Jake," said Gran. "Meet my granddaughter, Brooke Weatherby. Brooke, this is Jake McDonnell. He's working on financial oversight for the Inn. I thought you and he might want to work together on that. That is if Jake is willing to show you what he's done."

"That's a wise idea, Ellie." Jake turned to Brooke with a smile. "I'll be glad to work with you. There's a lot to go over together if you're okay with it."

"Sure," Brooke managed to say without sounding like a smitten fool, which is how she felt. When would she ever learn? Men who looked like that weren't interested in someone like her. She glanced at Gran.

Gran gave her a beaming smile of approval. "Then that's settled."

"Where's all your luggage?" Charlie asked.

"There are just two suitcases, a couple of bags. Not much else," said Brooke. In going through her wardrobe, she'd realized there were few things she thought suitable—several thrift-store items that were fine for work but not many beach-type pieces of clothing. Such was her life.

Brooke followed the others up the stairs, soaking in the peace that began to settle around her. Here, she had no worries; she could relax.

At the door to her bedroom, an unbidden sting of tears made her blink rapidly. The room's pale purple walls seemed to embrace her with memories of happy times spent with Gran and her cousins.

"All we need is for Livy to arrive," Brooke said.

Gran came up to her and wrapped an arm around her. "Livy should get here tomorrow."

"Great, huh?" said Charlie. "The Three Mouseketeers back together again."

Brooke laughed. When they were much younger, Gran had talked about the original Mouseketeers, and then they'd watched reruns of the later shows for a while during summer trips. Her cousin Livy imagined herself singing and dancing. However, what Livy had in enthusiasm, she lacked in musical ability. But the cookies she baked even back then? The best. Even now, a box of sweets baked by her was a favorite gift at Christmas.

"I can't wait to see her and have the three of us together again," said Brooke. "It's been way too long."

"Amen," said Gran. "We're going to have an incredible time." Her smile wavered, and Brooke wondered what was behind the invitation to spend time here together.

CHAPTER THREE

LIVY

Olivia Winters took a batch of cookies out of the oven and wiped the sweat from her forehead with a paper towel. She'd been up since four o'clock working in the kitchen of The Sweet Shoppe, the bakery she owned in Lexington, Virginia with Julie Hampton, her former roommate at the Virginia Culinary Institute.

Julie rushed into the kitchen. "Sorry Livy. I don't know what happened. Chris's alarm didn't go off. As soon as I realized what time it was, I came as quickly as possible."

Livy's lips thinned. "This is happening too often. It isn't fair for me to do most of the baking for our bakery and handle all the business, too. We're a partnership. Remember?"

"Oh, Livy, you're right. It hasn't been fair for a long time. Not since I met Chris. But I have some news. I was talking to him about his gourmet store next door buying us out. We haven't been happy with the bakery for many months now. What do you say? Are you ready to sell?"

Livy's breath caught in her throat. "You'd walk away from the business we worked so hard to get up and running and maintain?"

Julie gave her an apologetic look. "Chris has asked me to marry him and I said yes. He and I want to have fun, be able to party at night, not have me rush home to bed because I have to get up early every frickin' morning."

Livy sighed. One thing she was sure of. After five years of doing this, she didn't want to keep running the bakery basically on her own. And after what happened with Wayne, her overbearing ex-boyfriend, she was ready for a change.

Later, when Gran's invitation came to visit her, Livy knew it was the right decision to sell. She had to think of her future. One that didn't include a certain Wayne Chesterton.

Her mother, who was already in despair because Livy hadn't found a suitable husband, had protested both moves but had finally realized how sincere Livy was about the need to change her life. Now, she supported her decisions.

"Gran knows you better than I do," her mother admitted. "I'll never understand why you don't embrace genteel southern ways. You've gone from tomboy to kitchen worker."

Livy raised her eyebrows. "Kitchen worker?"

"Sorry, I shouldn't have said that." Her mother let out a puff of disappointment. "It's that I thought I'd be a grandmother by now. I can't wait to have little grandbabies to show off."

"Just because Maribelle Sutton has two granddaughters to fuss over, it's no reason for me to try to catch up to SueEllen in that department." She and SueEllen had been friends and competitors for as long as Livy could remember. The difference was that while SueEllen cared about winning, Livy didn't. One thing was for sure, Livy wasn't cut out for frills and silly "yes" conversations with men, just to please them. Talk about old-fashioned nonsense.

"I suppose you're right," sighed her mother. "But, darling, time is running out."

Livy forced a smile. "That's why it's a perfect time to head to Gran's. After working night and day for the bakery, I need a break."

"I agree with you. It wasn't fair. You did a lot more work than Julie. But you've always been a hard worker. I admire that about you." Her mother hugged her.

Livy allowed herself to relax in her mother's embrace for a minute before straightening. She rarely received this much attention from her. "Guess I'd better get things organized for the trip."

"How long will you be gone?" her mother asked.

"I'm not sure." Livy couldn't help smiling as a surge of anticipation raced through her.

Livy sighed with relief when she pulled her SUV into the driveway for The Sanderling Cove Inn. It had seemed a never-ending trip. She'd had to pull over twice to rest and walk around to shake off the sleepiness and boredom the highway driving had produced. Now, away from the business that had consumed her life, she realized how tired she was. She couldn't wait to get to her room and lie down. She felt as if she could sleep for days, not hours.

John, Gran's "special friend" as her mother called him, greeted her as soon as she pulled to a stop in front of the main building.

"Livy, my girl. Glad you've arrived." He kissed her on the cheek. "Your grandmother will be thrilled. Drive on over to her house. She and the others are waiting for you."

"Others?"

John grinned. "Hasn't Ellie told you yet?"

"No-o-o-o."

"The three of you terrors are back together again."

"Charlie and Brooke are here?" Livy's voice rose with excitement.

"You got it. Now get on over there."

Livy gave him a salute and pulled away.

She laughed when she drove behind the house and saw Gran standing there with her cousins, wearing a yellow T-shirt that read "*I Can't Adult Today*," navy shorts, and those flip-flops with the shiny pink bow that Livy coveted. Beside her, Charlie and Brooke were grinning and waving. The years melted away. Charlie, tall and thin, was as elegant as usual with her auburn hair tied back in a pony tail behind her classic features. Next to her and of medium height, Brooke looked the same as always with her brown, shoulder-length hair pinned back at her ears with clips and a wide smile that lit her hazel eyes in a pleasant face.

Laughing as her cousins pounced on her with hugs, Livy fought her way out of the car to Gran. After receiving a warm embrace from her, they all did a group hug. It felt so darn good.

"Let's get you settled in your room," said Gran. "Oh, here's Austin Ensley. Hi! Your grandmother told me you were spending some time here. You remember Charlie, Brooke, and Livy, don't you?"

Livy forced a smile, but for a moment, she felt frozen in time. When she was seventeen, she'd had a huge crush on Austin, but he'd had eyes only for Charlotte. She studied the man who'd replaced the boy and liked what she saw. Sandy-colored hair crowned his head. Blue eyes shone with interest and matched the smile on his face.

"I remember," he said. "But it was a long time ago. I'm sure a lot of things have changed for everyone since then."

"How long are you in town for?" Brooke asked.

"Not sure. My work was in Seattle, but I didn't like living there and figured it would be best to take a break before deciding on what to do going forward."

"You still the nerdy computer geek?" Charlotte said.

Austin laughed. "Guess you could say so. I had my own company and just sold it to one of the big guys. I'm trying to decide what to do next."

"If you need someone in marketing, I might be able to help. I just quit my job in New York and have no intention of moving back there."

His gaze rested on Charlotte, and Livy felt seventeen all over again.

"How about helping us with Livy's luggage?" Gran said.

"Sure." He reached into the open storage area of Livy's Honda SUV and lifted the canvas bag holding some kitchen items Livy would never be without—knives and other kitchen utensils she used daily.

"It's some of my baking and cooking equipment. Like you, I just sold my bakery to a competitor and am now considering my options."

He grinned at her. "I remember those cookies you used to bake. They were the best."

"Livy has her degree in Food Service Management and a certificate in Baking and Pastry Arts from the Culinary Institute of Virginia," bragged Gran, sending a flush of heat to Livy's cheeks.

"A real pro then," said Austin. "Nice." He turned to Brooke. "And what about you? What do you do?"

Brooke looked down at the ground and then faced him. "I work in an accounting office. Pretty dull, huh?"

Austin shrugged. "Numbers are important."

"Well, then," said Gran beaming at them. "Let's get Livy settled. Everyone, grab something, and let's take it inside."

Livy made sure everything was out of the car and then followed the others up the stairs to her room.

At the threshold, she caught her breath. The pale pink walls were just as she'd last seen them. A new bedspread covered with images of seashells lay atop the king-sized bed. But the posters of different chefs remained mounted on the wall.

"I've kept things nice for you," said Gran, putting an arm

around Livy.

"Thanks," Livy said softly, fighting tears. She could always count on Gran to be there for her. No judgment.

Austin left them with a promise to catch up later.

Charlotte turned to Livy. "Hurry and get settled, and then we can meet on the beach. I'm making margaritas to celebrate our being together."

Livy chuckled. Charlotte was full of fun. She was a little bit like Gran that way, no doubt because her mother was such an intense negative personality. It was a subtle form of rebellion for both of them. Livy was convinced Gran wore her T-shirts because Charlotte's mother detested them. On Gran, they'd become a perfect way for others to appreciate her sense of humor.

"Have fun, but remember, tonight we're eating dinner together here at eight o'clock. John is cooking up something special."

"Oh, I hope it's one of his grandmother's recipes," said Livy. "They're so delicious." As much as she loved baking, she was appreciative of all well-prepared food.

"Veal Piccata?" asked Charlotte.

Gran laughed. "I have no idea what he's doing, but let it be a surprise. That will please him."

"See you down at the beach, Livy. Let's go, Brooke," said Charlotte.

Livy waved them off and began the task of putting her things away and settling in. When she unpacked her bikini from last year, she sighed. Stress had added a pound or two to her body. She knew she wasn't fat, but she was no model-sized woman either. *Enough.* She was tired of the old "worrying about her figure" attitude.

CHAPTER FOUR

CHARLOTTE

Even as she made the frozen margaritas to take to the beach, Charlotte's thoughts remained on Austin. He was her first serious boyfriend and summertime love. While they hadn't gone "all the way," as her mother would put it, they'd come close several times. Austin had been frustrated but understanding when she'd explained she couldn't do it, that her mother had warned her time and time again that there would be no going back if she ever went ahead with it. Because her mother spoke from experience, Charlotte listened.

Seeing him now, she wondered at their innocence. He was still a handsome man though not one she was particularly interested in, especially after her breakup with Jeremy.

"It was great seeing Austin again," said Brooke. "I remember how in love with him you were."

"We were babies back then. How about you, Brooke? Any special guy in your life?"

Brooke shook her head. "It never seems to work out. Especially after they discover my responsibility to my mother."

Charlotte frowned and faced her. "Responsibility to your mother? Brooke, don't you think that's going too far? I know how close you are, but your relationship to her shouldn't destroy any chances for your happiness."

"You're right," sighed Brooke. "But I don't know how I can break Mom of the need to have me available. She's called me every day since I left. Sometimes twice."

A new understanding filled Charlotte. "That's why you're here. Right?"

Brooke gave her a sheepish look. "Yeah, Mom doesn't know it yet, but I told my boss I wasn't sure how long I'd be gone, that I might not come back."

Charlotte hugged her. "Good for you, Brooke. Your mom is a sweet person, but it isn't fair for her to hold you back from your own life."

"I know. Gran tells me the same thing. But my mother doesn't act this way to be mean to me. She just feels better when I'm around. Part of it is psychological because there are times when she feels so down and so sick. This visit is a test of sorts. I'm feeling a little bit guilty, but free too. You know?"

"I do," said Charlotte. "I broke it off with Jeremy, but there was no way I could marry him or out him either. Now, according to my mother, I'm the bad one who broke up a chance for a perfect marriage. Pretty sick, huh?"

"What's sick?" asked Livy coming into the kitchen.

Charlotte and Brooke filled her in on their dilemmas.

"I'm sorry. I'm not doing much better. My mother can't understand why I don't want the same kind of life she'd built for herself. But then, I've never been like SueEllen Sutton."

"Is she the girl who lives next door?" asked Charlotte.

"The one who's very competitive with you?" said Brooke.

"The one and the same," said Livy. "She's married and pregnant with her third child. Three strikes against me."

Charlotte lifted the blender filled with margaritas. "Brooke, grab the glasses. Livy, pick up the basket holding the napkins and crackers. Let's go. The beach is calling. I've already set up an umbrella and placed towels beneath it."

"Charlie's in charge. Just like always," said Brooke. But she was smiling.

Charlotte laughed. "I can't help it. I've lived under my mother's wings for too long. Not that I plan to continue. I've decided to leave New York. Being part of the social scene isn't who I want to be."

"Wow!" said Brooke. "The three of us rebelling. Who'd have thought it?"

They looked at one another.

"Gran!" they shouted, laughing.

At this time of day, the late afternoon sun was slowly beginning its journey to the horizon. Sunset wouldn't happen for several hours, but the mere hint of it took some of the heat from the day and the pace from everyone's steps. It was a perfect time to relax and catch up with her cousins. Charlotte was a bit surprised at her joy in seeing them again. Through the years they hadn't seen that much of one another. As grown women with jobs and other commitments, it had been challenging to coordinate convenient times to meet at Gran's.

They spread out towels and then covered themselves with suntan lotion. Brooke didn't have to be as careful as Charlotte and Livy, but still knew enough to follow suit.

"Okay," said Charlotte. "Time for a toast." She filled three plastic margarita glasses and handed out two to Brooke and Livy. Raising her drink, she said, "Here's to us. The three 'keteers!"

"No mouse?" Brooke said, grinning.

"No, we're our own threesome," said Livy.

They raised their glasses and sipped the cool, tangy drink.

"Don't let me get drunk," said Brooke. "Mom can't have alcohol, so I rarely drink."

Charlotte and Livy exchanged glances.

"Brooke, maybe it's time for you to relax a little and do your own thing for once," said Livy.

"I know, I know," said Brooke. "I've really needed this time." Her eyes filled. "I liked the last guy I dated a lot. Know what he said? He told me he loved me, but he already had one mother and didn't need another to try and please, that all my time was spent doing that."

"You and Aunt Jo," said Charlotte.

Brooke sniffed and looked out at the water. "I've always wanted a family of my own, and time is running out."

"Hold on. You're a year younger than I am," prompted Charlotte.

"And me," added Livy.

"Well, you know what I mean. Twenty-eight is damn close to thirty," said Brooke. "Do you realize how little traveling I've done, how few places I've seen?"

"Because of your mother," said Charlotte grimly. "It's a good thing we're here with you now. We're going to make sure it's a healthy break for you. Right, Livy?"

Livy bobbed her head. "Time to make some choices for yourself. I love your mother. She's very nice. But it's time for you to break the routine you've built around her."

They toasted Brooke's new life and talked about their jobs. Finally, conversation turned to Gran.

"Why do you think she invited us here at the same time? I have a feeling something's going on with her," said Brooke.

"I've wondered about that, too. We have to make sure everything is right with her," said Livy.

Charlotte had taken advantage of her time alone with Gran to ask her a few questions, but she'd been evasive, telling her that it was just a matter of aging.

Their conversation ended when Austin came by with another man from their past. Charlotte focused on the man's face, broad shoulders, and tight abs, and her body resonated with a tingling sensation. Austin's older brother, Shane Ensley, was a heartthrob. All the girls in the cove had drooled over the more sophisticated member of the Ensley family from time to time.

"Hey, do you remember my brother, Shane?" Austin asked. "He's come for a visit too. Thought we could get together sometime."

"That would be nice," said Livy in a breathy voice Charlotte understood. Shane was a tall, well-built man with classic features and blond hair—a real poster boy for the Gulf Coast.

Austin introduced Livy, Brooke, and her to Shane. He politely lifted his sunglasses and acknowledged them all with a smile, and then his gaze rested on Charlotte. She lost herself in a sea of blue. A smile played at his lips as they continued to stare at one another, oblivious of the others. It was, Charlotte would tell herself later, as if a web had been magically woven, tying them together in some weird way.

"We've got plans for tonight, but how about setting aside tomorrow night for one of Granny Liz's beach parties," said Austin.

Charlotte glanced at her cousins. "Sounds great."

Austin's grandmother was a close friend of Gran's and was usually agreeable to a party with the kids. When they were teenagers, Austin's Granny Liz, with help from the other four families in the cove, used to set up a table with hamburgers, hot dogs, salad, chips, and the fixings for s'mores and start a bonfire. She and Gran would cook for the kids and leave them alone after dinner. While no liquor was allowed because of the mix in ages, an occasional beer got through without any repercussions.

"Wholesome fun," is what Gran had called it, sitting with her friend and watching from a distance each time until the kids grew too old to want to participate. Now, as adults, the beach party took on a whole different aspect.

The last beach party in the cove Charlotte had attended was fun. Everyone brought food and booze and relaxed around the fire without getting disorderly even when one or the other had too much to drink.

"Who else is going to be there?" asked Charlotte.

Austin named several people—both male and female—and Charlotte's interest grew. She'd known most of the five families living here all her life. It was a tight-knit group.

"See you later," said Austin. "Better make it seven o'clock tomorrow."

"Need any help?" Livy asked.

Austin grinned at her. "How about bringing some of your cookies?"

Livy laughed. "I'll be happy to do it."

Austin and Shane left, and Charlotte turned to her cousins. "Wow. This visit is off to a great start. It seems like old times."

"What was going on with you and Shane?" Brooke said. "He couldn't take his eyes off of you."

"He seems like an interesting man," Charlotte said, not certain what to say.

"I guess," said Livy. "You were staring at him too."

"Who knew there would be this many attractive men around?" said Brooke. "I remember Austin as a boy, not the handsome man he's become. That dimple!" She turned to Livy. "Remember how you had a crush on him?"

Livy's cheeks flushed. "He's still pretty cute."

Charlotte gave Brooke and Livy a thoughtful look. "Doesn't it seem odd to you that so many of us are here at the same time? It makes me wonder if Gran and her friends planned it this way."

"That would be awful," said Brooke. "If so, I'm going to feel as awkward as I did back then as a teenager."

Charlotte wrapped an arm around Brooke. "You don't need to feel that way now. Livy and I are here for you."

"Yes," said Livy. "Of course."

"Thanks." Brooke patted her hair. "I want to do something different. I was going to get it cut, maybe color it, but time got away from me."

"I'll trim it for you if you like," said Livy. "I know how." She flipped her strawberry blond curls. "With hair like this, I've had to learn."

"Okay," said Brooke. "That would be great. I need all the help I can get."

The three women went inside to get ready for dinner with Gran and John. Charlotte inhaled the smell of lemon and garlic and grinned. John was cooking something delicious.

Upstairs, she and her cousins went into their rooms to shower and change. Later, as she emerged from her room, she noticed Livy and Brooke in the Jack-and-Jill bathroom between their rooms and went to check on them.

"What do you think?" asked Livy. She stood aside so that Charlotte could get a look at Brooke.

A thought occurred to Charlotte. "Are you feeling adventurous, Brooke?"

Brooke shrugged. "I don't know."

"Why don't you have Livy cut your hair to your chin level. That's the new look, and it would show off your neck and lighten the weight of your hair." She turned to Livy. "Do you think you could do that?"

"Yes. I attended beauty school for a while the summer after I graduated high school. That's where I learned to cut hair."

"I never knew that," said Brooke.

"As long as my mother knew it was temporary, it was all right with her," said Livy. "You know how she likes me to look perfect."

"Yeah, my mother too. You're lucky, Brooke. Aunt Jo doesn't care," said Charlotte.

"That says a lot, doesn't it?" said Brooke, her voice flaring a bit.

Charlotte heard the anger and thought once more that this time with Gran would be healthy for all of them. She sat on the edge of the tub and watched Livy go to work, surprised by her skill.

After cutting Brooke's hair, Livy blew it dry, using a brush to lift and control the ends. The effect was stunning. Brooke's brown hair, silky smooth, ended at the jawline, emphasizing the bones structure of her face.

"Now, let's get some mascara and eye shadow on you," Charlotte said, standing.

"You're making me feel like some kind of movie star getting made up for a red-carpet entrance," said Brooke, giving them a shy look.

"It's only practice for tomorrow," said Charlotte. "If Gran and her friends are setting us up to meet one another as if we'd never spent earlier years together, then the three of us are going to wow everyone. Right, you two?"

Livy laughed. "Count me in."

"Me, too," said Brooke, her eyes shining.

Charlotte realized then how much they needed one another to balance things out.

When they headed downstairs, they were giggling like old times.

Gran looked up as they descended the stairway and clapped her hands. "My! You look beautiful. Brooke, your hair looks fantastic. How did you manage that new style?"

"I didn't," said Brooke. "Livy did it for me."

"Well done," said Gran, giving Livy a quick hug. "I understand that the Ensley boys are putting on a beach party tomorrow. Won't that be nice?"

Charlotte studied her grandmother's satisfied smile and blurted, "Is this part of the plan you and your four friends have thought up?"

"What do you mean?" Gran said, eyes wide.

"Gran, you never could lie," said Brooke.

Gran lifted her hands in defense. "All right. All right. Elizabeth Ensley was the first to come up with the idea. Neither of her grandsons is married, and she thinks it's about time they found nice women to settle down with. And then, Pat Dunlap, Sarah Simon, Karen Atkins, and I all agreed it was time for most of you to follow suit."

"Gran, that sounds so ... archaic," Charlotte said, realizing she'd recently used the same word with her mother.

"Hold on," said Gran. "The families have been friends for years sharing this cove. As kids, you were all loved by each of us. It was nothing to feed a couple of kids from another family or to put suntan lotion on someone else's grandchild. We shared all of you among the five of us. Now that some of us are alone and facing old age, we'd like to see you happy and content with families of your own, if that's what you choose. Some may not. That's why we're leaving it up to chance by bringing you all together again. For old-time's sake, if nothing else."

Charlotte gazed at Livy and Brooke, unsure how she felt about the situation. It was true. Years ago, the five families had seemed like one before life interfered.

"It's an intriguing idea," Livy said, breaking into their shocked silence. "But I don't think any of you grandmothers should push it or feel disappointed if it doesn't work out. I'm not sure I ever want to marry. Especially after dealing with

Wayne. What a control freak."

"And you know my mother depends on me," said Brooke.

Charlotte, Livy, and Gran all frowned at her.

"Okay, okay," said Brooke, "I know it's time to be more independent. But I'll always be there for her."

"Of course," said Gran. "We all are and continue to be a support for her." She put an arm around Brooke. "Let's have a glass of wine with dinner. John is making a favorite for the three of you."

Charlotte followed the others into the kitchen, where the table had been set for dinner for the five of them.

Wearing an apron, John looked up from behind the kitchen counter where he was chopping something. "Ah, my beautiful ladies. What a pleasure."

He spoke to all of them, but Charlotte noticed his gaze remained on Gran. Someday, she hoped to share a love like that.

CHAPTER FIVE

BROOKE

Brooke awoke in a panic. *Mom? Where are you?* Her eyes flew open in alarm.

When she realized where she was, she sighed and rolled over. She'd had a dream about her mother calling for help. She stared up at the ceiling fan, rotating slowly above her. *Time to begin a new life,* she told herself, wondering how she'd allowed herself to become so trapped. Her ex-boyfriend, the last one who'd walked away, had told her that she and her mother had an unhealthy, co-dependent relationship. Brooke promptly made an appointment with a therapist and had been working on the issue ever since. It helped that Gran and her cousins supported her in this effort.

Feeling better, Brooke stretched and got out of bed. A walk on the beach was what she needed to clear her mind. She could hardly believe her good fortune in being here at Sanderling Cove, away from the life she'd grown to hate.

She slipped on a pair of shorts and a T-shirt and tip-toed out of the house. Outside, the sun was rising with the promise of another hot day. She moved quickly, eager to wiggle her toes in the sand. She noticed a guest leaving the Inn and gave her a friendly wave.

On the beach, she headed for the lacy froth at the edge of the water and let the waves rush to meet her. The water wrapped around her ankles with a cool embrace. She stood looking out at the Gulf water, inhaling the tang of the salty air, and listened to the cries of the seagulls and terns whirling in the sky above her. She'd never tire of this scene. She thought of her work back home, the rut she'd been in, and whispered a thank you to whoever might hear her.

"Morning," came a voice behind her.

She whirled around to find Jake McDonnell headed her way. "You're up early."

"I like this time of day." He grinned. "Besides, your grandmother likes to meet with me for coffee and an update every day at eight. Walking on the beach is a way to get ready."

"How do you feel about my helping you?" asked Brooke. The last thing she wanted was for him to consider her a nuisance.

"I think it's a good idea. Your grandmother wants to reevaluate the entire operation, and I think you should be part of it."

"Is something wrong with Gran to make her feel this way?" Brooke asked, suddenly worried.

He shook his head. "I think she's simply beginning to feel her age. Now is a smart time to reassess everything."

"Oh," said Brooke, taking in the information quietly. But her mind whirled, and she wondered how Charlie and Livy would feel about it. Did Gran intend to sell? The thought made her stomach clench. Sanderling Cove had always been a haven for her.

"Why don't you join your grandmother and me for coffee, and we can talk more about it," Jake suggested gently.

"Okay, I will," she said.

"See you then," Jake gave her a little wave and took off running.

Brooke watched him. Bare-chested and in jogging shorts, he sure looked ... healthy.

CHAPTER SIX

LIVY

Livy woke to find herself wrapped in the sheet that had covered her during the night. She glanced at the bedside clock and sat up with a start. Nine o'clock. She never slept this late—or hadn't in years. Owning a bakery meant rising at 4 AM and preparing fresh offerings for the day. But, once she'd gotten used to the routine, she hadn't minded those quiet hours with just Julie and her working together, listening to music on their earbuds, swaying to the beat as they mixed and kneaded and iced creations. Sometimes, Livy listened to books on tape. It was another way to spend time.

Julie accused her of being a romantic because of the kind of books she chose, but Livy didn't mind. She loved happy endings and promises of a life full of love. After all, real life wasn't usually that satisfying.

Livy climbed out of bed and went to the window. It looked like another perfect day. It would be fun to see so many of the Sanderling Cove kids again at the beach party tonight. Like Gran had said, it had always seemed like one big, happy family.

At the reminder of the cookies she'd promised to make, Livy washed up and went downstairs. Before it got too hot, she'd do her baking.

The kitchen was empty when she walked into it. But the smell of fresh coffee tantalized her nose, and she headed right to the coffee maker. Beside it, she found a note from Charlotte.

"Livy, Brooke is meeting with Jake, and I'm off doing errands for the party tonight. Catch up with you later."

Happy to have the kitchen to herself, Livy pulled out the equipment she needed. Gran had promised to have plenty of chocolate chips on hand for baking, and Livy found them, flour, sugar, and other ingredients in a cupboard. After pulling out butter and eggs from the refrigerator, Livy got to work. The secret to baking was using real, unsalted butter, not any substitute.

She was taking the last of the cookies from the oven when Charlotte walked into the kitchen carrying shopping bags. "Guess who I ran into in Publix?

Livy set down the pan of cookies. "By the grin you're wearing, I'm guessing it's one of the cove kids. Am I right?"

"Bingo! None other than Melissa Worthington herself. She couldn't wait to show me her enormous engagement ring. Seems she's going to marry a Texas oilman. According to her, he's very rich and ready to spoil her."

"I thought she was spoiled enough," said Livy. Of all the kids in the cove, Melissa and her sister, Morgan, were the most difficult with their need to flaunt all the material things they had. Their older brother, Kyle, was not that way at all.

"And guess what?" added Charlotte. "Morgan broke off her engagement."

"I didn't know she was engaged," said Livy.

"Apparently, Morgan's parents weren't happy with her choice of a boyfriend. Life goes on at Sanderling Cove."

Livy finished placing the cookies on a cooling rack and turned to Charlotte. "I'm sorry to hear that. Morgan is the nicer of the two of them." She peeked inside a paper bag. "What did you get?"

"A bunch of sturdy plastic plates, napkins, and plastic silverware for the party. Gran told Granny Liz we'd provide all that stuff, along with some food and your cookies." Charlotte gave her an impish grin. "It's going to be an interesting time. Brendan and Adam Atkins are here or coming soon, along with their cousin, Dylan Hendrix. Melissa says they've turned into real hunks."

"How about Grace?" Livy asked. Grace Hendrix and she had always gotten along. She could hardly wait to see her again.

"Grace is coming in this afternoon," said Charlotte. "That's as much news as I have."

"You're right. It's going to be a very interesting time," said Livy.

CHAPTER SEVEN

CHARLOTTE

As Charlotte dressed for the party, she told herself to have fun even though she wasn't going to play Gran's game. She wasn't interested in finding romance at this point. She didn't need to find a man; she needed to find herself. She drew a sleeveless aqua top over her head and straightened it above her white jeans. White might seem like the wrong color to wear to a beach party where she'd end up sitting on the sand, but she didn't care. She glanced at herself in the mirror to make sure she was ready. Tonight, she wore her hair up in an informal bun. People told her she was beautiful, but those words meant little to her. Her mother, a gorgeous woman, was more concerned about being proper, doing things right, her place in high society, none of which interested Charlotte.

She went downstairs to meet up with Livy and Brooke. They'd agreed to make an entrance together, carrying food for the party.

Brooke looked fabulous with her new hairdo, a little bit of makeup on her upturned nose, and what she guessed were new cropped pants and a peach top that enhanced the beginnings of a decent tan. Livy, cute as usual with her halo of strawberry blond curls, was wearing denim cut-offs and a pink top with ruffles at the V-neckline.

"You girls look wonderful," said Gran, coming into the kitchen. "I'll see you later. Elizabeth has asked me to help her."

"You mean help her spy on us?" said Charlotte, arching an eyebrow at her.

Gran laughed. "That too."

She gave them each a hug. "Have fun."

After Gran left the house, Brooke said, "I don't know about the two of you, but I feel about fifteen years old."

Charlotte laughed with Livy. "We've got to find something better for these grandmothers to do. Matchmaking is a dangerous business."

"Agreed," said Livy. "I'm anxious to see everyone and catch up, but that's it. I'm still taking a break before deciding where I want to live."

Brooke spoke up. "I'd like to meet a decent man, but you two know I'm not ready yet. I have to learn to be more independent from my mother first."

Charlotte gave her an encouraging smile. "You will. Sooner than you think."

"Thanks. That's what I'm hoping."

When they arrived at Elizabeth Ensley's house next door, the beach in front was filling up with people. Charlotte and her cousins placed their food offerings on the large table placed on the front lawn. After choosing something to drink from the ice-filled tub of canned drinks, they headed down to the sand.

It took Charlotte a moment to place the faces she saw with the memory of the people she knew when they all were younger. But when Shelby Simon approached, Charlotte joyfully hugged her. Shelby looked the same. Of medium height, she had a sturdy body, blue eyes, and reddish-brown hair.

"How have you been? You look wonderful. When is the

baby due?" Charlotte asked her.

"Thanks. The baby, a boy, is due in two months. Just in time for even hotter weather," said Shelby, caressing her round belly. "Mom and Dad and my grandmother are thrilled, along with me and my husband, Douglas. We're going to name the baby Joel after my grandfather."

"Oh, I bet your grandmother loves that," said Charlotte. Sarah and Joel Simon were lovely people. Joel died a couple of years ago from a heart attack.

"Come, let me introduce you to Doug. I know you couldn't attend our wedding, but I'd like him to meet you. Your cousins and you were so much fun when we were growing up."

Charlotte followed Shelby over to a tall, thin, brown-haired man with regular features. Observing them smile at one another, Charlotte felt a pang of envy. She'd told herself she wouldn't marry until she was good and ready, but, for the first time, she couldn't help thinking if that should happen sooner rather than later.

She and Doug chatted for a few minutes, and then Shane Ensley joined them.

After Shane and Doug were talking comfortably, Shelby and Charlotte headed over to where Melissa Worthington was standing with her sister, Morgan. The sisters looked alike with their dark hair, shapely bodies, upturned noses, and hazel eyes.

"Hi, Melissa," said Charlotte.

"Hi, Charlie," said Melissa. "Shelby, have you seen my engagement ring? I'm sorry my fiancé couldn't be here, but he sent me ahead, knowing how much it meant to me to meet up with everyone. It's been years since we've all been together. When's your baby due?"

Shelby grinned. "In August. It's a boy."

"My fiancé and I want at least three children," said Melissa.

Charlotte took this moment to slip away. Enough talk of babies. That wasn't something she could even think about. She grabbed another drink, walked over to the circle of chairs on the lawn, and sat next to Shelby's brother, Eric.

"Hi, Charlie," said Eric. "My grandmother said you and your cousins would be here. Guess that's why I agreed to come."

"It's nice to see you. What have you been up to?" Eric had a full head of red hair that he'd hated as a kid, but his classic features and green eyes were attractive.

Eric talked about the fact that he'd opened a medical practice in Tampa and worked with the Shriners Hospitals for Children. She soon became engrossed in learning about his work there, treating craniofacial conditions, cleft lip, and cleft palate.

"That's impressive," said Charlotte. As she began to answer questions about her career, she realized she wanted to do more than work in an office competing with men and women determined to do better than she, at any cost.

Shane Ensley pulled up a chair to join the conversation.

"What are you doing now, Shane?" Eric asked. "Last I knew, you'd graduated from law school."

"That's right," said Shane. "I'm in Miami, specializing in family law."

"That must keep you very busy," said Charlotte.

"Yes, I like it, though it can sometimes be depressing. But, Charlie, I understand you've been concentrating on marketing. Maybe you can help me on a campaign to build awareness of programs to help families in trouble."

"I'd like that," Charlotte answered honestly. "That's much more appealing than trying to sell things to people who don't want or need them."

"Whoa. Unhappy job experience?" Shane said.

"Yes, I knew I didn't like my life in New York, and I realize how much of it was related to my job. That, and my mother's hopes for me to be a New York socialite."

"You don't want that kind of life?" asked Shane, his blue eyes boring into her.

She shook her head. "No. You may remember what my mother is like."

"I do," said Eric. "Beautiful but remote, now that I think of it."

"So, you see why I've decided to leave the city, even though I don't know where I'll land."

Their conversation was interrupted when Morgan Worthington sat next to Eric and slung an arm around his shoulder. "I hear you're a famous, successful doctor," she said, batting her long eyelashes at him.

Shane and Charlotte exchanged glances and stood at the same time. Poor Eric would have to handle Morgan on his own. Maybe, by the looks of it, he didn't quite mind.

Charlotte went to find Brooke. She'd been a little nervous about the party, and Charlotte wanted to make sure everything was okay.

CHAPTER EIGHT

BROOKE

Brooke was sitting on a blanket beside the fire that had just been lit. Jake sat nearby on the sand, sipping a beer and looking relaxed as he talked to Melissa. Brooke couldn't help glancing his way now and then. He was a handsome man. She knew it would take a lot of willpower not to think of him as anything more than someone she'd be working with, but it was important for her to keep to business. She wasn't ready for more than that.

Austin came and sat down beside her. "How long are you and your cousins staying? I was sorry to hear that your grandmother is thinking of selling the Inn. It's a big part of Sanderling Cove."

Brooke straightened and turned to face Austin. "Selling the Inn?"

Austin returned her wide-eyed stare. "Crap! You didn't know?"

"No, I didn't. Neither do Charlie or Livy. The subject hasn't come up."

"I'm sorry, I shouldn't have said anything. I was talking with Granny Liz about my future, and it slipped out."

"I see," Brooke said. "I won't ruin the party, but tomorrow I'll have a talk with Gran and see how serious she is about selling." She shook her head sadly. "I'd hate to see it go out of the family."

"I hope I didn't mess things up by mentioning it," said Austin.

Brooke gazed at Charlotte and Livy. They'd be as shocked as she.

CHAPTER NINE

LIVY

Livy stood with Grace Hendrix discussing Grace's restaurant in Tampa. It felt comfortable to talk to someone who understood how much Livy had loved her career before her relationship with her business partner started to deteriorate. Grace had a partner in both business and in life. Together the two women had built a successful, intimate, upscale restaurant specializing in seafood.

"I can't wait for you to meet, Belinda." Grace's brown eyes sparkled. "She stayed behind to take care of the restaurant. But if you're going to be here for the summer, you'll be able to see her. Maybe there's some way we can use your services at the restaurant. 'Gills' could use some excellent baked items."

"We'll see. I'm taking a rest for several weeks at least. But thanks." Livy gave her a hug. "I'm glad I've had this chance to catch up with you and that the grandmothers have pulled us all together."

Grace laughed. "They can be a dangerous group. But I love them. Through the years, they've been there for all of us."

"Yes," said Livy. "The cove is a place where I've always felt welcome."

"To be honest, I've raised a few eyebrows, but they've accepted my choices, and that means the world to me," said Grace.

"I'm glad," Livy said. She glanced at Brooke talking with Austin. She thought about going over to say hi to them and decided to move on. Grace's brother Dylan looked a bit lonely standing by the cooler of drinks.

CHAPTER TEN

CHARLOTTE

When they returned to Gran's house after the party, Charlotte turned to her cousins. "Let's meet in my room. Girl talk time. I want to compare notes."

Livy and Brooke both agreed, but Charlotte noticed how quiet Brooke was and wondered what had happened to dim her mood. She'd been chatting with others but seemed subdued.

"Okay," said Livy. "Give me a few minutes. I can't wait to hear all the news from the two of you."

Brooke raced up the stairs ahead of them.

Charlotte turned to Livy. "What's wrong with her?"

Livy shrugged. "I don't know. I saw her talking to Austin, and she seemed upset, but I didn't want to interfere."

Charlotte followed Livy upstairs, deep in thought. When she'd spoken to Austin, he hadn't had much to say, but that wasn't unusual at a party like this. He was more of a one-on-one conversationalist. Right now, everybody was trying to get reacquainted and kept to broad topics.

She changed into pajama shorts and a tank top. As she brushed her teeth, Livy and Brooke entered her room and plopped down on her bed. Charlotte grinned with anticipation. It had been years since this had happened.

"Okay, give me a rundown on everything," said Charlotte, curling up on the bed beside her cousins.

"Before we begin, I have news that you need to know about," said Brooke looking grim. "I didn't want to say anything before now because I didn't want to ruin the party for you. But Austin let it slip that Gran is thinking of selling the Inn."

"Wha-a-at?" cried Charlotte. "Why would she do that without telling the family first?"

"Do you think that's why she invited us here together? To give us the news?" asked Livy.

"Let's find out," said Charlotte. "She stayed behind to help Granny Liz, but she should be coming home any minute."

Unusually quiet, they moved down to the kitchen. Charlotte was saddened by the idea of the Inn being sold and suspected Brooke and Livy were too.

While they waited for Gran, they chatted about Melissa's engagement and other news.

"Grace asked if I'd be willing to supply baked goods to her restaurant sometime in the future," Livy said.

"Shane thought I might be able to help him with some marketing for a charity he's involved with," offered Charlotte.

"I overheard Jake telling someone we were working together for a while," said Brooke.

"Seems to me like it's going to be a busy summer," Charlotte said, her mind whirling with ideas.

"Sh-h-h," Livy hushed them. "Here comes Gran."

"Surprise!" they cried when she entered the kitchen.

Gran clapped a hand to her breast. "Surprise indeed. I thought you girls would be upstairs chattering like old times sake."

"Actually, we're waiting here to talk to you," said Charlotte.

"Austin told me you're thinking of selling the Inn. Is that true?" said Brooke.

Gran sighed and took a seat at the kitchen table. "I'm not sure. I didn't want to discuss it with you until you'd had a chance to settle in. I needed to see if you all were going to be happy here for a while. John and I have planned an extended summer vacation. We hope you three will manage the Inn while we're gone. After that, we'll make a decision about selling it."

Brooke took hold of Gran's hand. "Are you okay? You've never taken much time off. What's the occasion?"

Gran let out another long sigh. "John's doctor told him his heart is failing. My lawyer informed me I'm of an age where I need to think of the time when I can no longer handle the work. Things haven't been running as well as they should or can. We need to have fresh marketing ideas, new computer systems for reservations, front and back-office accounting, and a better way of doing things. I know how talented you all are in different areas and thought you might help us. It would be a blessing if you're willing to stay and manage the Inn while we're away."

"Why didn't you come right out and ask us when you invited us here?" Livy said. Gran was usually very direct.

Gran patted her hand. "I needed to know you were happy to be back at Sanderling Cove. If I sensed you weren't, I wouldn't ask you for your help. It's that simple."

"You'd give up your trip?" asked Charlotte.

"We'd sell the property if we had to, then take the trip John has always wanted." Gran's eyes filled. "We've loved living here, and he's been so good to me that I want him to be able to drive through Europe for several weeks as he wants."

"When you say his heart is failing, what do you mean? How serious is it?" asked Brooke.

"He has weakening heart muscles. If he slows down and takes care of himself, he'll have longer to live than if he keeps to the schedule that he now has," said Gran. "You know, Johnnie, he's going to keep going until the end. That's why this vacation is so important. It's a way for him to slow down."

Her voice wavered. "I'd like to keep him with me for as long as I can."

Charlotte glanced at her cousins, saw the emotion on their faces, and said, "I'm in."

"Me, too," chorused Brooke and Livy.

"Tomorrow, we'll discuss details," said Gran. "Right now, I'm about partied out. See you in the morning. I love each one of you."

She kissed and hugged them individually before turning away and heading into her bedroom.

After she left, they were silent.

Finally, Charlotte spoke. "Gran's right. We can do this together. Even make improvements. Brooke, you can work the numbers, I can do the marketing, and you, Livy, can oversee the kitchen and food production. Does that sound about right?"

"Yes," said Livy. "We can all pitch in however and whenever we can. One of my favorite small hotels is here in Florida—The Beach House Hotel. The two women who put it together and own it had a unique way of setting up their hotel and growing it."

"I know that hotel," said Charlotte. "I stayed there once. It's a gem. They're more upscale than we are, but we can use some of their ideas to bring The Sanderling Cove Inn back to its former glory."

"We'll have a better understanding of what's happening after we get into the numbers," said Brooke. "I'm happy to work with Jake on that. Especially now that I know what the real situation is." She clucked her tongue. "I would hate to see someone outside the family take over the Inn. It just wouldn't seem right."

They studied each other.

###

The following day, the three of them toured the Inn's property from one end to the other, assessing it with fresh eyes. The two-story main building held sixteen guest rooms upstairs. Some had balconies that overlooked the pool below and the beach beyond. Others faced a garden view. In the two-story attached wing, another twenty rooms were available for guests, making a total of 36 guest rooms. Each room had a small refrigerator, a microwave, and a coffee maker in a mini kitchen with a sink and cupboards.

The first floor of the main building held a sizeable office, a small commercial kitchen, and a dining room that included a separate area for private parties. In addition, there was a small conference room and a large open area where guests could gather to relax, read, watch television, or play games. One wall of the gathering room held bookshelves loaded with books of all kinds. In an area called the "back of the house," there was plenty of storage space for cleaning supplies, pantry items, maintenance equipment, and the like, along with an employee coffee and locker room.

Outside the gathering room, a screened lanai offered a large pool with a spa at one end. Beyond that, a gleaming white gazebo sat in a flower garden designed for weddings and other occasions.

"Impressive," said Brooke.

"But no question that the guest rooms and public areas need sprucing up," said Charlotte.

"We should replace some of the patio furniture around the pool," said Livy. "The kitchen is another area of concern."

"Lots of opportunities for us to make it better," said Brooke.

"Oh yes," Charlotte quickly agreed.

When it came time to meet with Gran, Charlotte, like the others, was full of ideas. The family should've known that

Gran and John couldn't keep up with the work of managing an upscale Inn. If all rooms were filled, over seventy guests could be there.

Charlotte followed her cousins to Gran's house and into the kitchen.

"What do you think?" Gran asked them.

"It's going to be helpful for me to go over the numbers with Jake," said Brooke. "You've run a pretty tight operation in the past. There's no reason to think that can't continue. Maybe do even better. Especially if we're able to bring in new business."

"That's where I come in," said Charlotte. "After some refreshment to the property, I'm going to set up a whole new marketing campaign. I'll work with the PR people you've hired in the past and go from there."

Gran shook her head. "I haven't done anything new for a couple of years because a lot of our old-time customers have slowly stopped coming, and I wasn't sure what I wanted to do."

"Why didn't you say anything?" Charlotte said, distressed by Gran's apparent lack of concern. Then she remembered how many years Gran had worked at the Inn and understood her burnout.

"I remember when we were kids how people would make dinner arrangements here for special occasions," said Livy. "I used to hang out in the kitchen with the crew. That's when I knew I wanted a career in food production. I think we can take advantage of locals and visitors interested in small dining groups to improve visibility for the Inn."

Gran put a hand to her chest and exhaled. "You darlings. I think we might be able to carry off a renewal of the business with your help. I know your parents would ask me to sell it, but the Inn is how I've survived all these years. Your grandfather was a gambler. Something I didn't realize until after he died and left me with little means to survive on my own. That's when I had the idea for the Inn. And I started with only a few bedrooms in the house to rent out. After I discovered his insurance policies, that money and John's made it possible for us to build the Inn. We've had to make the business succeed in order for us to be able to stay here."

"And Johnnie has helped from the beginning," commented Charlotte.

"Oh, yes. He needed something to do and was willing to become a business partner after he closed down his restaurant." She shook her head. "If it weren't for him, I would've been forced to give up the idea. That's why it's so important to me that he has the vacation he's dreamed of. Running an Inn means working 24/7."

Charlotte studied her grandmother. She was wearing a green T-shirt that read "*Allergic to B. S.*" Somehow it seemed appropriate. This was a time for them to come together and plan for the future. She gazed at her cousins. Could they work together?

Time would tell.

CHAPTER ELEVEN

LIVY

Livy had hoped for a sister after her mother remarried. She'd received two younger brothers instead. Now, gazing around the table, Livy felt as close to her cousins as she would to any sister.

The idea of spending a summer lazing about was no longer her wish. She wanted to help Gran with the Inn. And the thought of possibly preparing a dinner once in a while was thrilling. She loved baking, always would. But now, she could try something different.

She glanced at Gran and wondered what a trip with Gran and John would be like. She could well imagine them interacting with others wherever they went. The hospitality business meant dealing with people every day, and they did that job well.

A sad look had crossed Gran's face when she mentioned John's health issue. Yet, the two of them shared a special love that not many people had. Livy recalled Melissa Worthington's joy over the size of the diamond ring her fiancé had given her as if that was the most important thing about her engagement. Then, her thoughts turned to Grace and her partner. Grace had quietly spoken of Belinda with an unmistakable loving tone. If the time came for her to consider getting serious with anyone, Livy wanted what Gran and Grace had. Not a big flashy ring.

Gran turned to her. "Is staying here and taking over the kitchen something you want? I know how tired you are, how much you said you wanted to relax and do nothing."

"I'm pretty excited about the idea," Livy said. "I'm also going to test selling baked items to restaurants. Maybe it would bring in extra money."

"No, sweetie, I don't want you to think we won't cover living expenses for you while you're here. We've set aside an account for that." She gave them each a steady look. "There's something else you should know. John and I are married. When we realized the legal ramifications of needing to be able to decide what to do for each other as far as health issues, we quietly took care of it."

"What?" cried Livy.

"But, Gran," said Brooke. "What about the family? Didn't you want to share it with us and our parents? Won't they be hurt?"

"Well, that's what we wanted to avoid. My daughters have not been comfortable with the idea of John and me living together, and I didn't want them to think I was getting married for their approval. I know that might seem harsh to you, but that's the way I feel."

"Bravo, Gran," said Charlotte. "I admire you for your independence."

Gran held up a hand. "I'm not trying to be difficult, you understand. I was married to your grandfather, but after finding out what he'd done by gambling away my future, I vowed to never remarry. But, I love John and want to be there for him when he needs me."

"I think you have every right to do as you please. You're not hurting anyone else by being independent," said Charlotte. "I can't wait to see my mother's face when you tell her."

"That's another thing," said Gran. "I'm not planning on telling anyone else. My four best friends here in Sanderling Cove already know, of course, but it shouldn't matter to anyone else." She shook her finger at them. "But if you think I'd approve of your doing something like this, marrying without your family, you'd be wrong. Your parents would just blame me."

"My mother is going to be disappointed to think she missed out," said Brooke. "But, don't worry, I won't say a word."

"Thank you," Gran said quietly, and Livy understood that this matter of independence was who she was.

After they discussed what role each would play going forward, Livy and her cousins headed out to the beach.

A summer storm was brewing, and they knew it wouldn't be long before a thunderstorm took away some of the heavy humidity that clung to them as they flipped off their sandals and headed to the water's edge.

There, Livy stood with the others facing the Gulf waves rolling in toward them then pulling away in a steady rhythm as old as time.

Life was taking on a new meaning. As she watched a trio of pelicans skim the water's surface looking for food, she thought it was right for the three of them to be together to help Gran and John. Through the years, they'd given her and her cousins a deep love and a sense of belonging that didn't exist in the same way outside of Sanderling Cove.

CHAPTER TWELVE

ELLIE

Ellie looked around with affection at everyone gathered in the dining room. She'd set up a staff meeting so that her granddaughters could meet the people who supported the operation of the Inn. Some of them had worked for her for many years.

Ambrose "Amby" Pappas and his wife, Beryl, descendants of Greek sponge divers who'd settled in the Tarpon Springs area of Florida long ago, had been with her the longest. Amby acted as landscaper and general handyman around the Inn, while Beryl headed the housekeeping staff. A smile tugged at Ellie's lips. No one could do a better job than Beryl. The Inn might need a little sprucing up, but it was spotless. She made sure the seven part-time staff members under her control were as diligent as she was.

Billy Bob Walker leaned against the wall by the entrance to the room, a bit stand-offish as usual. If one didn't know how gentle he was, they'd keep their distance. He was a big, burly man with large hands, sandy hair, and blue eyes that were so light they sometimes seemed spooky. He'd served prison time long ago for dealing drugs, but now he was as cold sober as anyone could be. His only vice today was his addiction to Tic Tacs in a variety of flavors. She'd been leery about hiring him to assist John, but John had insisted, and they'd been a splendid team ever since, along with two part-time kitchen helpers who came and went.

Ellie cleared her throat. "Thank you all for coming. I want

to introduce my granddaughters to you. They will be managing the Inn for John and me this summer while we're away. Brooke will be working with Jake in the office, Livy will work with Billy Bob in the kitchen, and Charlotte will be taking my place as morning hostess most mornings and redoing our website and marketing program."

Brooke, Livy, and Charlotte introduced themselves and told a little bit about their backgrounds and interests.

"Now, dear granddaughters," said Ellie, "meet the best staff anyone could have." She introduced each staff member by name and gave a snippet of information about them, ending with Billy Bob.

"So, there you have it, everyone. A new team for the summer. John and I have agreed to the upgrades our granddaughters are proposing, so expect some changes. We ask for cooperation among you. We've always considered you to be a part of our family. That won't change, even though we'll be gone."

John placed a hand on Ellie's shoulder. "We're grateful to you all. Without you, we wouldn't be able to make this trip. Thank you."

As people began to disperse, Ellie walked over to Billy Bob. "Livy will be working in the kitchen taking inventory. I trust you'll be willing to let her do her thing."

He bobbed his head. "Anything for you and John."

"Thank you," she said. Livy might be tiny compared to Billy Bob, but she was a force of her own.

CHAPTER THIRTEEN

BROOKE

When Brooke saw who was calling on her phone, she quickly picked it up feeling guilty she hadn't called her back. "Hi, Mom! How are you?"

"Missing you. When are you coming home?"

Remembering how the others had told her it was time to be more independent, Brooke drew a deep breath. "Not until sometime in September."

"Oh? I thought you might get bored at the beach."

Brooke chuckled. "I'm not bored at all. Charlotte and Livy are here too, and we're having a great time together." She didn't mention anything about the three of them helping Gran. That was Gran's story to tell.

"That sounds like a lot of fun," said her mother. "I'll have to thank Mom for having you all there at once. It's a lot of work for her, no doubt."

"Mother," said Brooke, "we're not kids anymore. We can be a help to her, not a hindrance."

"You're right. I sometimes forget that. You're all strong, independent women. Are any of your aunts planning to come there?"

"No," said Brooke, hating any suggestion that they might. "As Gran says, this is a time for us to have the opportunity to think about the future. How is the home nurse doing?"

"I've canceled any visits. I'm having one of my easier times, and I didn't want to spend the money. When it becomes necessary, I'll have them send a nurse to help. I'd better get back to work. Talk to you later. Love you."

"Love you too, Mom," Brooke responded, pleased her mother seemed to be doing well on her own. This was a transition for her too.

Brooke finished her coffee and headed over to the Inn to meet Jake. She reminded herself it was strictly a business relationship, and that no matter how attracted she might be to him, that's the way it should remain.

When she entered the kitchen, John looked up at her from behind the stove. Beside him, Livy was plating a dish with scrambled eggs and bacon.

"Looking fine, Livy," Brooke said.

Livy grinned at her. "Feels comfortable." She put an arm around John. "The real pro is here. How many years has it been, John?"

He shook his head. "More years than I can count."

Brooke left them and went into the administration office. Jake sat at one desk. An empty desk near his had been designated as hers.

"Good morning," she said cheerfully, happy to be doing something constructive. She was so used to working she had felt at loose ends from time to time.

"Ready to begin?" said Jake smiling at her. "I figured I'd show you the financials from four years ago and compare them year to year for you. The slowing trend will be apparent. It'll be up to us to mark certain areas that need improvement and develop a new budget that's reasonable. In the past, this has been a very lucrative business, which is unusual for a small operation like this. But it's doable, as Ellie and John have proved."

Brooke was soon lost in the paperwork they went through together. Finally, a couple of hours later, she sat back in her chair and sighed. "It will take time to go through the line items, but it's important that we do."

"Agreed," said Jake. "I've been working on insurance costs, investments, and financial management issues. But I'd like to turn the rest over to you. I've got other clients I need to pay attention to, but I don't want Ellie and John to think I don't care about their situation. I do. At Ellie's insistence, I've billed for my work so far, but I don't intend to charge them for more now that you'll be doing the bulk of the work."

"That's kind of you," said Brooke, impressed by him.

"John and Ellie have been kind to me, taking me on when I was first starting out. I remember things like that."

"Gran mentioned you've worked hard and done everything on your own. Did you grow up here?"

"Years ago, my mother was a housekeeper at the Inn. Unfortunately, it didn't last. She couldn't shake her drug habit. A friend of Ellie's living in Tampa took me in when I was twelve. She was wonderful to me, but John and Ellie saw that I got the extras a kid needs and helped me focus on college. I'll always be grateful to them."

"I'm surprised we didn't meet you earlier," said Brooke.

"I pretty much stayed away. It wasn't a happy time for me, but I've gotten past that," he replied.

Brooke had an urge to hug him. Instead, she gazed out the window of the office, touched by his story. Living with her mother, caring for her, Brooke had sometimes felt alone. She realized how much more difficult Jake's childhood had been.

Jake stood. "I'm going to leave you working on line items in the budget. I have a meeting in town. I'll check in with you later."

"Okay, hopefully, I'll have started a list of suggestions for all of us to discuss. My cousins and I toured the property earlier. Charlotte is making a list of things we need to do to refresh the rooms, and Livy is doing an inventory of the kitchen equipment and also reviewing menus."

Jake's smile lit his eyes. "Ellie told me she hoped to have the three of you help her. I'm glad you decided to do it. She said she and John are taking a much-needed extended vacation. That's a great idea. Most clients don't like change, needed or not. With them away, you'll have more opportunities to make those improvements."

Brooke basked in his smile. She was happy she'd decided to spend the summer here and even more pleased that she'd be able to help Gran.

CHAPTER FOURTEEN

LIVY

After clearing away breakfast dishes left by three couples staying at the Inn, Livy loaded the dishwasher, making a mental note that a second dishwasher might need replacing. Livy was a professional who understood that each cook, each chef had a personal way of doing things and protected it from change. She'd have to tread carefully with both John and Billy Bob, who clearly was undecided about having her in the kitchen to take John's place.

John was a talented short-order cook for the breakfast crowd and a better one for occasional dinners. But if, like her cousins, they hoped to improve the property, the kitchen needed upgrading, including adding to and rearranging space to accommodate two or more extra helpers as needed. Understanding how this might affect John, Livy wisely kept those thoughts to herself, instead merely taking inventory of what kitchen items were there now.

She was scrubbing out one of the cupboards when John and Billy Bob entered the kitchen.

"What are you doing?" Billy Bob asked.

"Just seeing what's here and cleaning a bit while I'm at it," Livy replied casually.

"Oh, I've meant to do that." John shook his head. "Ellie keeps telling me to slow down, so I've let a few things go."

"No, problem. I need to know what's here anyhow," she said as Billy Bob walked away. She turned to John. "As long as my cousins and I are staying, why don't you and Gran leave earlier than you'd planned? It's a perfect time to travel."

"Trying to get rid of us, huh?" John said, but a smile crept across his face. "As a matter of fact, Ellie and I talked about that earlier. She told me to stay out of your way, that the three of you are going to make some changes with her blessing, and I'd be sure to like whatever you girls came up with."

Livy gave him a quick hug. "You will. I promise. Where are you going to start this magical trip of yours?"

"We're going to England first since we speak the language. There's a lot to see. We're not going to plan the whole trip out day by day. We want to feel free to travel when and where we want."

"I traveled through Europe with a friend one summer and did just that," said Livy. "We never knew where we'd end up and saw enough to know we want to go back someday. Did you know they have a fantastic cooking school in Ireland? And there's a lot to learn about food and wine ... and cheese and bread ... and ..."

"Stop. You're making me want to pack right now," said John laughing.

"I'm happy you and Gran can make the trip. But, John, promise you won't overdo it."

John sighed. "Ellie's worried about me, but it's just old age and my heart telling me to slow down. This trip is as much for her as it is for me. She's not getting any younger, and neither am I."

Unexpected tears stung Livy's eyes. She wasn't ready to lose either one of them.

After John left and she finished wiping down the cupboard she'd been working on, Livy decided to take a walk on the beach. The sun had risen and was beating down on the white sand sending waves of heat shimmering across it. She sprinted across the stretch of beach in front of her and at the cooler water's edge, kicked off her sandals. The tang of salt air filled her nostrils, and her body relaxed as she slowly breathed in and out. The tension of the past several months receded as she studied the tiny fish darting about in the shallow water.

She lifted her face with contentment. Moments in nature like this were excellent for the soul.

"Hey, there," came a voice behind her. "I hoped to see you here."

Livy whipped around and faced Austin. "Hi, what's going on?"

"Charlie and I had lunch together. She told me you three will spend the summer managing the Inn for your Gran and John and hopefully doing some upgrades. I offered my services in setting up whole new computer and wi-fi systems for it."

"That seems nice but expensive," said Livy, wishing she wasn't disappointed by the news that he and Charlotte had been together.

Austin waved away her concern. "Not a problem. I'll do it for free. I'll even be able to get you a discount on any of the hardware you may need." He kicked a bare foot in the sand. "I have to keep busy. I promised Granny Liz I'd stay for the summer, but I can't just lounge around all day."

"I get it," said Livy. "I thought I'd be happy doing nothing all summer, but the idea of helping Gran and John with the Inn is something I'm quite really excited about."

"So, now that you've sold your bakery, are you going to open a new one? Maybe even here?"

Livy shook her head. "I don't want to be tied down to that schedule again. I might consider supplying a few restaurants with some items, but that's all. If we decide to offer dinner at the Inn for locals, that changes everything."

Kyle Worthington joined them. "Hey, strangers. Sorry I couldn't make the party last night, but I hear it was a fun one." He shook hands with Austin and quickly kissed Livy's cheek.

With straight dark-brown hair, chocolate-brown eyes, and an easy smile, Kyle was charming. Added years had made his features even more handsome. He and his sisters, Morgan and Melissa, were all beautiful people, but Kyle wasn't competitive or mean like them.

"Dating any more movie stars?" Austin asked.

Kyle laughed and shook his head. "All rumors. Though I've had a few patients in the business, I have no interest in actresses. Give me a down-to-earth woman any day." He smiled at Livy.

Livy willed her cheeks not to flush.

Austin looked from one to the other and said, "Guess I'd better be going." He took off.

Kyle and Livy stared at one another. "It was nice to see you," Kyle said.

"Come say hi sometime. Charlie and Brooke are staying with me at Gran's house."

"Will do," said Kyle. He gave her a wave and called to Austin. "Hey, wait up!"

She watched them go, telling herself she and her cousins had a busy summer ahead of them.

CHAPTER FIFTEEN

CHARLOTTE

Livy was in Gran's kitchen helping herself to a cold lemonade when Charlotte walked in.

"Oh, that looks delicious," said Charlotte. "I'm still getting used to the heat and humidity."

Livy handed her a glass of the cold drink and took a seat at the kitchen table. "John told me that he and Gran are going to leave earlier than planned. I think it's to give us the freedom to work on changes."

Charlotte murmured her thanks, took a sip of the drink, and gave her a satisfied smile. "I hope that's true. I've had a productive day and have lots to share with you and Brooke."

"Let's text her in the office now," said Livy. "I bet she's had enough of figures."

Charlotte quickly sent a message to Brooke asking her to meet them in Gran's kitchen and got a response right back. "She's on her way."

They sipped in silence, and then Brooke entered the kitchen. "Thanks for rescuing me. Jake left to meet with another client, and I've been stuck alone in the office looking at numbers until I'm about blind."

Livy handed her a glass of lemonade. "Margaritas later. Right now, Charlotte and I have news."

"So do I," said Brooke. "Gran told me she and John are leaving earlier than expected to give us time to work on the Inn. She's bubbling with excitement."

"John said he's making the trip as much for her as he is for himself," said Livy. "Isn't that sweet?"

"They're perfect together," said Charlotte. "I'd like to have that kind of relationship someday. Right now, I'm happy to be free from anything like that so I can concentrate on this summer's project. I've been doing some thinking. I want to make the Inn better than ever."

"Me, too," said Livy. "But it's going to take money to bring it up to its old standards. Especially in the kitchen. And if we're going to offer dinner as Gran and John used to, the kitchen can't wait."

"How are we going to get the money?" asked Charlotte.

"I have some good news," said Brooke giving them a triumphant smile. "Gran and John have wisely set aside money each year for renovations. We have approximately one hundred eighty thousand dollars to use. It seems like a lot, but it isn't. We're going to have to be super careful."

"Okay, but so far, I've discovered we need to replace a dishwasher in the kitchen with one that can handle a larger volume of dishes, and the commercial icemaker is iffy and may also need replacement," said Livy. "The other issues are smaller, adding to the inventory of some utensils, moving things around to make it easier for more people to work in the kitchen. Believe me. I try hard not to bump into Billy Bob."

Charlotte and Brooke laughed.

"The guest rooms need refreshing as we've already discussed," said Charlotte. "I was able to locate a hotel supplier in Miami, and when I talked to them, they were more than willing to work with us on new bedspreads, sheets, and towels for all thirty-six rooms," said Charlotte. "Discount prices on bulk purchases can make a difference. I told him we'd even be interested in overstock items."

"What about adding another washing machine and dryer for guests to use?" said Brooke.

"How about the coffee makers in the rooms? I think we should replace those with Keurig machines," said Livy. "I noticed some of the old ones weren't in the best of shape. This way, we can offer a variety of drink choices to our guests."

"I suggest we all price whatever we think we need, and then we'll make a decision together as to what we buy," said Brooke.

"We're lucky the rooms don't need to be repainted or recarpeted," said Charlotte. "We can make them seem brand new by giving each room different bedspreads and soft goods. I'll plan a trip to Miami to see what the supplier has available."

"And to meet a certain lawyer for lunch?" Brooke said, nudging her.

"She had lunch with Austin today," said Livy, giving Brooke an impish grin.

"Hold on, dear cousins," said Charlotte laughing. "It's all for business. Remember? Besides, it was worth a lot to meet up with Austin. He's going to help upgrade the wi-fi system for us and even work with us on updating the property management system."

"He told me he's going to do it for free," said Livy. "He wants to keep busy because he promised Granny Liz he'd stay for the summer."

"Wow. While you two are cavorting, I'm stuck in the office reviewing numbers," said Brooke. "What's fair about that?"

"Nothing," said Charlotte. "But I'm better at decorating and marketing work."

"And I'm best in the kitchen," said Livy.

Brooke grinned. "I'm better than either of you at bargain hunting. I can help Charlie with decorating."

"Great," said Charlotte with genuine enthusiasm. "All the public areas need to be taken apart and put back together again with a fresh look. Maybe even changing things from one room to another. There's lots of acceptable stuff to work with, and we can use any bargains you can find."

"Okay," said Brooke. "As the financial manager of this project, I say no expenditure will take place without the three of us agreeing. Before that can happen, we need to price out all equipment and other things and prepare a detailed capital budget so we can track expenditures. Agreed?"

Charlotte nodded alongside Livy, pleased to see Brooke take on that role. Brooke was the youngest and the past had allowed them to boss her around. This summer would be interesting with a rotating change of power because they each had enough of Gran within them to want to be in charge.

"I'm going up for a shower," said Livy. "I'm a mess after cleaning some of the kitchen."

"See you later," said Charlotte. "I'm going to take a walk on the beach. Let's meet up later for margaritas."

After they all agreed, Charlotte headed outdoors and onto the beach. It would be natural to get in touch with Shane while she was in Miami, wouldn't it? She shook her head and gazed out at the Gulf waters. She was fascinated by him, but this was a time to be away from all that social pressure.

"Hey, Charlie!"

Charlotte turned at the sound of the voice. Dylan Hendrix, Grace's brother, headed toward her, smiling.

"Hi, Dylan," Charlotte said cheerfully. Dylan was a nice guy, a little off-beat, and a successful artist who'd been lucky enough to have sold one of his early works to a movie star who featured it in a photo shoot of his house. With that, Dylan's career took off in a hurry.

"We didn't get a chance to talk at the party. What's going on with you?" Dylan asked her.

She filled him in on the plans to spend the summer helping Gran and John get the Inn back on track. "How about you?"

"Mimi asked me to spend some time here, and I thought it would be interesting to use this location for some interesting new projects. She's given me the use of her garage to make it happen."

"The colors here are so gorgeous," said Charlotte. "I can already imagine how beautiful your paintings will be." Dylan created large, bold abstracts, not like Jackson Pollock, but with the same free expression. She loved his work.

They continued talking about their lives. Dylan lived in Santa Fe and had a studio there. When he asked her about New York, Charlotte shook her head.

"It's such an empty existence for me. Sure, I'm social and like fashion, but not as everything in my life. That's how a part of society in the city lives. I'm just glad to be away."

"No men in your life?"

"Nope, and none in the foreseeable future," said Charlotte. 'I'm here to help Gran and to take a break from all that."

He gave her a knowing look and smiled. As he did, his blue eyes lit, changing his craggy features into a decidedly handsome face. His brown hair, highlighted from the sun, was pulled back into a ponytail and gave him an interesting appearance.

She chuckled. "How about you? Any girlfriends?"

"I broke up with a woman I'd been dating for a while. We wanted different things." He raised a hand to stop her. "No, it wasn't what you think. I want a family, and she didn't. Weird, huh?"

"Yeah, but I understand. Some women don't want kids."

He raised his eyebrows. "Like you?"

Charlotte shook her head and sighed. "Just haven't met the right person yet. My mother wanted me to marry a man I've known all my life. Only problem is, he's gay and has carefully hidden it."

"It's better for him if he comes out. Grace was a mess until she did, but we knew all along," said Dylan. "My parents, Mimi, and I are okay with it."

"Livy talked to Grace about her restaurant. She may do some work for her."

"Nice. Funny how we're all here. It was a great idea to get us together." He gave her a wave. "Gotta go. I promised to pick up my cousin, Adam, and his little girl at the airport."

He trotted away, and Charlotte remembered that Adam Atkins was a single father with a four-year-old girl. The poor child's mother had ditched them both. She thought back to times growing up when Adam, a big, athletic kid, had been the leader of most of the sports activities all the kids in the cove played together before everyone went their separate ways. Brendan, his brother, wasn't going to come to the cove until later. His wife just had a baby boy.

Still lost in thought about the people she'd known growing up, Charlotte stopped in surprise when she came face to face with Shane. Her heart skipped a beat. "What are you doing here? I thought you went back to Miami."

"Granny Liz asked me to return for dinner. She wants all of us to be together for this reunion as much as possible."

"I was going to ask you to join me for lunch tomorrow. I'm going to Miami to meet with a hotel supplier rep and thought I'd look you up. You mentioned maybe needing my help with a marketing campaign."

"Yes, I did. We're preparing for a fundraiser later in the year. If you're interested, I'd like to talk to you about the group."

"I'd like that," she said, pleased by the idea of using her talent in this new way.

A warm feeling washed through her when his lips curved, and she knew behind the sunglasses he wore, his blue eyes were shining with approval.

When she returned to the house, Livy and Brooke were in the kitchen.

"Glad you're here," said Livy. "Brooke and I were discussing whether we should go out tonight or stay in."

"Either is fine with me. I ran into Shane, and I'm going to meet him in Miami tomorrow. He's going to tell me all about the non-profit he's working on."

"Livy and I were discussing our ideas for the Inn, and we don't think Gran should know what we're thinking about for changes until final decisions are made," said Brooke.

"We don't want Gran and John to worry about anything. Especially now when they're beginning to pack for their trip," Livy explained.

"Agreed," said Charlotte. "No matter how much they might like the idea of changes being made, they might find it stressful."

Just then, Austin came into the room.

"I'm here to discuss..." he stopped when Gran appeared at the entrance to the kitchen.

The three women looked at one another in a panic.

Livy jumped to her feet. "Discuss my cookies?"

Austin gave her a surprised look.

"You men are all alike. Can't get enough of Livy's baking," said Charlotte, sending him a warning look to play along.

Gran walked over to them. "Everything all right?"

"Yes, Austin is here begging for more of Livy's cookies," said Charlotte hoping the others would continue to play along. Gran was suspicious of computers, didn't understand them, and got nervous with the lingo. If she knew what they were planning with new computer programs, she might rebel.

Gran beamed at them. "Cookies, huh? You know what they say. The way to a man's heart is through his stomach."

Charlotte laughed at the surprised glances between Livy and Austin.

"I'm on my way to Liz's house for a glass of wine. I'll see you later," said Gran.

"Have fun," Charlotte said, giving her a jaunty salute.

After she left, Austin took a seat at the kitchen table. "What was that all about?"

"We're trying not to overwhelm Gran and John with all the changes we want to make to the Inn," said Livy.

"I get it." He grinned at her. "But about those cookies ..."

CHAPTER SIXTEEN

ELLIE

As she had so many times over the past forty-some years, Ellie crossed her front lawn to Liz Ensley's house next door. Liz was sitting on the front porch of her home with Sarah Simon. In the distance, Pat Dunlap and Karen Atkins were walking toward them from the far end of the cove. Ellie lifted her arm and waved at them. These four women had seen her through a lot of ups and downs over the years. Having become a widow in her late thirties, she'd gratefully received their emotional support after she was left without much to survive on. She'd transformed her home into a small B&B and then enlarged the concept with the new buildings that created the Inn as it was today. Their husbands had been supportive too, which meant a lot. Sanderling Cove was a special place they all wanted to protect from visitors who wouldn't respect that. Sarah and Pat were now widows, and the survivors now rallied around them.

"Hey, there, Ellie. You're just in time. I opened a nice pinot grigio to share," said Liz as Ellie climbed the front porch stairs.

"Sounds delightful," Ellie said, taking a seat in one of the rocking chairs that had been drawn into a circle of five.

Pat and Karen arrived, and as soon as all the women had settled in their chairs and been served a glass of wine, Liz leaned forward. "Okay, everyone, how are we doing? Any sparks flying yet?"

"Austin is over at my house now," said Ellie. "Says he wants to talk to Livy about her cookies. I told her a way to a man's heart is through his stomach. What do you think?" A wave of hope rushed through her.

"An interesting beginning, I'd say," said Liz. "Shane told me he's meeting Charlie for lunch tomorrow. Another possibility."

"I saw Eric talking to Morgan," said Sarah.

Pat shook her head. "I'm sorry, but I have to say it. Even if Morgan is my granddaughter, that girl is as flighty as they come. I've tried to speak to her about it, but it's like talking to a stone wall."

Ellie exchanged glances with the other three women. Flighty wasn't the word they'd use for that spoiled young woman.

"I caught Dylan and Charlie talking together," said Karen. "And I'm hoping that Adam has another chance at happiness. The only good thing that came out of his marriage was my precious Skye."

"She's so adorable, Karen. I can't wait for my three granddaughters to produce some great-grandbabies for me to love," said Ellie. She'd encouraged Liz's idea for summer romances for the cove kids.

"Thank heavens Shelby is nicely settled," said Sarah.

"Yes, David is a wonderful man," said Liz, and they all agreed.

"Grace is happy with Belinda, and that's all that matters to me," said Sarah. "I don't worry about her or Brendan. Just Adam and Dylan."

"In addition to them, that leaves us with Shane, Austin, Morgan, Kyle, Eric, and Ellie's three granddaughters to worry about," said Liz.

"Seems to me, there's enough to get all of them settled," said Sarah. "Four young women and six young men."

Ellie laughed with the others. "Seven young men if you count Jake." She shook her head. "Only three great-grandchildren out of the bunch of kids so far. It's time for action."

A round of applause brought a smile to Ellie's lips. She loved these women.

The conversation turned to other things, and then Ellie announced, "John and I are leaving for Europe for the summer sooner than we thought. We're not going to take any chances on waiting. Charlie, Brooke, and Livy are going to manage the Inn for us. In fact, with our blessing, they're going to upgrade it. Charlie keeps referring to the upgrade as refreshing the property, but I suspect it will be more than that."

"So, all three will stay for the summer?" said Pat. "That's terrific."

"How's John feeling? He looks *fabulous*," said Sarah and then covered her mouth. "I didn't mean that quite the way it came out."

Ellie waved away Sarah's concern. Sarah's spouse, Joel, had passed on, and soon after, Pat's husband, Ed, died unexpectedly. Of the three men who were left, John was in the best shape. One evening, to the amusement of all of them, after two glasses of wine, Pat had called him a stud muffin.

"How will we keep in touch with you?" Liz asked Ellie.

"Your darling Austin is giving me lessons on uploading photos to my phone and computer, and we can communicate with emails," said Ellie.

"And we'll send photos of the kids and the Inn back to you," said Sarah. She was the savviest when it came to the electronics they all had to use.

"Look at that sunset," said Karen, bringing silence to the group. Sunsets were an important time of day on the Gulf

Coast as visitors and locals lined up to watch the sun slip below the horizon, hoping for a chance to see the "green flash."

After the sun disappeared, the women continued to sit, sip, and share news as they had so many times in the past.

CHAPTER SEVENTEEN

BROOKE

Brooke awoke with a sense of eagerness. Charlotte and Livy had put her in charge of the renovation, and she liked the idea. How many times at work had she bent to the wishes of others to keep peace around her? Here at Sanderling Cove, she felt herself come alive. Here, her grandmother encouraged her to do whatever she wanted instead of placing other people's desires before her own. It was so freeing. Not that she'd change that much. She'd dealt with selfish people and had no desire to become one.

Quietly, she got dressed and slipped down the stairs carrying her sandals so she wouldn't disturb anyone. Walks on the beach were times to reflect, to dream, to decide on action.

She got out of the house without anyone seeing her and headed for the sand. She was surprised to discover two figures already there—a man and a child.

Brooke approached them with a smile, intending to say hello and be on her way to the far end of the cove, where a small little inlet was an excellent place to collect shells.

As she drew closer, she saw that the child, a little girl around four, held a net bag for collecting shells. She admired the girl's blond curls and pink cheeks and remembered the joy of finding them at her age. "Gifts from the sea," Gran had called them.

"Hi, there," she said to the man. "I noticed your little girl might be looking for shells. I know a secret place farther down the beach that's the best place for collecting them."

The man, tall and well-built with broad shoulders, made her pause. She studied his face. Brown curly hair, classic features, a day-old beard, and a boyish grin. "Adam Atkins, is that you?" She'd had a crush on him fifteen years ago when he was in his early twenties. He looked older but even better.

"Yeah, I thought that was you, Brookie. You're all grown up."

Well aware she was wearing just her bikini and flip-flops, she felt as shy as she'd been back then. "So are you. And you have a sweet, little girl."

Adam put an arm around his daughter who'd run over to them. "This is Skye."

Brooke squatted down to get a better look. "Hi, Skye. I knew your daddy a long time ago. How old are you?"

Skye held up four fingers. "Daddy sometimes says I'm fourteen, but I'm really only four."

Brooke couldn't hold back a laugh. She stood and faced him.

Adam grinned. "What can I say? She's way ahead of herself."

Brooke let out a second laugh she'd been holding in. "If you're looking for something to do together, I'd be willing to show you my secret place for hunting shells."

Adam turned to Skye. "Ms. Brooke says she has a secret place for seashells. Shall we go there with her?"

"Yes," cried Skye, holding up the net bag. "I want to fill it to the top. Mimi said she'd put them in a glass jar for me."

"That's a great idea," said Brooke, charmed by this little girl. "Follow me."

Brooke and Adam walked together as Skye ran ahead of them like an eager, playful puppy.

"She's adorable. I know about your wife ... your ex ... and

I'm so sorry," said Brooke.

Adam grimaced and shook his head. "I don't like to talk about it. She was a life lesson I won't soon forget. What about you, Brooke? How are things with you? And your mother? I remember she always came here with you."

A stab of guilt hit Brooke in the gut. She hadn't thought about or called her mother for a couple of days now. "Mom's holding on. She still has her ups and downs but is able to work from home. Her health is usually a big question mark."

"I remember her being a nice woman," said Adam. "What about your cousins? I hear all of you are staying for the summer and will be fixing up the Inn. I'm a contractor. Maybe I can help."

"Oh? That might come in handy. How long are you staying?"

"I'm not sure. My brother Brendan and I own the business together, and he's told me to get away for a long-overdue break."

"Brendan's wife just had a baby, right?" said Brooke. "A boy, I heard."

"Yeah, he was the smart one, marrying a woman we all love. I should've listened to my parents." He shrugged. "The best thing to happen to me was having Skye. She makes all the misery worth it."

"Daddy, come look!" cried Skye.

Brooke watched Adam trot away from her and couldn't help wondering what it would've been like to have a doting father. Having been raised alone by her mother with few opportunities to have a man in their lives, she'd never know. She studied Adam and liked what she saw.

When they reached the little inlet, she saw that waves had washed many shells into a pile, just as she'd suspected.

"Be sure and search through them carefully to find perfect

shells for your collection," Brooke said, kneeling beside Skye. "They're all lovely but different, like snowflakes from the sky."

"Sky? That's my name." The little girl grinned at her, and Brooke had an urge to hug her. Skye was a beautiful child with her blond curly hair peeking out from beneath a sunbonnet and big blue eyes that shone with excitement.

"Go ahead and take your time, Skye," said Adam. "I'm going to sit right here on this log to watch you."

"And then will you help me?" Skye said.

"Of course, I just want to give you the chance to find some on your own. I remember what it was like to have no one else around me when I discovered shells by myself."

"Remember all the shell crafts our grandmothers set up for us?" Brooke asked. "Of course, you were much older than I was, so you often were away at school or summer camp."

"Much older? I'm thirty-eight. How old are you?"

"Twenty-eight. Not as different now, but back then, I remember how we all thought you were so old and wise," said Brooke.

"Well, I've proved that I'm not," said Adam, giving her rueful look. He looked out over the water.

"All I know is that you have a beautiful little girl, who I'm sure, is the envy of all the other grandmothers here," said Brooke softly.

Adam looked at her and laughed. "Mimi does love her. I do too, of course."

At that moment, watching the way his face lit with pleasure, Brooke knew the crush she'd had as a teenager was still lurking inside her.

CHAPTER EIGHTEEN

LIVY

Livy awoke to silence in the house and sat up with a start. Eight o'clock. She was supposed to have met John in the kitchen a half hour ago. She quickly got dressed, ran a comb through her hair, and took off, wondering at her lack of discipline. This time in Florida was what she'd needed, but she couldn't get too used to it. She had work to do for Gran. And it was Billy Bob's day off.

She hurried into the kitchen to the aroma of cinnamon and butter and sighed happily. Baking had always filled her senses with pleasure: touch, taste, smell—the whole works.

"Ahh, there you are," said John. "Thought you might not show at all."

Livy placed a hand on her hip and grinned playfully. "You know me better than that. I forgot to reset the alarm clock."

He laughed. "No worries. I've taken care of getting these cinnamon rolls made. Thought we could freeze what we don't use this morning. There are six couples coming in together right after Ellie and I leave."

"We should be starting on our project by then and having these ready will be helpful," said Livy while tying an apron around her waist. She slipped a baseball cap over her curls and went to the dining room to see if the table was set. With only two couples in the Inn, it would be an easy morning, giving her enough time to clean out kitchen cupboards and work on an inventory. Until Gran and John left, the regular routines would be done by them.

As she entered the dining room, she automatically made sure the sideboard was set up for self-service coffee and tea and that John had remembered to put out a selection of juice carafes in a tub of ice.

A man and a woman entered the dining room.

Gran rushed in from the living room. “Good morning, Bill and Sue. I hope you slept well. What do you have planned for the day?”

Bill greeted Gran and poured himself a cup of coffee while Gran and Sue chatted about sights in the area.

Livy quietly left them to help John.

Guests had the option of choosing what they wanted for breakfast ahead of time. It wasn’t a requirement, but it was helpful to John and Billy Bob in the kitchen.

“It’s Bill and Sue,” Livy told John, surprised how well Gran did memorizing people’s names.

John looked at the posting for the day. “Yogurt and fruit for her. Bacon and eggs for him.”

While John started to cook the eggs, Livy prepared a tray for Sue. She carefully arranged yogurt, fresh berries, sliced oranges, and granola. As soon as John plated the pre-cooked bacon and eggs for Bill, along with toast and jam, Livy carried the tray holding their breakfast into the dining room.

“Thanks, Livy,” said Gran when Livy walked into the room. She turned to the people at the table. “May I introduce you to one of my granddaughters? Livy is a professional baker and will be working here for the summer. It’s sure to be delightful for our guests. Please tell your friends.”

Livy said hello, answered their questions about training, and returned to the kitchen with a new respect for Gran. She had an easy way of making everyone feel right at home.

A short while later, the second couple staying on the property ordered a full breakfast of scrambled eggs, sausage, home fries, and plenty of juice. Gran greeted them by name and chatted with them before they got ready to go exploring.

"I don't know how you do it," Livy said to Gran after the guests left the dining room. "You know everyone's names and something about each one, making them feel as if they're friends."

Gran brushed a curl away from Livy's face. "You'd be amazed by how many do become friends. Some guests want their privacy and prefer to be left alone. I respect that."

"One of us will have to take over for you in the mornings," said Livy.

"You'll have to rotate, but to begin, I'd suggest Charlie act as hostess while you work in the kitchen, and Brooke and Beryl, head of housekeeping, review and schedule cleaning requirements for the day."

Livy laughed. "You've already thought this through. How did you know we'd all promise to stay and help you?"

Gran put an arm around her. "All three of you are treasures, and the timing was right for each of you."

Affection washed through Livy. "We all love you, Gran."

"To the moon and back?" Gran said, using one of her favorite sayings.

Livy hugged her tight. "And more."

CHAPTER NINETEEN

CHARLOTTE

Charlotte awoke with a sense of anticipation. While lying in bed, she reviewed her plans for the day. After her mid-day appointment to introduce herself to the hotel supplier in Miami, she was meeting Shane for a late lunch and to look at the non-profit he was working with. It would be a hectic day, but only the first of many trips to Miami, she suspected. She didn't mind the travel and was excited about new marketing ideas that didn't revolve around selling things consumers may or may not need.

When she went downstairs, Brooke was in the kitchen sitting at the table with a cup of coffee.

"Good morning. Another beautiful day. You're up early. What are you up to today?" Charlotte asked.

"Jake and I are going to work on a cash flow budget. Gran has been a shrewd investor, and John's financial contribution has provided enough funds for them to travel and for us to do the upgrades. But until they decide if they're going to sell or not, we need to maintain proper liquidity."

Charlotte agreed, unsure how she felt about Gran selling the Inn. As Gran had requested, neither she nor her cousins had mentioned a word about it to their families.

"You're going to Miami to meet with the hotel supply rep, right?" said Brooke. "We'll need you to get all the financial information about payments, delivery services and charges, and all those details." She gave Charlotte a sheepish smile. "Why am I even saying this? But of course, you will."

Charlotte shrugged. “No problem. What’s up with Livy?”

“She’s working in the kitchen today as usual, but she already texted me that we need to have a meeting soon to discuss equipment and staff assignments. She and Gran were talking about it earlier. Guess we’d better set aside time tomorrow.”

“Okay. I’m going to grab a cup of coffee and get ready to leave. I want to get as much done today as possible.”

“Does it have anything to do with meeting Shane Ensley for lunch?” teased Brooke.

Charlotte laughed but didn’t answer. She knew very well it did.

Charlotte pulled out of the hotel supply company’s parking lot in South Miami and drove to Coconut Grove. She was to meet Shane for a late lunch at one of the restaurants in the new CocoWalk. She loved the idea of a collection of shops, restaurants, and cafés dedicated to the idea of a waterfront neighborhood’s history with an emphasis on family.

His choice of a place to meet pleased her. Of particular interest was that they’d be discussing his non-profit, Family First, a cross between a Big Brother program and a guardian ad litem. She was anxious to hear more about it.

When Charlotte arrived at Theodore’s, she checked the extended outdoor patio but saw no sign of Shane. So, she entered the restaurant and gazed around. The interior was designed to make guests feel as if they were sitting in an outdoor garden. She loved it.

She saw Shane rise from a table in the back of the main room, and smiling, she headed for him.

“Glad you could make it. Have any trouble finding this place from the hotel supplier’s building?”

"No, the supplier's office isn't that far from here," she said, allowing Shane to seat her at the table.

A waiter hurried over to them. "Sorry. I should've seated you. What can I get the two of you to drink?" he asked, handing them each a menu.

Shane asked for water, and Charlotte ordered iced tea.

After the waiter left, Shane turned to her. "I'm glad you could meet me. If you could help with the Family First program, that would be terrific. Though not many people know about it, Family First provides a unique opportunity for teenaged boys. Let's order, and I'll tell you all about it."

Charlotte studied the menu. "M-m-m, everything looks delicious. Any suggestions?"

"They have great sandwiches. Sarita likes their salads," said Shane.

"Sarita?" said Charlotte.

He looked up from his menu. "Sarita is my assistant. A capable woman almost as old as our grandmothers."

"Nice, I didn't mean to pry," said Charlotte.

"You're not," he said simply and returned to his menu.

Charlotte made a quick decision from the menu and then took some time to look around the restaurant. Above the dark-stained wainscoting, the walls were painted a deep green, a perfect backdrop for the pictures of flowers of varying sizes and with different frames that dressed the walls. Live plants with colorful flowers were strategically placed throughout the room. She noticed grow lights hidden among the foliage keeping the plants happy. A simple arrangement of fresh flowers sat in the middle of each table. It was charming, Charlotte thought, taking a sip of her iced tea.

The server appeared to take their lunch orders.

While they waited for their food, Shane told Charlotte more about the Family First program that he and a friend had organized and supported with both time and money.

"With so many single mothers raising teen boys, there's a need for those boys to understand what role they can and should play in the family. In other words, how to be the man of the family in a respectful, loving way that benefits everyone. The idea is for a male volunteer to participate in some family functions subtly demonstrating things like quietly bringing order to younger children instead of screaming at them, holding the door for his mother, even working with the mother of the household to set up a daily schedule of activities, things a father might do if their situation was more traditional."

"How many families do you help?" she asked.

"At the moment, only twenty-five," he replied. "But, of course, we want to add more. Varying levels of help are handled. Sometimes a family needs a lot of help in getting organized. Some kids need tutoring or other activities to keep them off the street."

"Do you have a family you work with?" Charlotte asked, taking the first bite of her crab cake salad. The crabmeat, avocados, and red onions on lettuce topped with a creamy garlic dressing were delicious.

Shane nodded as he tasted his Grouper sandwich. When he could speak, he said, "It's a family with a single mom, a sixteen-year-old boy name Elijah, and three younger siblings in a not-so-great neighborhood. The boy is smart but needs some guidance. It's a lot for his mother and him to handle. She has to work nights so she can be at home during the day after the younger ones get home from their after-school program. The rest of the time, he's in charge." He sighed. "He gets bullied all the time because he's not part of a gang in the neighborhood. So far, he's holding on and remaining strong as he switches back and forth from being a regular kid to a stand-in dad. He's musical, so I'm paying for music lessons for him. Once a month, we have time together for something fun."

"It sounds like an awesome program, and he seems like an awesome kid," Charlotte said. "Where do you get your volunteers, and how many do you have in the program?"

"My law partner and I came up with the idea. We reached out to men in the Big Brother program to help us and have found volunteers and suggestions for kids through the guardian ad litem program. The Department of Children and Families is involved, as well." He grinned. "We have about twenty trained volunteers so far and more in training. We hope to add many more. A lot of young men could use our help."

Charlotte sat back in her chair. "I'm impressed, Shane. Growing up, I thought you were a neat kid, and now I know how right I was."

"Thanks. Even though my parents went through a nasty divorce and my mom wasn't the best, I was pretty lucky growing up. It can be really difficult for some kids. Especially with the way alcohol and drugs have affected families. It seems only right for me to do what I can to change things."

Charlotte was touched by the color that crept into Shane's cheeks and realized that though he was the image of a young, successful man, he was much more. And a little vulnerable at that.

Shane reached into the briefcase sitting on an empty chair at the table and handed her a folder. "Here's more information and some early ideas we had for promotion. We know you can do better."

"I can't wait to begin," said Charlotte. "I'll be doing work for Gran and John, too, trying to upgrade the image of the Inn."

"We can't pay you, but we'd be happy to spread the word if

you're thinking of setting up business here in Florida."

Charlotte's eyes widened in surprise. His words had opened a door into a future she hadn't considered. She wasn't sure what she was going to do after the summer was over, but the thought of staying was something new.

"Right now, we're using an empty space in my office to handle the administrative stuff for the program, but that's about to change," said Shane. "Maybe when you come back, we'll have a new office for you to see."

His cell phone rang. "Excuse me." He clicked onto the call. "Hi, Morgan. Yes, I know I promised to meet with you sometime, but it can't be this evening. I have plans. Okay. Talk to you later."

Charlotte sat still, refusing to let her feelings show.

Shane ended the call and gave Charlotte a sheepish look. "Sorry about that. Granny Liz asked me to be extra nice to Morgan because she's had so many disappointments."

"Oh," said Charlotte, her mind spinning. Was Granny Liz trying to set up something between Shane and Morgan? If so, didn't she understand how awful Morgan could be? The thought of Shane ending up with someone like Morgan caused Charlotte's stomach to fill with acid. But then, it wasn't her business.

"It's been great having this time with you," said Shane, giving her a smile that sent her nerves aflutter. "Thanks for agreeing to help with the program. I apologize, but I have an appointment and can't stay. I look forward to getting your thoughts on the program."

"Fine," she said agreeably.

Shane paid for the bill, walked her to the restaurant's front entrance, gave Charlotte a kiss on the cheek, and waited with her until the valet delivered Charlotte's car to her before walking away.

###

On the drive back to Sanderling Cove, Charlotte thought about Shane. He was different from the men she'd dated in New York. There, appearance, position, money, and power played a big part in their lives. Shane, who had the looks and the background, cared little for money and power. He'd been a natural leader, someone others liked.

She recalled the rush of attraction that had gone through her when he'd smiled at her, praising her willingness to help him. Charisma. That's what he had. He could make anyone want to help him. Lord, she hoped he'd never go into politics. That would ruin him. He was perfect just as he was.

Charlotte forced herself to review her meeting with the hotel supplier. She'd been right with her idea to take advantage of overruns on the supplier's orders. Some of those items were simply not needed; some were experiments that didn't work. But the salesman she talked to at Hotel Supplies, Sol Goldstein, had assured her that he'd be happy to help. He'd already agreed to put together a catalog of sorts for her to consider. All guest rooms had walls painted in one of three colors: sand beige, a pale turquoise, and a soft green, suitable backgrounds for different color combinations for bedspreads and artistic accents. The sheets and towels would remain white. She could hardly wait to get started.

She hadn't yet reached the Inn when she received a phone call from Livy. "Hi, Charlie. I'm on my way out for the evening, but I wanted to tell you that I've set up a meeting for tomorrow morning at eight to talk about various roles for each of us to assume. I want you and Brooke to know what Gran and I discussed and then have her demonstrate a few things."

"Okay. Where are you going? "There was a pause, and then Livy said, "Austin invited me to dinner. As payback for the cookies. Nothing more."

"I see," said Charlotte. "Well, go and have fun. As soon as I can, I'm going to get out of these clothes and into something more comfortable and relax."

"Okay, see you tomorrow," said Livy with a lilt to her voice.

CHAPTER TWENTY

LIVY

Livy waited at Gran's for Austin to pick her up. It seemed silly, really, when she could've easily walked next door to Granny Liz's house. But manners had been an important part of her upbringing, and she liked the fact that he'd suggested it.

Brooke came up beside her. "You nervous?"

Livy laughed. "Not really. It's just Austin."

Brooke elbowed her. "But I know how much you used to like him. No leftover feelings?"

Livy sighed. "I'm not sure, but it wouldn't matter anyway because I'm honestly not interested in a relationship with any man. Wayne did a number on me, almost making me wonder if I could make any decision on my own. I'm never going back to that."

"Austin doesn't seem that way at all," said Brooke. "I'd find that dimple hard to resist."

They laughed together, comfortable sharing their feelings.

Austin pulled into Gran's driveway, and Livy went out the door to greet him. Manners be damned. She wasn't going to stay inside like a damsel in distress waiting to be rescued.

At the sight of her, Austin grinned. "You look great. Hope you're hungry. I've reserved a table at Gavin's at the Salty Key Inn."

"Oh, how nice," said Livy. "I've heard wonderful things about it. I like the story about the three sisters who own it, too."

"Yeah, pretty cool," he said, assisting her into his low-slung, silver Audi A5 convertible. "I've left the top down. Is that a problem for you?" he asked politely.

Livy patted her curls. "Between the breezes and the humidity, I don't think it could get much worse."

He looked at her and laughed. "I like it like that," he said, getting behind the wheel. "Don't worry. I won't go fast enough to make it a mess. The traffic on Gulf Drive doesn't allow it."

Austin drove with confidence, allowing her to study the landscape as they drove by. She loved this unpretentious area of the Gulf Coast with some buildings painted funky colors. But when they drove through the entrance to the Salty Key Inn, she admired the upscale look of the buildings. Standing apart from the guest rooms, Gavin's, the restaurant named after the three owners' uncle, had an excellent reputation for outstanding food.

Austin parked the car and helped her out of it. Then, walking toward the building, they spied a peacock strolling across the lawn heading to the bayfront.

Inside the restaurant, Livy paused, fascinated by what restauranteurs did to make their place unique. The rich paneling on the walls, the crystal sconces matching the sparkling chandeliers, and the crisp, white-linen tablecloths all lent an air of elegance that matched the reputation of the food.

A hostess greeted them, pausing a moment to smile at Austin, and then led them to a table in the corner of the main dining room. "A note was made that you wanted privacy. Hope this table will do," she said smoothly, casting a glance at Livy.

"Thanks," said Austin as a waiter came right over to seat them.

"Welcome," the waiter said, helping Livy get settled in her

chair. He stood aside as a server approached and poured fresh water into their water goblets.

"We're glad you chose to dine with us tonight," said the waiter. "Will you want the wine menu in addition to these?" he asked Austin. He handed menus to Livy and Austin.

"By all means," said Austin.

"Very well, I'll send the wine steward over to you. In the meantime, I'll be happy to answer any questions you might have about the dinner menu."

"Thank you," they said together, and smiled at one another.

Livy eagerly looked over the menu. She loved seeing what new things chefs were creating. She read through the selections carefully, delighting in the possibilities. But her eyes came back to the snapper almondine and rested there.

Austin ordered the rib-eye steak, medium-rare, topped with sautéed mushrooms. He and the wine steward chose a merlot that would go with the steak and not overpower the snapper.

Satisfied that all was set, Austin said, "I'm glad you agreed to go to dinner with me. It's a nice chance for us to talk about ideas for the wi-fi upgrade for your grandmother's inn without her or John overhearing us. When are they leaving on their trip?"

"Next week. It's cute to see how excited they both are. I'm hoping we can get everything done at the Inn that we want this summer." She kept her tone upbeat, but a part of her was fighting disappointment over the fact that he'd invited her for a business dinner, not a social one.

"And then what happens? Any ideas about where you go from there?" Austin asked.

Livy shook her head. "I'm keeping all options open."

"Me, too," Austin said. "I started my business while I was still in college. It took off, and I've been working day and night ever since. Now that it's been sold, I have a lot of choices as to what I'm going to do next. Something in the computer industry, probably."

"Does that mean you'll go back to California after the summer?"

"Not necessarily. Research and development can happen anywhere."

Their wine came, temporarily halting conversation while Austin sampled it. With his approval, the waiter poured a glass for her and then filled Austin's glass and left. After sipping the wine, Livy studied Austin. He looked nothing like a stereotypical geeky guy. He was of average height, muscular, and nice-looking with gray-blue eyes that drew attention.

"So, you don't know what you're doing after the summer," he commented. "What about Charlie?"

"You'll have to ask her yourself," said Livy, realizing he must still have a thing for Charlotte. If that was the case, she wanted nothing to do with Austin's plans to pump her for information. It was good to know where she stood. Livy decided to relax and enjoy the evening.

They easily fell into a conversation about what she perceived was needed in the Inn, especially with new computer programs.

By the time they finished the last of their key lime pie, Livy was as relaxed as she'd been in ages.

The ride back to the cove was pleasantly quiet. Livy liked the fact that she had no need to impress anyone, keep a conversation going, or think about any future dates. Austin had been fun but honest about the reason he'd asked her out. She'd already made a mental note to tell Charlotte that Austin was still interested in her.

CHAPTER TWENTY-ONE

CHARLOTTE

Charlotte met with her cousins in the kitchen the next morning, eager to see what new roles they each might have. She was already excited about the idea of a fresh look at the marketing, and she and Brooke were working together on décor for the rooms.

"What's going on? Why did you want us to meet with you and Gran?" she asked Livy as she helped herself to a cup of coffee.

"In order to make this work, we all need to take over for Gran in addition to the jobs we created for ourselves," said Livy. "Gran is waiting for us at the Inn. Let's go."

Charlotte was impressed by the way her two cousins had taken on leadership roles. She didn't mind. She was used to being in charge with a personal assistant at the office. This was much easier.

Gran met them when they walked into the Inn. "Glad to see you here. Our first two guests of the eight in-house couples will be arriving for breakfast soon. Greeting them is something you all need to do on a rotating basis. Livy, of course, will be limited in what she can do if she's cooking, but she can have her turn too. And I suggest Brooke work with Beryl in scheduling the cleaning staff and inspection of the rooms. That leaves you, Charlie, with the bulk of greeting breakfast guests. But, as I said, all of you need to become comfortable with the task.

"After all the guests have eaten and have either departed or left for the day, we'll meet again, and I'll re-introduce you to Beryl and the two women who will be cleaning the rooms today. You all have to know all the routines so you can establish schedules to make sure everyone has some time off. Of course, if we have a full house, nobody gets much time off."

"And if we want to provide special dinners for small groups or special nights for locals, we'll have to hire more temporary help," said Livy. "After seeing how dining is handled at Gavin's, I am full of new ideas."

"Gavin's? Is that where Austin took you?" said Brooke.

Livy smiled and held up a hand. "It was a business dinner. He's still caught up in Charlie."

"Me?" said Charlotte. "Why would he be? I admit he's adorable, but he's not for me."

"Of course not," said Livy. "You're hooked on his brother."

"Shane?" Charlotte shook her head. "I'm not interested in anything more than helping him with the non-profit he formed with his partner." She knew she might be lying, but if she admitted it, her cousins would be impossible with their teasing.

"We'll see," said Brooke, giving her a knowing look. "Shane is a great guy."

It was a moment before Charlotte noticed Gran on the sidelines beaming at them and realized she and her cousins sounded like high school girls before an upcoming prom.

"Okay, everyone," said Charlotte. "Guests are heading this way."

She stood in the background with Livy and Brooke, listening as Gran greeted them cheerily.

Gran spoke as if she was a gracious hostess to the guests she'd invited to her special home. Soon, she had them chatting about some of the local restaurants, where they lived, the purpose of their trip, and the details of their lives the woman was more than happy to share. When Gran offered to make reservations for them at the restaurant they'd talked about, Charlotte noticed the look of delight that crossed the woman's face.

Charlotte and Brooke followed Livy into the kitchen, where Livy and John began to work on the food order.

"Gran sure is smooth," said Brooke. "It's perfect that you'll more or less be in charge of that, Charlie. I'm better at working with Beryl and the housekeepers."

Charlotte realized that running the Inn in addition to handling the upgrades and marketing was going to be a full-time job. She looked at John helping Livy prepare the breakfast and wondered how John and Gran had managed to do all the work they did. No wonder they wanted an extended vacation.

Later, as they observed Gran and Beryl working with the cleaning crew, she realized how important it was to have high-quality bedspreads, sheets, and towels. She also understood that though it might be nice to have different colored towels in the rooms, it was much more practical to have towels of one color, so they were interchangeable between guest rooms.

When Beryl handed out her checklist for the cleaning of any room, Charlotte appreciated the details. But then, you couldn't expect guests to pay top dollar for a room that wasn't spotless. She decided to make a call to The Beach House Hotel to see if she could speak to one of the owners. She had a question or two to ask them.

That afternoon, Charlotte sat in the office with Brooke and Livy. She'd made arrangements to speak to Ann Sanders at The Beach House Hotel at three o'clock. Both Brooke and Livy had paper and pen in hand. She punched in the number she'd been given and waited.

“Good afternoon, Ann Sanders speaking,” said a soft, pleasant voice.

”Hello, Ann. This is Charlotte Bradford from the Sanderling Cove Inn. You agreed to answer some questions for my cousins, Olivia Winters, Brooke Weatherby, and me. The three of us are doing an upgrade to the property this summer and have admired what you and Rhonda Grayson have done with The Beach House Hotel and wanted to get your perspective on the success of it.”

“I'm happy to answer any questions you have. I've heard of the Inn. It has an excellent reputation.”

“It did, but it's fading a bit. May I put you on speaker phone so my cousins can hear?”

“Of course. You must know I love the idea of three women working together to put a little shine on your place.”

“Why do you think The Beach House Hotel is such a success?” Charlotte said, reading off a list they'd put together.

“Rhonda and I believe that each guest is important and should be greeted with genuine warmth. Unfortunately, we don't always have the time, but when we do, we welcome our guests in person.”

“Yes, my grandmother believes the same. What about including the local residents? Your restaurant is open for both hotel guests and locals. Is it worth the effort?”

“Yes,” said Ann. “It's important for us to welcome everyone for both the revenue it produces and the goodwill it generates in the community. There are some people on the neighborhood association board who think we overdo it at times, but we've managed to avoid any real interference.”

“I see,” said Charlotte. “We're lucky to have the support of the other four families who live in the cove. Normally, we wouldn't provide dinner, but it's an idea we're working on.

First, we have to take care of a few other things. How about your rooms? Do they all look alike?"

"While they have some of the same soft goods like bedspreads, we add different touches to each room to make it unique. Each room is tasteful without overdoing the beach theme, if you understand what I mean."

"Oh, yes," said Charlotte, echoing her cousins. "What about cleaning the rooms? Do you do anything special?"

"We make sure each room is clean, of course, but again, we do something special in each room—fresh flowers, turn-down service, and chocolates on the pillows at night, the usual."

After completing their list of questions, Charlotte said, "Thanks a lot for your help. The Sanderling Cove Inn has had an exceptional reputation in the past. Rather than allowing it to become something less, my cousins and I want to make it something more."

"Oh, yes," said Ann, with a smile in her voice. "Never be ashamed to state you have a high-end product. But if you advertise it that way, you must follow through to make sure it lives up to its reputation. It's something Rhonda and I work for every day with our staff."

"You both are an inspiration to us. Thank you for your time," said Charlotte, thrilled with Ann's answers. It was everything she'd been thinking all along.

"Good luck to the three of you," said Ann. "We're wishing you the best. Let me know when you're in town. We'd love to meet with you. We women have to stick together." She chuckled. "Rhonda's here. She says, 'Damn right' on sticking together."

Laughing, Charlotte said, "Thanks again," and ended the call.

She turned to Brooke and Livy. "What do you think? She answered all our questions and that's exactly what we had in mind. Right?"

"Yes," said Brooke. "I like the idea about adding meals when the time is appropriate."

"It will be a lot of work, but I think it'll be well worth it," said Livy. "But only when we're completely ready to do it."

"Now we need to get to work on our upgrade budget," said Brooke. She turned to Livy, "Are you sure Austin will do all the consulting for free and provide equipment and products at his discount?"

"That's what he said, and I believe him," Livy replied smiling. "Should we draw up a contract with him anyway?"

Brooke added something to a list in front of her. "Oh, yes. That's exactly what we're going to do. We need to document any free labor and supplies. Adam Atkins is a contractor and has offered to help with any projects."

"Fantastic" said Charlotte. "I haven't seen him yet. I heard he's here with his little girl."

"Yes," Brooke said. "Her name is Skye. She's four and is adorable."

Charlotte noticed the way Brooke's eyes lit but didn't say anything. She was getting as bad as the grandmothers trying to match up everyone.

"By the way," said Livy, refilling her glass of water from a pitcher of water, "I ran into Morgan. Guess who she has a date with tonight?"

"Shane," said Charlotte, careful to keep her voice even. Though he was doing it to be nice to Morgan as his grandmother had requested, the thought of Shane with Morgan made her unhappy.

The next morning, after Charlotte had greeted three couples staying at the Inn, she went into the office to work on some ideas she had for the non-profit. Brooke was working with Beryl and the cleaning staff, and the office was quiet.

Charlotte had thought a lot about the Family First program, liking it more and more. She wanted to make it easy for anyone interested in volunteering to have a single number to call, a website to go to, and an easy way to text a message.

She lifted the business card Shane had handed her and punched in the number for his office.

A musical voice answered. “Ensley and Jenkins. How may I help you?”

“I’d like to speak to Shane Ensley, please,” said Charlotte.

“I’m sorry, he’s not here. May I connect you to his partner, Jed Jenkins?” she asked.

Charlotte paused. “Yes, thank you.” Shane’s partner, she knew, was as involved in the Family First project as Shane.

“Jed Jenkins. How may I help you?”

“Hello, I’m Charlotte Bradford, a friend of Shane. I’m working on marketing for the Family First project, and I need to ask him, or you, about setting up contact information.”

“Oh, you’re the Charlie that he told me about. Sure, shoot. What do you need?”

Charlotte explained that she’d revise the website and would need to be able to list ways for interested parties to contact them for volunteering and further information.

“It’s important to make it easy for them to reach someone within the organization. We need to build interest for not only volunteers, but also those who want to reach out for help and those willing to donate money. What do you suggest? Is someone going to be available to help? Can you provide confidentiality? That sort of thing,” said Charlotte.

“At the moment, our office assistant, Sarita, takes down any information that comes in and passes it on to the head of volunteers or Shane and me,” said Jed. “But I get that if we’re going to expand, we need to have someone in charge of the entire operation. Interested?"

Charlotte laughed. "I guess Shane didn't tell you that I'm working with my two cousins at my grandmother's Inn, about to do a lot of upgrades to it as we manage it this summer."

"Ah, I know something about Sanderling Cove and the Inn there. Tell you what, how about I discuss how to set this up with a few people, and then I'll come to your coast to talk it over with you. You can show me what you have in mind for the website. I need a break anyway."

Relief filled Charlotte. "That'll work. I believe Shane will be here this weekend. We can all discuss it then. Thanks for the idea. That'll save me a trip to Miami."

"No problem," said Jed. "I'm grateful for any help you can give us. Shane said you're superb at this."

"We'll see. I'm excited about this program and hope it does well. Goodbye. See you soon," said Charlotte.

"Thanks again," said Jed and clicked off the call.

Out of curiosity, Charlotte googled Jed Jenkins. He didn't have the movie star looks of Shane, but he was an attractive man with chestnut hair, hazel eyes, and a friendly smile. Better than that, he seemed a kind and humble man.

Next, Charlotte took a look at the website for the Inn. She'd wait until after the rooms were redecorated before photographing them. In the meantime, she thought she could get some better shots of the outdoor areas.

The landscaping for all five houses and the Inn was overseen by Ambrose Pappas and his two sons, who owned Pappas and Sons Landscaping. Amby had been working on the property for over twenty years and took pride in his work, resulting in a beautiful outcome.

Charlotte went outside and walked over to the gazebo. It was the perfect place for a small wedding ceremony. White paint gleamed on the spindles of the balustrade that enclosed it and on the gingerbread corner braces that hung down from its green roof. Inside, benches lined the perimeter of the building, leaving plenty of space for activities. One of her favorite memories was the tea parties she'd shared with Gran and her cousins there.

She was wondering what to focus on when she heard a voice behind her. "Hey, Charlie, what are you doing?"

She turned. Dylan was walking toward her, his shorts and T-shirt covered in splashes of colored paint.

"I'm taking some photographs of the Inn for the website I'm redoing."

"Want any help? I brought a few of my cameras with me. I often take photographs of scenes I like to use in an abstract way for my paintings."

Charlotte grinned. "Would you be willing to take photographs both outside and inside the Inn? I'd work with you on exactly what I want."

"Sure. It would be fun to spend some time with you. Everyone is so busy doing their own thing, and we don't get to see much of one another until evenings on the beach together."

Charlotte had always liked Dylan. Quieter than some of the other kids, he had a sense of fun they'd all enjoyed. "Your help would be appreciated."

"Okay, deal. Let me get one of my cameras for outdoor shots of the gazebo."

"Thanks. I don't want any photos of the pool area until we bring in some new furniture."

"See if you like what I do, and we can go from there. This will give me a break from painting."

Brooke saw her from the patio and came over.

Charlotte explained what she was doing and how Dylan

was helping.

"He's a great guy," said Brooke. "Very creative. I think you'll make a terrific team."

Adam joined them. "What's up?"

Charlotte told him about the new photographs she wanted and how Dylan had promised to help.

"I told Brooke if there's any construction work you needed to be done, I'm available," Adam said. He glanced at Brooke.

Brooke beamed at him, her smile lighting her face. "I have some ideas, but I haven't presented them to my cousins yet. Nothing major but a lot of little touches that will make a big difference."

"Want to show me?" said Adam.

"Sure, but no decisions until my cousins approve," said Brooke. "I'm in charge of the finances, and that's what we agreed on."

"Go ahead and show him around," said Charlotte, aware of their interest in one another.

Dylan arrived, and she and Dylan spent the next hour working with his camera, talking about ideas for photo shoots for the Inn.

Later, hot from the sun, they retired to the Inn's kitchen where Livy was making a coffee cake for the next morning.

"Smells delicious," said Dylan taking a seat at the small table in the corner of the room.

"Sorry. I can't give you any of this, but there are some muffins left over from this morning. Help yourself," said Livy as she placed the coffee cake on a cooling rack.

"Livy, you're one in a million," said Dylan taking a bite of muffin and rolling his eyes with pleasure.

Livy and Charlotte exchanged amused glances. Charlotte was aware that Livy would never settle for a man who didn't see her beyond her fabulous treats.

CHAPTER TWENTY-TWO

ELLIE

Ellie stood in the central yard of the cove, scarcely believing the time had come for her to leave with John for their extended vacation. Where had the days gone? The girls had already been here for two whole weeks, sizing up the situation at the Inn, learning the ropes of being hostess and businesswoman combined. At one time, she'd wondered if she'd be truly comfortable having others tend to her "baby." Now, she was content to hand it over to her granddaughters. They'd all proven to be more than capable.

"Ellie, we're going to miss you." Liz stepped forward out of the crowd who'd gathered to give them a farewell. Liz put her arms around her and whispered, "Don't worry. Now that Austin has set up my computer, I'll let you know what's going on. Looks like we might have a few possibilities."

Chuckling, Ellie returned her hug and glanced at the people around them. On this Saturday morning, most of the young people had joined their elders in wishing them farewell. It did her heart good to see them. As she'd mentioned to her granddaughters, Sanderling Cove was a special place where all the kids had been treated equally by all the adults. Even now, Ellie knew how others were stepping in to help Charlotte, Livy, and Brooke with their plans for the Inn.

Larry Atkins and Sam Ensley were talking with John while the others took turns hugging her. Tears filled Ellie's eyes. It would be nice to get away, but she'd carry these people and this place with her.

CHAPTER TWENTY-THREE

CHARLOTTE

Charlotte walked with her cousins beside Gran and John as they headed to the limousine they'd hired to take them to Miami. From there, Gran and John would fly to London's Heathrow Airport.

As much as she loved Gran's independence, Charlotte had sided with her cousins that the family needed to know that Gran and John were married before taking off on their trip. Gran surprised them by agreeing, even announcing that she'd host a family party in the fall when she and John returned from Europe. Gran had waited to make the calls to the family until last night to ensure there would be no fuss, no family visits before they took off. Charlotte was glad Gran had stood firm on this decision. She could imagine what her mother might say, or even Aunt Leigh. Propriety was so important to them. Aunt Jo would simply be hurt not to be a part of it.

Charlotte kissed Gran and John goodbye and stood by as they slid into the backseat of the limo.

As the limo eased out of the driveway, Charlotte waved and held back tears until the car carrying its passengers disappeared. In the quiet that followed, she noticed her cousins were as emotional as she. The three of them were now on their own, working and living together to make things happen at the Inn.

"Are we all set for our guests?" Charlotte asked Brooke. Six couples were arriving within hours of one another for a week's stay—a reunion of some sort.

Brooke gave her a little salute. “All guest rooms have passed inspection.”

“Cookies have been made and set out, along with ice water and iced tea,” said Livy.

No sooner had those words been spoken than a car came down the driveway toward them. The three of them exchanged nervous glances. This was it. They were beginning the journey.

Charlotte hurried inside to get ready to register and welcome the guests. She agreed that a personal appearance was in order, just as Ann and Rhonda practiced at The Beach House Hotel.

Behind the small registration desk, Charlotte greeted their arrivals. From outside Atlanta, this middle-aged couple with pleasant smiles were repeat customers. Dave and Lindy Lewis had arranged for five other couples in their neighborhood social group to come to the Inn for the beginning of a summer break.

“Last year, we went to New Orleans for a week,” Lindy explained. “This year, with our kids older, we’re here for a rest before our summers explode with activities. Some of our kids are driving, some working, and others are going to camp.”

“We’ve delighted you’ve chosen The Sanderling Cove Inn for your vacation. I’m Charlotte Bradford, here to serve you along with my cousins, Livy and Brooke. We all hope you’ll have a delightful time here.”

“The guys and I have arranged to go deep-sea fishing,” said Dave.

“How exciting. St. John’s Pass is a great place to line up a captain for a day of fishing,” said Charlotte, glad she’d read up on all the local activities.

“We gals will have a day at the spa right down the road from here,” Lindy said. “I can’t wait.”

"It all sounds fabulous," Charlotte said. "Help yourself to fresh cold drinks, coffee, or tea along with Livy's famous chocolate chip cookies any time throughout the day. At five o'clock, hors d'oeuvres and wine will be available for you and our other guests." She looked at Dave's belly and quickly added, "cold beer too."

"Perfect," said Lindy. "I hope you've put us in downstairs rooms as we requested."

"Oh, yes. They're all reserved for you," said Charlotte. She looked up as Brooke entered the room. "Here's my cousin, Brooke, to help show you the way."

"No worries, we can find the rooms," said Dave. He turned to Lindy. "I'll get the things from our car and meet you there, honey,"

"Why don't I walk you there to make sure everything is in order?" Brooke said to Lindy, who smiled her thanks.

After they left, Charlotte noted what she wanted included in a simple online check-in system for guests. It would become part of the reservations system Austin was already working on.

Over the next two hours, the rest of the guests arrived in pairs. They seemed a happy group and were already talking about meeting on the lanai for drinks and a swim.

After the last arrival, Charlotte checked the pool area.

With Gran's blessing, they'd ordered some new pool furniture and had also bought inexpensive but tasteful extra side chairs for gatherings on the pool deck. In addition, they'd picked up some cute plastic stemware and plastic glasses for pool and lanai use.

Satisfied things were in order there, Charlotte went into the kitchen to see how Livy was doing with hors d'oeuvres for the group. Usually, whoever was on duty would simply set out cheese and crackers, pretzels, nuts, and other easy snacks for cocktail hour. But they'd decided to experiment with a new routine to see what worked and what didn't.

Livy was taking a tray of cheese puffs out of the oven. "If these are a hit, I'll make more tomorrow and freeze them, so they're available at all times."

"That new freezer you wanted is moving up the list of wants, huh?" said Charlotte.

Livy laughed. "It's not going to be easy to stick to our budget, but Brooke will make sure we do. She's a taskmaster, for sure."

"Me?" said Brooke. "I heard that. Just sticking to my job. What's going on with you two?"

"I'm going to open the cocktail hour, and then I have a date," said Livy. "Eric Simon asked me to go out to a bar he likes. He couldn't get Morgan to go with him, so I said I'd go. We're not into each other except as friends. Besides, tomorrow he has to go back to his condo in Tampa because he has some surgeries scheduled this week."

"I admire him and his work," said Charlotte. "When you think about it, there are a lot of interesting people in the cove families. Have fun. I'm staying in tonight because I have to get up early for breakfast time tomorrow." She shook her head. "I don't know how you did it, Livy, getting up at 4 o'clock each morning to bake."

Livy laughed. "This is a lot easier."

"I'm going to babysit Skye tonight," said Brooke. "Mimi Karen had plans for the evening. Adam and Dylan are hitting a couple of bars, and I agreed to watch her. I don't mind. She's adorable."

"You'll make such a fabulous mother one day," said Livy.

"Yes, and you're so loving with Aunt Jo," Charlotte said.

"How are things going with her and you?"

A shadow passed over Brooke's features. "She's not calling me every day like she usually does. When we talk, she seems to be down, but we've agreed to talk no more often than every three days, and I think it's best that way. She can't rely upon me as her social life."

Charlotte placed an arm around Brooke. "I envy your relationship with your mother, but I know it's been hard on you. I'm glad you're here with us."

Brooke's face brightened. "Yeah. Gran told me in no uncertain terms to change the old pattern of constantly checking on her as she wants, making sure she's happy. 'Time for both of us to be independent,' she said."

Charlotte exchanged glances with Livy. "Livy and I support you. Let us know if we can help."

"Thanks." Brooke's eyes were shiny with tears. "I can't tell you how happy I am to be here."

"Group hug," said Livy, and the three of them wrapped their arms around one another.

Later, Charlotte checked to make sure no phone calls had come in to the office, and then she left the Inn to go for a walk on the beach. Outside, the early evening sun was playing hide and seek with puffy white clouds. She slipped off her sandals and wiggled her toes in the sand, her thoughts drifting to what she'd told Brooke. It was true. She wished she had a different kind of relationship with her mother, a kinder one, a gentler acceptance of one another.

She walked into the frothy foam at the water's edge and took another step, allowing the water to swirl above her ankles. Its coolness refreshed her even as her mind spun. Brooke wanted a family; Livy wanted to continue her cooking in a different setting, in a different way. But what did she want for herself?

Charlotte thought of her work with the Family First group and realized she'd been happier doing that than she'd been in a long time. And she was learning to love the hospitality business even as she wondered if she wanted to work 24/7. Maybe she was spoiled as her mother thought. Many people had to work long hours. Some had to work two jobs, or even three to get by. Why did she feel so restless?

Staring out at the movement of the waves, she realized what had been bothering her. She wanted a real relationship with a man she liked before she even loved him. Maybe this idea of Gran and her friends to bring all the cove kids together wasn't a bad one. They were people she could trust, people who might help her understand her previous reluctance to get involved in a deep relationship. In New York, she was sometimes shallow—someone she didn't necessarily like. Here, she could be the person Gran had always loved.

She turned at the call of her name and faced Shane. Her lips curved happily. "Hi. What are you doing here?"

He shrugged. "Morgan and I are going out. She's been asking me, and I think she's feeling a little left out."

"Morgan can be a lot of fun," said Charlotte, surprisingly protective of her. Even though Morgan could go overboard on getting noticed, Charlotte understood how hard it would be to compete for attention when her sister Melissa was around. Melissa was a presence that Morgan couldn't match.

"Yeah," said Shane. "It's no big deal. Just for one evening." He stood by as she emerged from the water. "I spoke to my partner, Jed. He told me he's coming here to meet with you on Saturday. Something about the website and contact information."

"Yes. I spoke with him the other day. He wants to see what I'm doing to the website, and we're going to get all the contact information squared away. Want to join us?"

"I wish I could, but I promised my Family First family that I'd do something special with them. I can't back out of it. I'm sure Jed will fill me in." He studied her and then kicked at the sand with the toe of his running shoe. "Maybe we can go out sometime."

She studied him. He was a puzzle to her, remote from time to time. "That would be nice."

"Did your grandmother and John get a respectable sendoff?" Shane asked. "I couldn't make it here in time to see it."

"Yes. It's really happening," she said. "I'm so excited for them."

"Me, too," said Shane, with a note of sincerity in his voice. "They are two of my favorite people. I hope they have a wonderful trip."

"I'm sure they will," said Charlotte. "I'd better get back. We have guests in-house, and I want to make sure all is okay."

Shane went on his way, jogging along the sand with an easy lope. She watched him for a minute and then headed up to the Inn.

CHAPTER TWENTY-FOUR

BROOKE

Brooke loved when Skye greeted her with a hug. She knelt beside her.

"We're going to have fun tonight. I'll tuck you in with stories. Your Daddy said you like books. I do, too."

"Can we read a Charlie and Zeke story?" asked Skye.

"Sure. Do you have one here?" Lee Merriweather had written a series of books about a boy named Charlie and his dog Zeke and all the discoveries they made about the world around them.

Skye raced away.

"I appreciate your doing this for me," said Adam facing her. "It's been a while since I've been able to get away for an evening."

"I'm happy to do it," Brooke said, smiling at him. "I like kids, and I didn't have any other plans."

"Mom said she was sorry she couldn't be here to thank you herself," Adam said.

"No worries. As I said, I'm happy to do this." She turned as Skye came running toward her holding a book. "Here it is."

"Terrific. We'll read it later. I thought we'd play a game or two before bedtime." She held up the deck of cards she'd borrowed from the Inn.

Skye's eyes rounded. "Really?"

"Sure," said Brooke. She knew several card games after playing so many of them with her mother when she was young.

"Sounds like you two are going to have fun, Punkin. Give Daddy a kiss goodbye," Adam stooped to hug Skye, who threw her arms around his neck.

" 'Bye."

"Where's Dylan?" Brooke asked as he straightened.

Adam gave her a teasing grin. "Waiting for me to pick him up. I'm driving. Safer that way."

He and Brooke laughed together. Dylan would never live down the night he'd snuck booze out of his grandparents' home when he was fourteen and had proceeded to get drunk, even driving their car in the driveway and on the road around the cove. He'd never been much of a drinker since.

Even though Skye was asleep, Brooke continued reading aloud the last page of a book about a pig who wanted to fly. The story, and the moral behind it, was adorable. Then, carefully, she closed the book and placed it on top of the pile of books they'd read together. In the morning, Skye would find them nearby.

She went downstairs and out to the porch. There, she drew in a breath of fresh salty air and lowered herself into one of the rocking chairs. Skye was a lovely child who made Brooke realize how much she wanted children of her own, but she was hesitant about the idea of commitment. This summer was her time to find herself, to be free to do what she wanted, and when. Charlotte and Livy might think they knew her, but they'd be surprised at how determined she was to step away from any relationship that might become serious. Maybe, like Livy, she'd be willing to socialize with so-called friends, but that would be all.

CHAPTER TWENTY-FIVE

LIVY

The best thing about being just friends with a guy was that she could truly relax. And being away from her mother's expectations was even better. As far as her mother was concerned, Livy was spending a summer working at the Inn with no prospects in sight. That's how she intended to keep it.

Sitting with Eric in the Pink Pelican restaurant, Livy laughed at one of his corny jokes. If you didn't know that he was a doctor held in high regard, you might guess he was a computer nerd.

The restaurant was cute, with its pink walls displaying a collection of pictures and photographs of pelicans. Pelican salt and pepper shakers, glasses with images of pelicans on them complemented the "neighborhood bar" feel to the place. Livy sipped her beer and ate her grouper sandwich.

"I talked to Shelby last night," Eric said. "She's hoping you'll consider providing baked items to her restaurant. She tasted your cookies and loved them. I did, too."

Livy returned his smile. "Thanks, but I'm not sure what I'm going to do in the future. Right now, my cousins and I are concentrating on the Inn. We'd like to turn things around there, bring it back to its former glory."

"What happened to it?" asked Eric. "It's been a nice place, an acceptable addition to the cove."

Livy shrugged. "Nothing serious. I think Gran and John are just tired of running it. And they haven't done much to keep it up to speed in the wi-fi arena."

"Austin said he's donating time and equipment to help you. He's generous."

"Yes," Livy said. "All of us cove kids are pretty good guys."

Eric's eyebrows lifted. His gaze swept over her, and he grinned. "Guys doesn't refer to some of us."

Even as she felt heat rise to her cheeks, Livy laughed. It felt so satisfying to be appreciated for something other than her cooking.

CHAPTER TWENTY-SIX

CHARLOTTE

Charlotte waited anxiously for Jed to arrive, curious to see what kind of person he was. She'd already seen pictures of him online, and he looked nice, with a pleasant smile. She reviewed the changes she'd made to what had been an uninteresting website. She'd added color, switched photographs around, cleaned up the way people could react by volunteering, donating, or simply requesting more information. The important thing was to make sure all those contact points were ready.

At the appointed hour of eleven, Jed pulled up in a beige Lexus SUV. Charlotte left her post in the reception area and went to greet him.

He climbed out of the car and waved as he walked toward her carrying a briefcase. "Hello, Charlie. We finally meet."

Charlotte returned his smile and shook his hand. "Thanks for coming on a weekend day. How was the drive?"

"Pretty boring crossing Alligator Alley, but that's okay. Gave me time to think about this work. You're right. We have to set up the proper structure for the group, get more volunteers, more funds."

"Come on in. What can I get you to drink? Coffee? Tea? Lemonade?"

"Just plain water, thank you," he said, following her inside.

In the office, he set down his briefcase. "Let's see what you've come up with." He pulled a chair up next to hers, and they both sat down.

She showed him some different banners they could use and talked about establishing clear lines of communication.

He sat back in his chair. “I like what I see. Your banner showing children of all ages is catchy, and I like the color scheme of blue and gold. The way you’ve organized the material is great, with easy links for more action. But, after seeing this, I’m more convinced than ever that we need to hire and fund a director for the project. We’ve talked about it, of course, but we can’t continue as we have been with Sarita doing much of the work.”

“Can you get government funding for your project?” Charlotte asked.

His face lit. “I hadn’t thought of that. Let me work on that and get the word out that we’re looking for someone to run the program. Until then, Shane and I can fund a temporary person. I’m sure he’ll agree with me on this.”

Charlotte studied him. “How did you and Shane meet? And when did you decide to go into business together?”

“We met at Stetson University, ended up becoming roommates and decided to open an office together. We each chose Family Law for different reasons, but we’ve worked well together.”

“Is your family from Florida?” Charlotte asked, genuinely interested.

A shadow crossed his face. “My mother and I lived in Gulfport, where the school is located. Unfortunately, she died before I graduated.”

“I’m sorry,” said Charlotte. “That must have been difficult.”

“It still is,” he said, gazing out the window. “Drug overdose.”

Saddened by the pain in his voice, Charlotte decided to change things a bit. “I’d like to show you the Inn if you’re interested. My cousins and I are working on upgrades for it.”

"Including its website?" asked Jed.

She laughed. "You checked it out?"

"Yup," he said. "Wanted to know what we were getting into, hiring you."

"I'm doing this for free," countered Charlotte.

"Oh, I know, but it still has to be right. Shane sometimes leads with his heart."

"And you don't?" she asked him, giving him a steady look.

"Sometimes I do," he answered with a shrug.

"I've always admired Shane," said Charlotte. "All of us kids in the cove still do, he being the oldest and a natural leader."

Jed smiled and nodded. "He's a great guy, but he can be a real heartbreaker."

"What do you mean?" she said, surprised.

"Women go crazy over him, but he ends any relationship that becomes too serious. I'm not sure why. Maybe something to do with his mother." Jed pulled his fingers through his brown hair. "Don't know why I said that. Let's see the rest of the Inn. A lot of people I know like to get out of Miami once in a while. This might be a nice place for them to stay."

Charlotte pushed aside thoughts of Shane. "Well, then, let's take a look."

After showing Jed around the Inn, Charlotte led him into the office once more to discuss what to look for in hiring a head of volunteers for Family First.

Livy surprised them by bringing in a plate of cookies and iced water. "Here. You can be my testers. It's a new recipe for molasses cookies."

Charlotte made the introductions, amused by the admiring looks Jed gave to both Livy and the plate of cookies.

"Wow," said Jed, biting into a cookie, his hazel-eyed gaze

settling on Livy.

"Enjoy," she said and turned to go.

"Wait! I know we just met, but are you free for dinner?" Jed asked. "Charlotte and Shane can vouch for me."

Livy paused, studied him, and nodded. "Make it early. Let's say six."

"Okay, thanks," said Jed. He turned to Charlotte. "Do you have an available room for tonight?"

She laughed. "I'm sure we do." Charlotte admired Livy's cool attitude. In her own way, she was as magnetic to men as Shane apparently was to women.

That evening, Charlotte was sitting on Gran's porch reading a book to escape the pressure of trying to come up with new ideas for the Inn's website. As she'd discovered working with the Family First project, things behind the scenes had to be in place before the website could be completed. Until the rooms were renovated, she couldn't take new photographs of them for the Inn's website.

The same held true for the rest of the property. She needed to meet with Brooke and Livy as soon as possible to finalize the purchase list for the Inn so she could move forward.

She sighed and stared out at the water moving in its usual rhythmic pattern. If she were honest with herself, she'd admit that more than websites were on her mind.

She was in the middle of her cozy mystery when a face appeared at the porch railing. She jumped. "Shane, what are you doing here? I thought you were in Miami."

He chuckled. "Sorry to scare you. I came back for the rest of the weekend. Have time to go out for a drink?"

"No, thanks," said Charlotte. "I'm staying in tonight and relaxing."

"How about something right here, then?" His smile was engaging.

"Okay, come on in. I'll get something for both of us," she said, rising. "How about a glass of red wine?"

"Fine with me. I'm going to turn in early, too."

After hearing Jed's words about him, Charlotte wanted to know more about Shane. She went into the kitchen to fix their drinks.

Shane came inside and followed her there. "How did it go with Jed?"

"Pretty well. I'm sure he'll talk to you about it, but it's apparent you need to hire a fulltime coordinator for the project."

"Makes sense. We're getting busier and busier," said Shane accepting the glass she handed him. "Glad you had a chance to meet Jed."

"I liked him. He was sincere and straightforward. Even about you."

His brow creased. "Me?"

She smiled playfully at him. "It seems you have a reputation as a love 'em and leave 'em sort of guy."

Shane shook his head and set down his glass. "I just haven't found the right person yet, and I don't want to lead anyone on."

"How did it go with Morgan the other night?" Charlotte asked, curious in spite of herself.

"I've already told her we're just friends, nothing more." He sighed. "She's one mixed-up woman. If she isn't an alcoholic now, she's on her way."

"I've wondered about that," said Charlotte. "I'm glad you were honest with her." She hesitated. "The man my mother thought I should wed and I agreed that we'd be honest with one another. It made things easier for us, even though our parents were disappointed when we told them we'd never marry."

"Yeah, honesty is the best policy," Shane said. "After seeing how destructive a bad marriage can be, I don't want even to be in a relationship with any woman unless I'm sure about her. My parents were miserable; it got pretty ugly."

"Okay. We've agreed to be just friends," said Charlotte.

"Friends," said Shane, clicking his glass against hers.

They sat on the porch and stared out at the water. The moon lit a bright path atop the moving waves making Charlotte think of the yellow brick road in the Wizard of Oz. So many possibilities lay ahead of her. If only she knew what it was that she truly wanted.

"A penny for your thoughts," said Shane smiling at her.

"I was thinking of all the possibilities ahead. I don't know what I want to do in the future, only what I don't want," she said. "What about you? Where do you see yourself in another couple of years?"

He was silent, and then he spoke, staring out at the empty beach. "I will be continuing my work with family law. Hopefully, the Family First project will be fully supported by then. Personally? I'm not sure. Granny Liz keeps telling me I need to settle down and raise a family, but she doesn't realize how much my parents' marriage made a lasting impression on me. I know friends who are happily married, but I'm not sure that's for me."

"I understand. I've wasted a lot of time floundering, wondering why I couldn't get excited about marrying someone and realized it was because I never wanted to stay in New York. Being here has proved that to me."

"Granny Liz and her friends, including your grandmother, think it's a clever idea to bring us all together," Shane said. "But it might be a waste."

Charlotte shook her head. "I'm not sure about that. Everybody here is pretty special. We're a mixed group, but unique." She held up her hand. "I'm not saying it will work, but in the meantime, I intend to enjoy seeing everyone."

"You and Austin?" Shane asked.

"No," said Charlotte, "that was a long time ago. Maybe he and Livy?"

Shane laughed. "Jed texted me that he's taking Livy out to dinner. That almost never happens. He doesn't usually move that fast."

"Livy is a nice person ..."

"... and a wonderful cook," said Shane.

She chuckled. "There might be something to that old adage about winning a man's heart."

"Those cookies of hers are damn good," said Shane. "Can't beat that. What about Brooke? She's as attractive as the rest of you."

"She's a lot like me in that she isn't looking for anything except a chance to be away from caring for her mother."

Shane finished his wine and set the glass down on the table between them. "I'd better go. It was nice just to sit and talk. Thanks for all you're doing for Family First."

"My pleasure," Charlotte replied honestly. "It's a special program."

She walked Shane out of the house, watched him trot next door, and went back inside to read. As she picked up where she'd left off, the hero on the page morphed into a tall, blonde, man with a smile that made her happy.

CHAPTER TWENTY-SEVEN

BROOKE

After spending time with Eric sitting by the bonfire the group had been building every night, Brooke headed back to Gran's. Eric was an interesting man, she decided—a skilled physician, a nerdy guy who was a gentle soul attuned to people. She knew what it was like to take care of others and loved that he did it with such grace and attention to detail.

Others had joined them by the fire. Even though her pulse raced at the sight of Adam walking toward them, she reminded herself not to get involved. He'd made it clear to everyone he was glad to see them, but that's all this break was to him—a chance to heal after over two years of being on his own with a small child.

When Eric asked, she quickly agreed to help him move his sailboat from Tampa to the cove. He wanted to moor it inside the cove, safely away from swimmers. When she and her cousins were little, Gran kept a sunfish for them so they could learn how to sail. With more than one sunfish in the cove, a lot of races had taken place. She'd forgotten how much she'd loved it.

Brooke found Charlotte reading on the porch. "Good evening," she said, lowering herself into a chair next to Charlotte. "You didn't want to join us at the bonfire?"

"No, I'm reading an interesting book and need the break. You know how that is."

"Yes, I do," Brooke said. "Nothing better than a book."

"Unless it's Adam Atkins?" Charlotte asked, giving her a saucy smile.

Brooke chuckled and shook her head. "He's off limits. But I'm going to help Eric move his sailboat here to the cove tomorrow. I can't wait to get aboard. Should be a fun way to spend a Sunday."

"I'm glad we're all getting along so well," said Charlotte. "It's been marvelous to remember all the happy times we've had here at the cove."

"At the time, I didn't realize how special it was," Brooke admitted. "But now I see why Gran is so excited to have us here helping her. Hopefully, the Inn will stay in the family, a tribute to all we've been given."

Charlotte straightened in her chair. "That's such a nice way to look at it."

"I mean it," said Brooke, suddenly tearful at the thought of losing this place, having others take it over.

Charlotte stood and hugged her. "Thanks for the reminder."

Brooke hugged her back, hoping she'd never have to go back to her old life.

CHAPTER TWENTY-EIGHT

CHARLOTTE

The next morning, when Brooke didn't come downstairs for breakfast, Charlotte went to check on her. She was curled up on the bed.

"Brooke? Are you okay?" Charlotte asked.

"I've got one of my migraines," Brooke said in a soft voice.

"I'm sorry. Can I do anything for you?" asked Charlotte.

"Yes, you can fill in for me on Eric's boat. I promised I'd help him sail it down here from Tampa. We're supposed to leave at ten to go get it."

"Okay, I can do that. I'll ask Livy to take care of any guests having a late breakfast. The crew of six couples should be through eating by then."

Brooke took hold of her hand. "Thanks. You're a sweetheart. I didn't want to disappoint him."

"I'm happy to do it. I haven't sailed in years, but I remember how much I used to love it," said Charlotte, excited about the idea.

She left Brooke and went to the Inn to talk to Livy, checking her watch as she walked.

She'd found she liked greeting guests, chatting with them. It was a pleasant way to begin the day.

Livy looked up at her. "Glad you're here. One of the couples decided to get an early start. I'm fixing their breakfast now."

"Okay. I'll go in and talk to them. Brooke has a bad migraine and is in bed. I promised I'd take her place on Eric's boat today. He's bringing her down from Tampa. We're leaving here at ten. Will you take over for me then?"

"Sure. I'm going to need a morning off next week. We'll discuss it later. As soon as the last guest leaves this morning, Austin will start his project working on the new wi-fi network."

"I'm glad we don't have other guests coming in until next weekend," said Charlotte. "I don't want to begin advertising until the website is up and other printed materials are ready. We can't do that until we finalize the shopping list and I'm able to purchase some upgrades to the rooms and public areas."

"Okay, tomorrow we'll meet to discuss it," said Livy. "Hopefully, Brooke will feel better by then. Migraines are so awful."

"Yes, she was really hurting. I'll text Eric to let him know of the changes." Charlotte left the kitchen and went to the dining room to talk to their guests.

"Hello. I understand you're leaving this morning. I hope you had a nice stay."

"Oh, yes." Margie Nichols said. "It's a lovely place, and I liked the feeling that this was our private home with service from you as we requested it."

"I'm so glad," said Charlotte making a mental note to add this to her advertising campaign. Something like "No place like home away from home."

Margie and her husband talked about their life in Alpharetta and what it was like living in the Atlanta area, and then Livy came in carrying a tray of food. Charlotte helped serve it and offered more coffee and juice.

Once they were settled, Charlotte went into the office to check for phone messages and scanned the reservations chart. Looking over the calendar, she wanted to see more advertising coincide with holidays both big and small. Little things like

Donut Day or Love Your Sister Day could be made into cute ads for the Inn. She'd work with Brooke on vacation package prices. Summer days full of possibilities lay ahead.

She heard the ping on her phone indicating a message and picked it up.

"Thanks for letting me know about Brooke. I'll pick you up at ten and we'll head to Tampa to my boat. Eric."

Shortly after that, the rest of the guests entered the dining room in a group, laughing and chatting, their voices high with excitement and full of travel plans.

As soon as she could gracefully do so, Charlotte left the Inn and hurried to Gran's house to get ready for Eric. She knew from past experience to take plenty of suntan lotion, a sun hat, bottles of water, and a light coverup. The sun's rays reflected off the water could be surprisingly hot, a real danger to an unprotected body.

She changed into a bathing suit, pulled on a pair of shorts over it, gathered her beach bag, and went to check on Brooke.

The room was dark when she walked inside. "Hey, hon, how are you doing?"

"Not so well. I'll be fine tomorrow, but today is a lost cause. If I try to hurry it, the pain will only get worse."

"Before I go, can I bring you some water? Anything?" Charlotte asked.

"Water. No ice. Just water," said Brooke.

Charlotte left and returned with a glass of water and a few saltines. "Here you go. Feel better soon."

"Eric's okay with you taking my place?"

"Yes, he seemed fine with it. Get your rest. See you later."

When she went downstairs, Eric was waiting for her in his car in the driveway.

She gathered her things and went to join him, surprised to find Shane sitting in the passenger seat.

"Hi," she said, sliding into the backseat of the silver Mercedes sedan. "Thanks for letting me take Brooke's place. I'm looking forward to a nice sail."

Eric greeted her with a smile. "Welcome aboard, Charlie. I asked Shane to come because the water's a little rough today with the cold front coming in later. Hopefully, we can beat it."

"Is Brooke okay?" Shane asked.

"She has a migraine," Charlotte said. "She just needs a day of rest and quiet."

"Yes, that's the best way to handle one," said Eric.

Charlotte sat quietly in the back, content to listen to Eric and Shane talk about the last boat show in Miami. She tuned them out and let her thoughts linger on publicity campaigns for the Inn. If they worked, life would become much more hectic. She wondered if she or her cousins were ready for that. Brooke had remarked that she wanted the Inn to stay in the family, but that meant that one of them would have to be willing to remain to help Gran.

"Hey, Charlie, you hungry? Want to grab lunch at the marina?" Eric asked.

"Yes. I was up early and I'm ready for lunch," she replied.

"Well, it can't compare to Gracie's at the Salty Key Inn, but it'll do," said Eric.

She laughed. They'd all been to Gracie's for breakfast or lunch at one time or another and agreed it was unbeatable.

The marina near the mouth of Old Tampa Bay was a well-organized operation with seemingly every facility one would want, including a bar and a restaurant. They parked, and while she and Shane found seats at the bar, Eric went out on the dock to check on the boat.

Charlotte looked at the menu and decided on a grouper

sandwich and a bottle of beer.

Shane ordered the same, and while they waited for their food, Eric joined them.

"We've got plenty of gas. I ordered ice, water, and beer to be delivered to the boat. Things look clear for a nice sail. Wind is up a bit, but we'll be all right," said Eric sliding onto a stool beside Charlotte.

Without even looking at the menu, he ordered the bar special—grouper sandwich and fries. "And add a hoppy beer to that," he said to the bartender.

"This is a happening place," said Charlotte. "Do you do a lot of sailing?"

"Not as much as I'd like," said Eric. "Depends on my work. I try to have a light schedule on Wednesdays and the weekends, but it's pretty busy most of the time. My specialty is outside of normal plastic surgery."

Charlotte's attention was drawn to Shane chatting with a waitress who was all but climbing into his lap. She sometimes forgot what effect he had on women.

After they ate, they walked down the dock to Eric's boat.

"She's a beauty," said Shane. "A Catalina 355. Sweet!"

Eric grinned. "Yeah, she's awesome."

"I love her name. *Destiny's Smile*," said Charlotte. "With your medical specialty working on mouths, you've chosen a name that suits her."

"Come aboard," said Eric, stepping onto the deck and signaling for them to join him.

Charlotte stepped onto the deck and down into the cockpit. Eric had installed a black bimini over the cockpit to provide shade, for which she was grateful.

A delivery boy from the grocery rolled a wagon onto the dock beside them.

Eric greeted him, and then he and Shane off-loaded the ice,

drinks, and a couple of bags of snacks into the galley.

Charlotte kept out of their way, taking pleasure in sitting in the cockpit. A breeze fingered her hair, cooling off the nape of her neck. She re-tied her ponytail and pulled it through the hole in the baseball cap she placed on her head.

Eric started the engine, gave instructions to Shane to toss the docking lines into the boat, and then with him aboard, they eased away from the dock.

They motored some distance from the marina, and when at last they had plenty of sea room, Eric handed her control of the helm and set to work hoisting first the mainsail and then the small genoa jib. The southeasterly breeze caught the sails, and flapping noisily, they filled as Charlotte fell off to port onto a close reach.

Eric asked Shane to cut the engine and took over the wheel from Charlotte.

In the quiet that followed, Charlotte listened to the hiss of the water as it caressed the boat's hull moving through it. As always, it was peaceful.

"We'll go to the end of Tampa Bay, under the bridge and out into the Gulf," said Eric. "It should be a nice sail north up to Sanderling Cove."

"Perfect," said Shane. "Anybody want a beer?"

Both Charlotte and Eric raised their hands.

Shane went to the galley below and returned with three cans.

"Nothing tastes better than a cold beer with the sun roasting my skin," said Shane. "A slice of heaven."

"Nothing better," Eric quickly agreed.

Charlotte sipped her cold drink and looked out over the water to the land around her. Tampa was an interesting place, and this part of Florida was her favorite. Most of the Gulf Coast from St. Pete Beach north to Clearwater Beach was without much indentation—another reason that Sanderling Cove was so unique in the area. Having the sailboat moored in the cove would be a treat for everyone, especially when other family members came to visit.

She glanced at Eric. Because of his red hair and fair skin, he wore a long-sleeved shirt to cover his arms and keep his back from burning in the sun. Beside him, Shane wore bathing trunks and nothing more, his skin already brown. The men had been friends from boyhood and were enjoying the sail together.

Feeling sleepy, aware that things were being handled well, Charlotte gazed out at the water, letting thoughts of work slip away. Not knowing what lay in her future was something different. She'd thought she knew what she'd wanted. Now, she would set aside planning and let life unfold. That thought brought a smile to her lips.

They sailed under the Sunshine Skyway Bridge, clearing Fort DeSoto Park. Then they ran downwind to the northwest along the coast.

The breeze grew stronger and shifted slightly to the south.

"We'll be sailing dead downwind, so let's allow the wind to work for us," said Eric.

Shane stood to go below for water just as a sudden gust of wind swirled around the boat. The main boom jibed, hitting Shane on the head and knocking him overboard.

Shocked, Charlotte stared into the rough water where Shane had landed. She waited for him to move, expecting him to swim toward them. She counted to ten, and when he hadn't moved, she yelled to Eric, who had quickly brought the boat head to wind, started the engine, and was struggling with dropping the sails. Charlotte grabbed a flotation cushion and jumped into the water, keeping an eye on Shane. She was an excellent swimmer. It was one thing Gran had insisted on for everyone in the family.

Swimming hard, she moved through the water. Though she knew it was only seconds, it seemed to take forever to get to Shane.

She grabbed hold of him, turned him onto his back, and rested his head on the cushion to keep his head above water. While Charlotte was swimming out to Shane, Eric steered the boat upwind so he could bring the boat close to where Charlotte was holding onto Shane.

Eric hollered to her and tossed her a life ring, holding onto the line with one hand while keeping the boat heading into the wind.

"Grab hold," Eric shouted.

Kicking with all her might, she swam toward the orange circle, dragging Shane with her. So far, he hadn't struggled against her movement. Not a healthy sign.

With one last effort, she grasped the life ring and continued kicking to help Eric pull them to the boat.

"Hurry! Grab him!" Charlotte shouted when they reached the boat.

As Eric bent over the swim platform at the boat's stern to lift him, Shane gagged and began thrashing.

"Stop it, Shane," Charlotte said. "We're helping you." She pushed, and Eric pulled, lifting Shane out of the water and onto the boat.

Charlotte clung to the life ring, exhausted.

In moments, Eric reached for her, and, relieved, she felt him pulling her upward and onto the boat. She lay there a moment, gasping for breath. Shane lay beside her, coughing up water.

She sat up and faced him. "Are you all right?"

Shane gazed at her with eyes that didn't look quite right. She looked up at Eric.

"We need to get ashore," said Eric. "I think he's had a severe concussion. I don't like what I'm seeing."

They helped Shane onto a bench in the cockpit and wrapped a towel around him.

"Hey, buddy. What's your name? Do you know where you are?" asked Eric, kneeling on the cockpit floor beside him, looking into his eyes.

Worried, Charlotte put an arm around Shane.

"I'm in a boat. A mermaid saved me." He gazed at her in a daze. "It was you."

"Who are you?" Charlotte asked, insisting on an answer. It scared her to see him like this.

"Shane Ensley," he answered, lifting a hand to the large bump on the back of his head. "Ouch! Damn, that hurts."

Eric held up three fingers. "Okay, how many fingers do you see?"

Shane blinked and studied Eric's hand. "Three. One, two, three. I'm okay. Just bumped my head."

Eric and Charlotte exchanged worried looks.

"Do you think it's okay to continue, or should we try to make it to shore and get help?" Charlotte asked Eric.

"Let's keep going, but I insist on having him checked at a hospital in St. Petersburg. Better to be safe than sorry."

"I can hear you," said Shane. "And I'm not going to any hospital."

Eric put a hand on Shane's shoulder. "We won't worry about that now. Let's get this boat moving again. It's lucky a mermaid did save you, buddy. You were out of it for a few minutes."

Shane looked at her. "You're beautiful, you know."

"He's still out of it," said Charlotte to Eric.

Eric looked from Shane to her and shrugged. "Maybe not."

Shane held an ice pack to his head as Charlotte stood at the wheel, keeping an eye on him. Eric reefed the mainsail to keep it under better control and then hoisted the sails and brought the boat back onto a northerly course.

As they headed north, Charlotte called Austin to tell him about Shane's accident and ask for his help in getting him to the hospital.

"I'll drive the cove boat to pick you two up. I'll bring one of the other men to take over for Shane and help Eric," said Austin.

She clicked off the call and relayed the news to Eric.

Shane overheard her. "No. You guys are overreacting. I'm fine. I'm fine."

"Relax. Austin's already on his way," said Charlotte. She'd never forget the few minutes Shane had seemed so lifeless. He said he was fine, but she still wanted to be sure he wouldn't have any future problems.

A short while later, they saw a Boston Whaler headed their way, and soon Austin and Adam pulled up beside the sailboat.

Charlotte caught the line they tossed up to her and wrapped it around a cleat to secure it.

Adam climbed aboard. "Okay, let's get Shane into the Whaler. You should go too, Charlie, after your swim to save him. I'll stay here and help Eric get the boat to the cove," he said with an undeniable note of authority.

Neither Shane nor she objected as they were carefully loaded into the smaller boat.

"The fact that he was unconscious and the pain he's experiencing now are indicators that it would be best to do a CT scan to assess the brain," the ER doctor said after examining Shane.

"We'll wait here," said Charlotte. "And then what happens?

Can he come home?"

The doctor gave her a professional smile. "Let's wait to decide that, okay?"

A shiver crept down Charlotte's back. What if the doctors discovered something horrible?

When a nurse arrived with a wheelchair to take Shane to imaging, Charlotte and Austin said goodbye. She blinked back tears as he was rolled away.

"Pretty scary stuff, huh?" Austin said, taking her elbow and leading her away to the waiting area.

"Yeah, for a minute, I thought ..." She shook her head. "I can't even say it."

"You saved him, Charlie. I can't ever thank you enough. He's the best big brother anyone could have."

She was too emotional to speak.

A short while later, the doctor entered the waiting area and came over to them. "Looks like a bad bang on the head but nothing more serious. However, he's going to have to rest for several days. We don't want him to do anything to change that status."

"Okay," said Austin. "We'll both keep an eye on him." He turned to her. "Right?"

"Yes," said Charlotte, her emotions in a turmoil.

As Austin drove them into the cove, Eric and Adam ran toward the car, followed by a group gathered to greet them.

Charlotte stepped out of the car and stood aside as everyone spoke to Shane, asking how he felt.

Granny Liz threw her arms around Charlotte and hugged her tight. "Thank you, Charlie. Eric told us all about how you saved Shane. I can never thank you enough for what you did. Shane is so special to me."

Tears filled Charlotte's eyes as she faced Granny Liz. There was so much she wanted to say but wouldn't.

Later, alone in her room, Charlotte lay in bed thinking. She couldn't deny her feelings any longer. After thinking she might lose Shane, everything had fallen into place, unsettling her. She'd never think of him as just a friend any longer. He was much more than that. Saving him had changed everything.

CHAPTER TWENTY-NINE

ELLIE

Ellie sat in the reading room of the inn they were staying at in the English countryside and gazed at Liz's words on her computer screen with shock.

Charlie had saved Shane's life in a near-drowning incident. When pressed, Charlotte had thanked Gran for making sure she and her cousins knew how to swim and had taken lifesaving courses.

"That dear, dear girl," whispered Ellie, dabbing at her eyes with a tissue before focusing on the screen once more.

"Charlie and Austin are tending to Shane, making sure he gets to rest for the next few days. It's so inspiring to see Charlie's concern. You and I have often talked about what a wonderful pair they'd make. I'm not sure, but maybe our dreams about them could come true. Only time will tell. But if the sparks between them ever burst into flame, it'll be undeniable. I'm rooting for that to happen, as I'm sure you are too."

Ellie let out a long sigh. Life was so tenuous. They had dreams for all their grandchildren. To think they'd almost lost Shane was horrifying.

She turned back to the screen and read about the wi-fi upgrades Austin was putting in, the way Skye and Brooke had taken to one another, and the dates Livy was going on. For a moment, she longed to go home.

John came into the room. "Ready to go?"

She smiled at his enthusiasm. "In a second. I'll catch you

up on the family news as we travel."

This trip with John was turning out very well. Most of the time, they felt like a young couple on their honeymoon, eager to see and do everything. Other times, they simply relaxed.

CHAPTER THIRTY

BROOKE

Brooke sat with her cousins in the office, the checklist in her hand. "Okay, time to get serious. Charlie, you want to go ahead and order the soft goods for the rooms. That would mean bedspreads, towels, and sheets. Right?"

Charlotte nodded and handed her the list she'd drawn up of expenses for those items. "I want to get this done as soon as possible so we can photograph the updated rooms."

"I've pulled together a list of bathroom accessories like soap dishes and toothbrush holders and the like," said Brooke. "Small, inexpensive things but needed."

"I've been searching Craig's List for some furniture I thought we could use for the gathering room," said Livy. "I've also found a commercial ice maker there for a more than fair price. I'd like to call today to get it."

Brooke consulted her list. "Okay, let's go ahead and do the linens for the rooms, the ice maker for the kitchen, and the freezer that Livy found online the other day. After we get those items, we'll reassess for other things. This afternoon, I'm going to a couple of consignment shops I've heard about. I saw a wooden card table we could use for games in the gathering room. The old table needs refinishing."

"Good luck." Charlotte stood. "Sorry to run off, but I promised Granny Liz I'd stay with Shane for a while this morning. She insists on having someone on hand to make him take it easy. I'll place a call to the hotel supplier in Miami and order what we want. We've already agreed to have his company provide linen service."

"Before you go," said Brooke, "one more thing. Livy wants to have Sunday off. We'll have eight couples here. Billy Bob will handle the kitchen, but one of us needs to be here to welcome guests. Are you game to do it, Charlie? I promised Skye I'd go with her to Disney World on Saturday. I know we'll be exhausted by the time we get home late Saturday night, and I'll want to sleep in."

"Sure, I'll do it, but I think we'd better draw up a schedule so we all have the freedom to do what we want within reason," said Charlotte. "This business is tough. That's why I want to think of ways to make things easy for Gran or whoever takes over the Inn." She paused and gave Brooke a steady look. "I'm not sure how we're going to work it out, but I, too, want to keep it in the family."

"Definitely," said Livy. "That's why we're staying for the summer, isn't it? Maybe even beyond that."

"That's the hope," said Brooke.

Charlotte gave her a saucy smile. "Have fun with Adam at Disney World."

Livy nudged her. "Skye is a convenient excuse for being with her hot father."

Brooke shook her head. "Not going to happen. Adam is a wounded warrior not about to get serious about anyone. He told me straight out."

"Too bad," said Livy, "because Skye loves you."

"I know. That's why Adam and I are playing it cool. We don't want her to get any wrong ideas." Brooke knew she was right, but it still hurt. For the first time in forever, she was comfortable with a man. Maybe because she had no expectations beyond being with an old childhood friend.

CHAPTER THIRTY-ONE

CHARLOTTE

Charlotte trotted over to Granny Liz's house with mixed feelings. Her emotions had been on a roller coaster ever since she'd thought Shane might die. It was then that she realized how devastated she'd be if he hadn't recovered. Though they'd talked of being just friends, she realized that deep down, she hoped their friendship might grow to something more meaningful. But it was way too soon to do more than wonder about it. Ever since the accident, Shane had become withdrawn.

He was sitting on the porch in a rocking chair when Charlotte arrived. "Hi," she said cheerfully. "I'm going to be your companion for a while. Granny Liz asked me to come over to visit with you so she can go out on errands with Austin."

Shane shook his head. "It's foolish, all this business of someone being around to make sure I don't pass out or something. I got a bump on the head. Big deal."

"I know," said Charlotte taking a seat in the rocker next to his. "Granny Liz is the one who needs watching. She's been in a tailspin ever since the accident. We scared her. Even Grandpa Sam is worried about her. So, let's just humor her for a while longer."

"But I'm fine on my own," said Shane pushing back. "In fact, I'm heading to Miami tomorrow. I have some things to take care of with the Family First family of mine."

"Is it safe for you to drive? It's been less than a week since the accident." She saw his eyebrows form a Vee of frustration and added, "I'll drive you if you want."

He studied her. "I don't know why you're both so upset over all this."

"Granny told me you're special to her. And since you are the oldest of all the grandkids, she treasures you maybe more than the rest of us. It's been a wake-up call for all of us to realize that anything bad can happen at any time."

"I've decided as much as Granny wants me to spend most of the summer here, I can't. Not with everyone watching over me. Thanks. I accept your offer to drive me back to Miami." He took a sip of water. "I'm sure Jed will be happy to drive you back here on the weekend. He really likes Livy and will return on Saturday. In the meantime, you can stay in my condo on one condition. No hovering. Got it?"

Charlotte raised her hand. "I promise."

"There's plenty of room, so we don't need to bump into one another," said Shane.

"Okay. I'll see what I can work out," she said, rising. "I'll leave you now."

"Thanks." Shane leaned back in his chair and closed his eyes.

As she left him, she was more than a little worried. He seemed so depressed. She'd read up on concussions and near-death experiences and knew depression could sometimes follow.

Charlotte met with Livy and Brooke and told them about her need to help Shane for a couple of days. They both agreed to her plans, especially when she mentioned that Jed would bring her back with him when he came to the cove to see Livy.

"Is anything serious going on with you two?" Brooke asked

her. "You're staying at Shane's condo."

Charlotte caught her lip and sighed. "My staying there is just to help him out. I'm not sure what happened, but this accident has changed him. I'm going to suggest he see a counselor to work some things out."

"I have noticed he's become very quiet," said Livy. "Jed told me he's asked for several days off."

"It was a close call," said Brooke. "People tend to say it was just a bump on the head, but if he was unconscious like you say, then who knows how long it will take him to heal."

"He wants to be at home, but I'm hoping to convince him to come back to the cove for Granny Liz's sake, if not his own," said Charlotte. "But if he feels forced to stay here, it won't go well."

"You're right," Livy said, shaking her head. "I can understand. My mother went crazy when my brother, Thad, got a concussion playing football. But this is more difficult because Shane is that much older, that much more independent and can't be told what to do."

"Thanks for understanding," said Charlotte. "Now, I'm going to get to work finalizing the purchase of bedspreads and linens and towels. The laundry service is giving us a discount for switching over to them. An added bonus."

"I was able to get the ice machine. Amby is going to pick it up for us this afternoon, along with the other pieces of equipment we talked about," said Livy. "I've warned Billy Bob about changes in the kitchen area, but this will be the first big sign of it."

"You're brave to work with him. When he stares at you, he's so scary," said Brooke.

Livy grinned. "I've discovered he's a gentle giant with a large sweet tooth. So I'm keeping him well supplied with cookies. That and his favorite Tic Tacs keep him happy."

"He's a softie," Charlotte agreed, "but he likes to pretend he's tough. I suspect he's actually a little shy."

"Gran and John are grateful he's worked for them for so long. I'd like to keep him here for as long as we can," said Brooke.

"Me, too," said Livy. "That's why I'm being careful about getting his approval for the changes we make in the kitchen. He's been here so long he thinks of the kitchen as his. I get it."

"Seems like things are moving along. Be sure and give me all your receipts because we'll need to reassess. I'm going to the consignment shop today." Brooke waved and left them at Gran's house to go back to the office.

"I'll call Jed and reconfirm the new arrangements for Saturday. Thanks again for covering for me on Sunday morning," said Livy. "Jed says he's taking me out of town somewhere special. He's already made plans through Shane to spend the night at Granny Liz's."

"Is it getting serious between you and Jed?" Charlotte asked, unable to hold back.

Livy shrugged. "I don't know. Like you, I just want to have fun."

Charlotte returned Livy's smile but wondered if she genuinely felt the same way. She was so confused.

The following day, as planned, she carried a small suitcase over to Granny Liz's house. Shane had insisted on taking his car to Miami. Charlotte understood his need for independence.

Granny Liz greeted her on the porch. "Shane is packing now. I want you to convince him to come back here. I'm not sure what's going on, but some childhood memories he's tried to bury in his subconscious have resurfaced. Unhappy things.

Maybe his injury is at the root of it. But I think it's important for him to be here among friends and family."

Charlotte had no chance to do anything but nod when Shane appeared with his duffle bag.

"Ready?" he asked her and bent to give Granny Liz a kiss on the cheek. "Thanks for everything. I need to get back home."

"Your true home is here, Shane. Like always," Granny Liz said softly, cupping his cheek with her hand.

He sighed before turning away.

Charlotte followed him to his car, a white Lexus coupe, and placed her suitcase into the trunk along with his. "I'm driving," she said with a firmness he couldn't deny.

He studied her and then reluctantly handed her the keys.

She got behind the wheel and waited while he got settled in the passenger seat.

"Pretty fancy car," she said, studying the dashboard, getting used to it.

"A real splurge with money from my mother and Ricardo." As he spoke, a shadow crossed his face, and Charlotte wondered what was behind it.

"That's a nice gift," she said.

"Yes, but I told them I didn't need it."

Her curiosity piqued even more. Charlotte knew Granny Liz was right. Something was going on with Shane—something to do with his family.

They pulled out of the driveway and headed down I-275 to I-75, where they could connect to Alligator Alley, which would take them from the Gulf Coast across the peninsula to Miami.

Charlotte was glad for the opportunity for them to be alone. They'd vowed to be honest with one another, and this was an excellent time to test that resolution.

She broke the silence in the car. "Granny Liz thinks you're

dealing with old issues in your family. Is that right?"

He clasped his head in his hands. "You're going to think I'm crazy, but in the water after the accident, my mind filled with memories. They flashed before me like camera shots, just as some people have reported before they died."

Charlotte clutched the wheel so hard her knuckles turned white. "So, you had a near-death experience?" Her heart plummeted at their close call. "I almost lost you."

"This is even stranger. At the end of those dreams or whatever they were, I saw a mermaid. And it was you," said Shane.

"That's what you said on the boat," Charlotte said. "I thought you were dazed."

"Yeah, I finally realized that no one would believe me and decided not to tell anyone what happened. But those things, those images did run through my brain."

"I believe you, Shane," Charlotte said calmly. "From what I've been reading about head injuries, it can happen. They will go away as a part of the healing process. You're not crazy."

Shane stared out the window and was quiet.

Charlotte continued driving, allowing him privacy.

When he spoke, his voice was soft, full of pain.

"My parents grew to hate one another. Before they got a divorce, they used to fight all the time. It got pretty ugly. My job was to keep Austin away from them. He was four years younger and didn't see or hear what I did, mostly because I made sure he didn't."

"I'm so sorry," Charlotte said. "How awful for you. How old were you when they divorced?"

"I'd just turned ten," he said. "Granny Liz was the one who took Austin and me in for summers and vacations. Understandably, I didn't want to spend much time at home. So, when my mother placed Austin and me in a private school with lots of afterschool activity, I was more than happy to attend, so I didn't have to be with her."

Charlotte glanced at his haggard expression, and her heart went out to him.

Shane let a long sigh. "I've been to counseling and thought I'd put all that behind me. But after seeing those images of them fighting, their hatred, I realize it's never really over."

"But wasn't their wedding one of those big society ones?" Charlotte said. "It was touted as a fairytale come true."

"Oh, yes. A big deal in Miami," he snorted. "As if that means anything."

Charlotte thought of her mother in New York and their differences. She answered with more anger than she'd wanted. "Now you know why I want out of New York."

Startled, he looked at her.

His confession had stirred something inside her. Feeling free to speak her mind, she said, "I had the opposite situation with my mother growing up. Guess everyone at the cove knows I had a brother who drowned not far from there. That's why my mother doesn't like to come to the cove to see Gran. I never really knew him. I was pretty much a baby when it happened. But I understood from an early age that no matter what I did, I wasn't the child my mother wanted, that given a choice, she would've saved him, not me."

Charlotte felt her lips tremble. She blinked back tears.

"I'm sorry, Charlie. I can't imagine anyone not wanting you. That must have hurt."

"Oh, my mother and I are friends of a sort now, but that feeling of not being wanted has never left me." She blinked harder and then let out a sob that shocked her.

Charlotte quickly pulled over to the side of the road. Embarrassed, she unstrapped her seatbelt and struggled to get out of the car.

Shane's hand came down on her shoulder. "It's all right, Charlie. I understand."

She turned to face him, and his arms came around her. Pain tore at her insides, and she gulped air in between sobs that racked her body. Years of hiding feelings of inadequacy emerged in a torrent of pain. Though she told herself to stop, she couldn't.

Shane rubbed her back and let her cry.

When she finally lifted her face, she saw tears in his eyes.

She sat up and wiped her face with the tissue he handed her. "I'm so sorry. I don't know where that came from."

"You don't?" he said.

Charlotte caught her breath, took a sip from the bottle of water he offered and sighed. "Actually, I do know. After hearing your story, I felt safe telling mine. Weird, huh?"

"No," he said. "We were honest with one another. Like we promised. Remember?"

She nodded, feeling relieved. "I do."

"That kind of friendship is what we need right now," said Shane. Then, with a thumb, he wiped the last of her tears off her cheek.

"Yeah. Life is complicated," she said, still surprised by how easily she'd let her feelings out with him.

Charlotte sighed, straightened, refastened her seatbelt, and then eased the car onto the highway. She concentrated on driving, hoping to settle her emotional outbreak. She was here to help Shane, not be a burden to him.

CHAPTER THIRTY-TWO

CHARLOTTE

Shane's condo was as classy as his car. In a gated community of townhomes near the water, it was ideally located within walking distance of CocoWalk. With three bedrooms and two baths, it was a rare find for what Shane told her was an excellent price.

"It's lovely," Charlotte said, liking the contemporary feel to the two-story condo. Outside, palm trees offered shade, and colorful flowers added texture to the landscaping.

Shane patted his stomach. "I'm suddenly hungry. How about something to eat? We can walk down to one of the restaurants."

Charlotte frowned at him. "You're supposed to be taking it easy."

"I won't be doing anything strenuous. Just walking to the restaurant. After we eat, I promise to come home and rest." Shane's voice had an edge to it, and Charlotte realized he was right. Better for him to be up and out than forced to lie still with the memories that haunted him.

"You're right. But let's choose a place close by. Maybe even do takeout and bring it back here," she said.

"Okay. That's a fair compromise. I'll wheel your suitcase to the guest room for you. We can leave whenever you're ready."

It wasn't until Charlotte went into the bathroom and took a look in the mirror that she realized how red and swollen her eyes were. Mascara had even run a bit.

Charlotte ran a washcloth under cold water and rinsed her

face, still amazed by her breakdown. In retrospect, she realized her feelings might seem silly. So, her mother remained twisted by grief over her son's death, and while dealing with her demons had never made Charlotte feel as worthy as the son she lost. In today's world, with all the cruelty and abuse of children, it wasn't that serious, was it? Charlotte shook her head, remembering what she knew to be true. Neglect was just as emotionally harmful as physical abuse. The bruises just weren't visible.

She quickly restored her eye makeup and headed out to the living room where Shane was waiting for her.

"I'm sorry for being so needy," she said, approaching him.

His eyebrows drew into a frown. "What do you mean?" He stood, lifted her chin, and gave her a steady look. "We're all entitled to our feelings, Charlie. Growing up under a shadow left by someone you didn't even know is hurtful. I understand. You have every right to feel the way you do."

They stared at one another. The atmosphere in the room shifted and became charged. For a long, tense moment, Charlotte wondered if he was going to kiss her, but he turned and walked away.

Later, carrying their Chinese food back to Shane's condo, Charlotte was well aware of the attention Shane drew to himself. He didn't seem to notice until a tall, attractive brunette threw herself into his arms. "Shane, where have you been? You promised me a dinner, and I intend to make sure I get it."

"Oh, hi, Amanda," he said, smiling and gently disengaging from her. "It's been a while. I've been busy with family."

She cast a sour look at Charlotte. "Who is she?"

Shane glanced at Charlotte and turned back to Amanda.

"This is Charlotte Bradford, a family friend."

Amanda narrowed her eyes at him. "M-m-m, this is what's keeping you busy?"

"No, not really. My other family too."

"Oh, the one you're helping?" The creased lines on her forehead softened. "Oh, well, then I expect you to call me soon." She kissed him on the cheek. "See you soon, Shane. Don't forget."

Charlotte remained quiet as they continued their walk back to his condo. A family friend, he'd called her. What could she say? They'd agreed to it, but it still stung. Still, she couldn't deny the way her stomach had curled inside her at the sight of Amanda in his arms. In truth, she had no right to be jealous.

"Sorry about that," Shane said. "I've tried to tell Amanda that it wasn't working, but she doesn't want to hear it."

"She seems pretty determined," Charlotte commented.

"That's the problem," he said, rubbing his hands through his blond hair, wincing when he got too close to the bump on his head.

"Let's get home, have lunch, and then we can both rest. I'm going to do some work on my computer."

Shane smiled at her. "Thanks."

The next morning, Charlotte awoke to the aroma of coffee. Smiling with anticipation, she threw on a pair of shorts, straightened her cami, and went into the kitchen.

Shane was sitting at the small round table in the kitchen dressed in a dark suit.

"Hey, what are you doing?" Charlotte said. "You're supposed to be resting, not going into work."

"I have to meet with Elijah's principal at his school. We're working on a plan to get him into a charter school out of the neighborhood. I won't disappoint him."

"No, of course not. Do you want me to drive you? I can do that for you."

He shook his head. "No need to disturb your day. I promise to come home right after the meeting. I asked Sarita to send any messages at the office here, but Jed has already told me he vetoed that idea. Everyone wants me to get some rest, and it's driving me crazy."

"We all want you better," Charlotte said, wondering if she should mention the idea of talking to a counselor about his visions.

He grinned up at her. "I've called Dr. Gleason, my old counselor. She'll see me at three."

Charlotte gave him a quick squeeze. "I'm sure you'll feel better about things after you talk with her."

She poured herself a cup of coffee and sat at the table opposite him. "I'm glad you're helping Elijah. Just having your support must mean a lot to him."

"I sometimes think it's the people outside your family who can give you the most help," said Shane. "But, as I mentioned, Granny Liz is the one who supported Austin and me when we needed it. I'll never forget it."

Charlotte gave him a thoughtful look. "That's why I think it's important for you to agree to go back to Sanderling Cove for more days of rest. The longer you're away, the more Granny Liz will worry. I understand both points of view, but she asked me to help convince you to do it."

He stirred restlessly in his seat.

Charlotte held up a hand. "That's all I'm going to say about it."

Shane grew still. "Okay, I'll think about it."

They sipped their coffee quietly, then Shane rose. "I've got to go. I'll talk to you later. I'll stop and get a few things to eat.

My cupboards are bare, and the refrigerator isn't much better."

"If you want me to cook, I'll try. But, I'm not like Livy, who can create a feast out of nothing."

"No problem. I'll grill up some chicken. Then, you can fix a salad. All right?"

"Okay. I make a great salad."

Shane laughed. "Then, we're good to go. See you later."

Charlotte waved to him, finished her coffee, and, restless, walked through the condo studying each room.

In the den, Charlotte found a framed photo of Shane, Austin, and Granny Liz smiling. In another, a man Charlotte recognized as Shane's father posed with a pretty woman and two young children. Still another showed a woman sitting in a chair by a window, her back straight, and her face turned toward the photographer with a smile that looked forced. Studying it, Charlotte almost shivered at the lack of warmth. Years ago, she'd seen Shane's father at the cove, even his step-family, because he was close to Granny Liz, his mother. But she couldn't remember ever seeing his mother there. No doubt she wasn't welcome at the cove after she and Shane's father had finally divorced.

Understanding the family history, seeing more than just pictures of people in the photos, Charlotte realized the damage parents could do, even unwittingly. She and her mother had danced around the issue of David's death without discussing how it had affected each of them. Maybe, next time she had a chance to talk to her mother about it, she would.

When Shane came home at noon with groceries, Charlotte took one look at him and saw how exhausted he seemed. "Let me help you with these. I'll put them away."

Expecting a bit of a pushback, she was surprised when he sighed and said, "Thanks. I'm going to change."

"Can I fix you a sandwich?" she said, eying the Jewish Rye bread and sliced ham he'd bought.

"Sure, thanks." He turned and headed out of the room.

Charlotte fixed sandwiches for both of them. Hopefully, after lunch, Shane would take the time for a short nap. She was worried about him.

During lunch, she asked Shane about his meeting for Elijah.

He smiled and leaned forward. "It went well. Next fall, he'll be attending a charter school that specializes in musically gifted kids. He plays the piano and sings."

"Marvelous," she said, excited by the progress made for one of many kids who needed help. "One step after another."

He grinned. "Hey, I like that. We should use that phrase in our publicity."

Pleased, she shrugged. "Okay. I can work that into some of the promo stuff I'm designing for your group."

His gaze settled on her. "I like that you're so willing to help. I know you've been successful in the business."

"I like this kind of work better. It's making me realize it was time for a change."

"Change can be a good thing." He got up from his chair at the kitchen table. "Thanks for lunch. I'm going to lie down for a while."

"I'm going to read," she said. "And then, if you'd like, I'll drive you to see Dr. Gleason."

"Okay, I've got a killer headache and don't want to be bothered to drive again."

Hopefully, after talking to Dr. Gleason, he'd decide to return with her to Sanderling Cove, where he could be assured plenty of rest.

Later, when Charlotte picked him up from his appointment, she gave him a questioning look.

He was quiet as he settled in the passenger seat and hooked his seatbelt.

"How'd it go?"

His expression was sad as he turned to her. "I was able to talk to her about the visions I had. As you said, it's not that unusual under the circumstances, but we talked about them in depth, and I've agreed to go back and see her after I feel better. She thinks it's a wise idea for me to go back to Sanderling Cove and rest there, to reassure Granny Liz."

Charlotte couldn't help the smile that spread across her face. "When do you want to leave?"

"Tomorrow morning, first thing. I know you need to get back, and that will give you time to get organized for your Sunday morning crowd."

"That'll be perfect," Charlotte said. "While you were napping, I mixed up a little barbeque sauce for the chicken. We'll have a nice easy dinner and a relaxing evening before heading to bed." Hearing her words, Charlotte felt heat rise to her cheeks. She knew she shouldn't be thinking of Shane and bed together, but the thought had intruded, and now she couldn't get rid of it.

He noticed her discomfort and winked at her, making her turn away in confusion. She felt a hand on her shoulder and faced him. "It's silly, I know. We're just friends. Right?"

His blue-eyed gaze rested on her, and then he slowly nodded.

"Thought so," she said, forcing a smile. "The last thing either of us needs right now is something more than that."

"Agreed," he mumbled without looking at her.

They'd just finished dinner when Jed arrived. "Did I miss anything?" he asked, glancing at their empty plates.

"Have you had dinner?" Charlotte asked.

He shook his head. "Too busy at the office. Got any leftovers?"

Shane got to his feet. "There's more chicken keeping warm on the grill. I'll bring it in."

"Thanks." Jed took off his sport coat and loosened his tie. He turned to Charlotte. "How are things going? Are you making sure he gets some rest?"

"Yes. Better yet, Shane has agreed to go back to Sanderling Cove. Did you get the message?"

"Yes, that's why I'm here. I just wanted to make sure everything's all right. We need him back in the office, but not until he's healed." Jed turned as Shane walked in carrying a plate of grilled chicken.

"Talking about me?" he said, setting the plate down on the table.

"Yeah. How are you doing?" Jed asked him.

He glanced at Charlotte and then let out a long breath. "Apparently, this bang on the head did more damage than we thought. But I'll be fine. I've agreed to take it easy for a few more days. But I'll be back in the office as soon as I can. Anything I should know about?"

Jed shook his head. "Everything's under control. No more business talk until you come back. Sarita would have my neck if she knew I'd said even this much to you."

Shane laughed. "Sarita runs the show. I get it."

They grinned at each other before Jed accepted the napkin, knife, and fork Charlotte handed him. "Livy says you're taking her to a special place tomorrow."

Jed face lit with excitement. "There's a Spanish restaurant on St. Armand's Circle in Sarasota that I think she'd like.

Thought we could make a day of it, maybe have dinner there and then head back to St. Pete Beach to one of my favorite bars."

"Sounds like a lot of yummy food," Charlotte said.

His lips curved into another happy smile. "It's fun to be with someone who likes to eat, try new things." His expression grew serious. "I like her a lot."

He gave her a questioning look, but Charlotte didn't respond. She wasn't going to speak for Livy. They'd have to work things out for themselves.

"Have a beer," said Shane, handing Jed a cold can.

"Nice to see you, Jed. I'm going to leave you two alone and get back to my book," Charlotte said.

Jed gave her a little salute. "Thanks for taking such good care of my buddy."

Charlotte and Shane exchanged amused glances. They both understood Shane would do only so much relaxing.

Later, after Jed had gone and Charlotte said goodnight to Shane, she lay in bed thinking about the unlikely events of the past two days. Spilling her guts to Shane and having him tell her things he hadn't told others had brought them a lot closer as friends. This is what they both needed. But, was this what they really wanted?

CHAPTER THIRTY-THREE

BROOKE

Laughing, Brooke was glad she'd worn comfortable sandals as Skye tugged on her arm, urging her forward. She understood how excited the little girl was. Disney World was a child's dream come true. Mickey Mouse had waved at Skye, Minnie had danced in front of her, and Cinderella had hugged her back. Moments Skye would never forget.

Brooke glanced at Adam and noticed his smile was as wide as hers. As the advertising proclaimed, it was a magical place for a child full of imagination. Though she didn't want to admit it, Brooke had secretly oohed and ahhed at seeing Cinderella. But then, she liked fairy tales. They were so far removed from reality.

"Skye, honey, we need a break. How about a cool drink?" said Adam.

"Okay, and then can Brooke and I go on the Small World ride again?" said Skye.

Adam gave her a sympathetic look. "How about it, Brooke?"

She laughed. "Okay, after the cool drink."

Adam leaned closer and whispered. "I owe you big time, don't I?"

"Oh, yeah," she said. "I'm going to have this song running through my mind for at least a month."

"C'mon," said Skye, giving Brooke's arm another tug.

"Okay, here's a place for a drink right here," Brooke said.

“I’ll grab a seat. Dad will get us drinks.” A shiver ran through her. Was this what it was like to be part of a family of her own? She glanced at the happiness on Skye’s face and knew she wanted this someday.

CHAPTER THIRTY- FOUR

LIVY

After a delicious dinner of tapas shared with Jed, Livy strolled around St. Armand's Circle, glancing at the shops, letting her meal settle. She didn't know which she'd enjoyed more—the shrimp sauteed in olive oil, fresh garlic, and chili pepper, the chicken croquettes, or the baked stuffed mushrooms. It was much more convenient to have small delicious bites than eating a large meal.

"I'm glad we didn't do a full dinner," she said, smiling at Jed. "I got to sample lots of different tastes. That 1905 dressing on your tomato salad was fabulous. It's amazing what a little Worcestershire sauce can do."

He stopped walking and faced her. "You made that meal fun, Livy. I'm glad you're not one of those women who don't dare eat anything because they might get fat."

"I decided not to worry about that. I care, but not enough to give up tasty food," she said, well aware of other women—sleek, well-dressed ones—around them.

"What about you? Have you always appreciated a variety of food?" Livy asked.

For a brief moment, a shadow crossed his face, then he smiled. "My mom was an excellent waitress ... during the times when she was sober. She worked in several different restaurants, and when she could, she arranged for me to have meals in the kitchen. I learned early on the difference between okay food and great food." He shrugged. "I guess I should be grateful for that."

"It's a lovely gift to give a child," said Livy. "Enjoyment of food is one of life's pleasures." Her tone became bitter. "Not that my mother sees it that way. Gran is the one who told her to back off from making comments about my love of cooking and eating."

"You're lucky to have someone like Gran in your life. I don't have any grandparents that I know of," said Jed.

"I'm sorry," said Livy, patting his arm. "I don't know what I'd do without Gran and John. They've been big supporters of mine. My cousins, too."

"Yeah, they're nice people. Shall we head back?"

"Okay. It's a perfect night for a swim in the pool at the Inn or cooling off in Gran's splash pool. I'm glad you're staying overnight with Shane."

"Me, too," said Jed, taking hold of her hand.

Walking together, feeling more comfortable with him, Livy wondered what the rest of the summer would bring.

CHAPTER THIRTY-FIVE

CHARLOTTE

Sunday morning, Charlotte smiled at a couple who joined the others in the dining room. "Good morning. I hope you had a nice sleep."

"Oh, yes," said Nellie Greene, an older woman with white hair and a ready smile. "Better yet, I found a couple of special shells I've been looking for. It pays to get up early." She held up a pretty tulip shell.

"Let me see," said a woman already seated at the table.

Carrie ... Corrie? Carrie ... Sutton? Yes! That was her name. "Isn't it pretty, Carrie?" said Charlotte smoothly. "With one more day here, you should be able to find some nice shells yourself. And remember, we have several handbooks on shells. You can carry them with you and check for yourself."

"You do? I'll do that today. My granddaughter wants to make shell jewelry with me. I've bought some shells at one of the stores, but this will be even better." Carrie beamed at her. "This is one of the reasons Greg and I like to come here. For the little services like this."

"That's what we hope to give our guests." Charlotte knew Gran would be pleased with her.

By the time all eight couples had been served and the dining room cleared, Charlotte was happy to see the end of breakfast. Dealing with them and Billy Bob in the kitchen was enough of a challenge for any day. It made her wonder if managing the Inn was what she wanted to do in the future. Livy and Brooke seemed more suited to it and had already talked of staying on.

Charlotte talked with Beryl about housekeeping for the day and went into the office to check for emails and phone calls. She'd placed a couple of ads in the Miami and Tampa newspapers as well as travel websites reminding readers that a beachside stay was a pleasant way to relax. So far, they'd gotten a few reservations as a result from them.

As soon as things were in order, Charlotte headed back to Gran's house. She hoped to see her cousins, maybe have time for girl talk.

She found Brooke and Livy in the kitchen. "Hey, you two. What's going on? How did your dates go last night?"

"Wow. Look at you," said Livy.

"You really are taking Gran's place," Brooke said.

Charlotte looked down at the orange T-shirt she'd borrowed from Gran and laughed. The shirt read: *Life's Good!* "I've decided to make some changes. While I was with Shane, I told him about trying to be up to my mother's standards. It brought back a lot of feelings I've stuffed inside. So, from now on, being here, helping Gran, I'm going to do what's right for me, not my mother."

Brooke laughed. "Your mother hates those shirts."

"Exactly," said Charlotte with a satisfied smile. "One tiny step in trying to free myself from the past."

"Like Brooke and her phone calls to her mother," said Livy. "I understand."

"How about you, Livy? What are you doing to change?" said Charlotte, genuinely curious.

"That's easy. I'm going to do what I want and to put myself first without worrying about my mother's expectations. I want to be able to enjoy the time we have together," said Livy.

Charlotte looked at her two cousins. "Gran would be proud of the changes we're making. What else is going on?" She grabbed a glass of iced water and sat down at the table with them.

Brooke sighed. "I was just telling Livy that Adam, Skye, and I had a wonderful trip to Disney World, but if I never hear the "It's a Small World" song again, it will be fine with me." She laughed with them. "Adam's a great guy, but we both know we're not going to pursue any real relationship other than through his daughter. I adore Skye, but as I've mentioned before, neither of us wants to hurt her by pretending to be something we're not."

"And you, Livy? What have you been doing?" Charlotte said, setting down her glass of water and giving her a steady look. Jed had mentioned he liked her.

"Jed and I went out to dinner in Sarasota, walked around the area, and came back here to Gran's splash pool. It was nice. Really nice. That's it."

Brooke grinned at Livy. "I bet there's more to it, but I'll let you off the hook." She turned to Charlotte. "You and Shane must be more than casual friends if you're discussing things like your mother."

Charlotte nodded. "My mother ... and David."

"Your brother who died young?" Livy said, her eyebrows arching like a question mark.

"Yes. We both talked about very personal things. Now, I understand a little bit more about why Shane is the way he is," said Charlotte, remembering the pain in Shane's eyes when he talked about his parents.

"Wow, that's deep, Charlotte," said Livy. "Seems as if a real friendship is forming, like you want."

Charlotte hesitated to respond. It's what she'd told everyone she wanted.

###

Later, Charlotte was in the kitchen at the Inn organizing the hors d'oeuvres for the guests when Shane surprised her. "Hi, what are you doing here?" she asked, aware of the smile spreading across her face.

"Granny Liz sent me here, said you might need the help because of all the new guests checking in. It's something Grandpa Sam used to do for your grandmother from time to time." He grinned. "Guess she knows how bored I am."

She took a moment to study the dimple like his brother's that showed up occasionally. "Okay. I'm working on the hors d'oeuvres; you can get the drinks set up. We're trying out different things for cocktail hour. Tonight, I thought we'd offer some margaritas to those who want them."

"Okay. Show me where to find what I need, and I'll get it ready. Five o'clock is the time, right?"

"Yes," said Charlotte, checking her watch. "Fifteen minutes to go. Just wait. Suddenly everyone will appear. My guess is all thirty-six people."

"Even if they're going out for dinner later?" asked Shane.

"Oh, yes. You'll see. It's one of the extras here at the inn that guests love. Even if it's just wine and peanuts. But Livy, Brooke, and I want to make it even better."

"Did you know I was a bartender in college?" said Shane. "I make a mean margarita."

"Yeah? What's your secret?" she said.

"A touch of orange juice and an extra squeeze of lime." He reached into the cupboard she'd indicated and pulled out a bottle of tequila. He turned to her and grinned. "By the way, I like your T-shirt. Is that your new motto – *Life's Good*?"

Charlotte shook her head. "One of them. Gran's got a lot of cool shirts. I'll take it day by day, and then I'll see."

He laughed. "I've always liked Gran, thought she was a free spirit. Maybe working and living here is helping you to change like you wanted."

Charlotte grew serious. "I want to thank you, Shane, for allowing me to be open with you the other day. I've stuffed my feelings for so long I'd forgotten what it feels like just to be me. I want this fresh start. Talk about being in a rut."

He put an arm around her and pulled her close, making her pulse surge ahead. "I'm happy I was there to listen to you. You helped me, too. I need to be able to let go of the past. Like you, I'm hoping for a fresh start."

She stepped back, and they faced one another, smiling.

After a minute, Shane broke eye contact and turned away. Charlotte reminded herself they were just friends and went back to putting together a blue cheese dip for the carrots she'd peeled and sliced earlier.

Just before seven o'clock, Charlotte cleared away the empty plates and bowls used for the cocktail hour and started the roundup of empty glasses scattered around the gathering room and outdoor pool deck. This was a valuable time for her to connect with the guests, to make sure they were having a nice time. The work was worth the effort, she thought. Guests were happily chatting with one another, making friends and memories. From here, they'd go their own way or, perhaps, decide to dine out together. There were a number of nearby restaurants to choose from, including the Pink Pelican Bar down the road and Gavin's at the nearby Salty Key Inn.

Charlotte loaded glasses into the bus tubs on the small rolling cart used for this purpose. She and her cousins had talked about hiring one or two people to help with this social hour in the future, but until they decided they could afford it, they were committed to doing it themselves.

She glanced at Shane talking to one of the guests about the

Family First program. It was an opportune time to discuss many things with interesting people.

After everything had been cleaned up, Charlotte sat in the kitchen with Shane, sipping a margarita.

"Refreshing, just as you said," she told Shane. "Tell me about your job in college. Did you have to work your way through?"

"My parents paid for my tuition and books. Everything else I had to cover myself. Jed and I shared a small apartment, and we didn't go out a lot, but we still found time for fun in between working stints. He worked in the same bar as I did."

"Nice," said Charlotte.

"Yeah, we're different, but we get along well," said Shane. "Neither of us did a whole lot of partying. Not with our family backgrounds."

"That made it easy then," said Charlotte. "Being in the city at NYU, I was more interested in food than getting smashed at a bar. There are so many small, neighborhood places to get take-out that it made living easy. Guess that's why I'm not a great cook. No need."

He winked at her. "But you make a damn good salad."

She laughed. "That's not hard to do."

"What about tonight? Do you want to get something to eat?" Shane asked her.

"Sure," Charlotte said happily. "What do you have in mind?"

"I was thinking of a burger. Maybe some fries with it. Nothing fancy."

"Perfect. I'm ready as soon as Rico gets here." Rico Torres was the evening manager available to guests until 11 PM. She brushed off her T-shirt. In the past, she'd offer to go change. Not anymore. Shane was a friend who understood what she was trying to do.

Charlotte made sure the answering machine was active on the phone, and things were in order in the gathering room. As soon as Rico arrived, she updated him on the day's activities and left him to study in the office until it was time for him to leave. Rico was the college-aged son of one of the housekeepers and was more than happy to earn money spending his study time at the Inn. Gran adored him and had for many years.

Charlotte drove Shane in her car to the Pink Pelican. It was a cute place to have a cold beer and a sandwich during the day. In the evening, the place morphed into a cool night spot with live music and dancing.

Sitting in the passenger seat of her car, Shane was quiet, staring out the window at the scenery. She didn't mind the silence. It had been a busy day, and she was still mentally sorting through conversations with their guests.

The parking lot was full when they arrived. Charlotte inched her way into a spot at the edge of the property.

"Busy night," said Shane, managing to get out of the car.

She climbed out onto the pavement and locked the car. The sound of music rocked its way to them, and she felt her spirits lift.

A small crowd headed their way, laughing and talking.

Shane took hold of her hand to bypass them and then kept hold of it as they walked to the front entrance.

At the door, Shane spoke to the hostess, who, Charlotte noticed, fluttered her eyelashes at him as she announced a bunch of seats had opened up out on the deck. She handed him two menus. Then Shane led her through the throngs of people who filled the indoor space.

Out on the deck, they found a table at the outer edge and

quickly grabbed it.

Shane handed her a menu. "I know what I want. How about you?"

"You're having the Pelican Burger and a beer, right?"

He grinned and nodded. "A local IPA to go with the burger."

She set down the menu. "That's easy. I'll have the same."

A waitress came over to them wearing the uniform of black shorts and a pink golf shirt. "What can I get you?"

Shane gave her the order and sat back. "Looks like a good crowd."

Charlotte's gaze roamed over the multitude of people on the dance floor and stiffened when she noticed a familiar, dark-haired woman. "Morgan's here."

"Who's she with?" Shane asked, looking to where Charlotte was pointing.

"No one I know," said Charlotte. "Let's hope she doesn't see us. Looks like she's been here partying for a while."

"Forget her," said Shane. "This is our first real date."

"Date? Is that what this is?" Charlotte said before she stopped to think how that might sound. "I'm sorry. That came out wrong. I thought we were just friends."

Shane's gaze settled on her. "Can't friends have a date now and then?"

At the way he was smiling at her, a tingling sensation filled Charlotte. "Sure, we can," she answered, telling herself she and Shane were being honest.

The waitress came with their beers and burgers, stopping any chance for further conversation.

She'd taken the last bite of her burger when Morgan appeared beside their table. "What are you two doing here?" She placed a hand on her hip and faced Shane. "I thought you told me you and Charlotte were just friends?"

"We are," Shane said smoothly.

"Friends with benefits?" Morgan asked, narrowing her eyes at Charlotte.

"Absolutely not," said Charlotte, upset at the way Morgan was speaking to her.

Shane placed a hand on Morgan's arm. "Just settle down. Who are you here with?"

"No one," said Morgan. "I asked Dylan to come, but he said he was busy." Her lower lip formed a pout that might have been cute if her lips weren't lax from the alcohol.

"How are you going to get home?" Shane asked. "You can't drive."

"Well, then," said Morgan, pulling up an empty chair. "I'll get a ride with you two."

Charlotte and Shane exchanged resigned looks.

"Okay, I'll drive you home," said Charlotte. "Tomorrow, someone can bring you here to pick up your car."

"Thanks," said Morgan, leaning toward Shane. "I'm glad you're just friends with Charlotte." She turned to Charlotte. "What happened to you? Why are you dressed like that? You used to be so pretty."

"She *is* pretty," said Shane.

Charlotte brushed off her T-shirt. "I happen to like what I'm wearing." The fact that her mother would be appalled at her outfit gave Charlotte a little thrill. With a little help from Gran, she was becoming her own person.

As she was driving Shane and Morgan home, Charlotte thought how silly it was that she felt she had to defend herself because of what she was wearing. It was all so shallow. She chalked it up to another summer learning experience, certain there was more to come.

Back at the cove, Shane thanked Charlotte for the ride. "I'll walk Morgan across the cove and be back. All right?"

Charlotte checked her watch. “It’s getting late, and I have the morning shift tomorrow. Can we postpone it until tomorrow night?”

“Sure. That might work out better for me, too.” He touched the back of his head. “That music was loud.”

“Gawd! You act like an old man,” muttered Morgan.

“He’s still recovering from his injury,” Charlotte reminded her, though she was becoming more and more irritated at the way Morgan leaned against Shane, holding onto his arm.

“Thanks again for everything,” Shane said and walked away with Morgan, leaving Charlotte staring at them.

CHAPTER THIRTY-SIX

CHARLOTTE

Charlotte sat in on a staff meeting after lunch on Monday afternoon, eager to tell her cousins the news.

She glanced at Beryl, whom she had invited to the meeting to help with scheduling. Gran had a way of attracting excellent people to her devoted staff. Beryl was no exception. Of average height and medium weight, she was in her late fifties, like her husband. Her black hair, streaked in the front with a natural white strip, surrounded a strong-featured face. More handsome than pretty, her kind nature showed in her dark-brown eyes.

"Pretty exciting for Ellie to have you girls here helping her," said Beryl. "We'll work together to make it right for her."

"Oh, yes," Charlotte said, waiting for Brooke to sort the paperwork in front of her.

When Brooke finally looked up, she smiled at them. "Thank you, Beryl, for being here. Gran said you're indispensable, and we've already seen it."

"I've got exciting news," said Charlotte. "I can't wait any longer to tell you that all the soft goods will be delivered next Monday. Then we can begin to change out bedspreads, sheets, and new towels for the old ones."

"We will need to launder the sheets and towels first," reminded Beryl. "And we'll need a double crew to change everything out and prepare the old spreads that are in decent enough condition for delivery to a charity."

Charlotte turned to her cousins. "We decided on the charity

helping women in shelters. Right?"

"And the homeless shelters," Brooke reminded her. "With that in mind, I'd like to address the dining room issues. Livy and I have taken an inventory and want to get rid of some of the smaller items and order more."

"It ties into the kitchen," said Livy. "We need to replenish glassware and mugs. We discovered some old ones partially hidden in the back of the sideboard in the dining room and want to get rid of them to make space for updated ones. Also, some silverware needs to be added to our supply, especially if we go ahead with plans to serve occasional dinners."

"I found a company online that will give us bulk discounts for ordering mugs. I've found beige pottery mugs imprinted with the outline of a sanderling on it," said Brooke.

"I want to add the name of the Inn to them for no cost and be able to sell them to guests," said Livy. "Several women in one of the groups wondered if we had things like that for sale."

"What is all this going to cost?" asked Charlotte, pleased that Livy and Brooke were working together on this.

"Not as much as you might think." Brooke handed out a list she'd made. She turned to Beryl. "We need to schedule a deep clean for the dining room."

"I don't think we need any new furniture for that room," said Charlotte. "Do we agree on that?"

Brooke and Livy nodded.

"Why don't I schedule the deep clean for Wednesday?" said Beryl. "We'll devote Thursday and Friday to cleaning the gathering room. Are any new furnishings or decorations on order for that room?"

"None that I know of. I'd like to suggest moving some of the photos and paintings around between the dining room and the gathering room. I've mentioned it to Dylan, and he's offered to look at everything we have and make some suggestions." Charlotte beamed at them. "He's even promised to give us one of his pieces of art."

"That would be fantastic," said Livy.

"I'm going to talk to him about some ideas I have for notecards using his artwork," said Charlotte. "Maybe we can use the one he gives us for special cards, and we can write a little story about it on the back of them. A PR kind of thing for both him and the Inn."

"That would be perfect," said Livy. "We can add them to the collection I want to set up next to the registration desk. I figure we can sell things like hats, T-shirts, mugs, and cards that promote us. Nothing that isn't tasteful, but things our guests have been asking for."

"It's an easy way to spread the news about the Inn," said Charlotte. "There's a lot of competition out there."

"As long as we don't invest a lot of money in it," said Brooke, holding up the budget she had given to them.

"What about a fresh coat of paint in the dining room?" said Beryl. "Amby told me the other day that he thinks it needs it."

Charlotte looked to her cousins, and they all agreed. "Okay, now, I've been working on banners for the website and have several to show you."

"Thank you, girls, for inviting me to the meeting," said Beryl, rising. "Don't worry. The team and I will take care of the dining room and the gathering room for you. Any questions about what to do with what we find, we'll ask you."

Charlotte got to her feet and impulsively gave Beryl a hug. There was something so real, so kind about her that she couldn't resist.

After Beryl had gone, Brooke and Livy stood looking over Charlotte's shoulder as she showed them some ideas for the updated website. The banner they chose was a simple one of sanderlings, which look like sandpipers, on the beach as waves washed ashore. A picture of the Inn inside a circle was included to the left. On the home page, the background of the website picked up the color of the water. Charlotte was developing other pages for things like attractions, special events, and the like.

"Simplicity is the key. We must make it easy for people to reach us, to know what we offer, and how they can make reservations both online and with direct calls," said Charlotte. "I'm trying to do the same thing for the Family First project for Shane."

"Speaking of Shane, what happened to your date last night?" said Livy. "Morgan was talking about how she rescued Shane. What is she talking about?"

Charlotte drew in a deep breath. "The only rescue that took place was our rescue of her. We met at the Pink Pelican. She'd had too much to drink to drive. We ended our so-called date early so I could drive her back here." She shook her head. "Besides, Shane and I aren't dating. We just went out for a quick burger."

"Charlie, you're either dating or you're not," complained Brooke.

"I'm as confused as you are, but Shane said we're just friends out on a date. He's not ready for anything more, and right now I need to concentrate on me. How do you like this one?" Charlotte tugged on the green T-shirt she was wearing. It said, "*I Forgot My Designer Shirt at Home.*"

Livy laughed. "Another of Gran's shirts?"

"Until I can buy some of my own," Charlotte said. "You can't imagine how freeing it is for me to wear them."

Livy's expression grew serious. "Actually, I can. My mother buys me clothes thinking it will make me change my mind about wanting to date, get married, and have kids. I'm not ready for that."

Charlotte and Livy turned to Brooke. "What's going on with you?"

Brooke shrugged. "Nothing. Absolutely nothing. I tried calling my mother and had to leave a message. Okay by me. I had no real news at all."

"You were supposed to go sailing with Eric. Has that been rescheduled?" Charlotte asked Brooke.

"I'm going sailing with him on Saturday. Why don't you come along?" said Livy.

"And be a third wheel? I don't think so," said Brooke.

Livy took hold of her arm. "Listen to me. It's not like that between us. I refuse to leave you behind."

Brooke's face brightened. "Okay, I'll do it. Charlotte's working that day, and I'll be free to go."

Charlotte momentarily felt a bit jealous of their carefree afternoon, and then she rallied. It would be good for Brooke to get out. She'd been more or less stuck with Adam and Skye.

After the meeting, Charlotte headed outside excited about the changes beginning to take place at the Inn. The new icemaker and extra freezer Livy had bought were installed in the kitchen, and a new dishwasher was coming next week. In addition, Brooke had purchased the card table for the gathering room, and she was about to meet Dylan to discuss shifting the artwork in the Inn.

She saw Dylan walking toward her and waved to him.

Smiling, he jogged over to her. "Glad you called. I've been thinking about some of the paintings in the Inn. You're right. A few need to be changed around. While it was quiet, I looked them over in the dining room, gathering room, and other locations. Your grandmother has an exceptional eye for interesting, original work."

"She likes to go to the art shows in the area," said Charlotte. "I used to love to go with her."

Dylan studied her and then said, "I like your T-shirt – "*Sorry, I'm Not Alexa – Don't Tell Me What to Do!*" Your grandmother usually wears shirts like that."

Charlotte laughed. "This is hers. I borrowed it."

He grinned. "Bet she'd like to see that on you."

As they headed over to the Inn, Shane called to them. They turned and waited for him to approach.

"What are you two up to?" Shane asked.

"We're about to do some work inside the Inn," said Charlotte.

"And I'm about to ask Charlotte to join me on a trip to the Dali Museum tomorrow," Dylan said, grinning at her. "I'll even buy lunch. How about it, Charlie?"

Surprised but pleased, Charlotte said, "I'd like that. Thanks."

"Want to join us, Shane?" Dylan asked.

"No, thanks. I have plans with Morgan," he said.

Charlotte hid her surprise. Was this a favor for Granny Liz, or had Morgan finally convinced him she wasn't as difficult as they sometimes thought?

"You're welcome to come with us now to do an inventory of the artwork in the Inn," Charlotte said. "I noticed that you have some nice paintings in your condo."

"Thanks anyway. And, Charlie, I can't get together with you tonight as I'd mentioned."

"All right," said Charlotte. "Maybe another time."

As Shane walked away, she turned to Dylan. "After reviewing the interior, you're invited for margaritas with Brooke, Livy, and me. We can discuss it then." Shane stopped, glanced back at them, and then trotted away.

"I didn't know you were seeing Shane," Dylan said to her.

"I'm not. I'm helping Granny Liz by driving him back and forth to Miami when he needs to go there. That's it," said Charlotte realizing it was all too true.

Once she and Dylan entered the Inn, all her attention was on Dylan and his suggestions. Listening to him talk about the colors, shapes, and textures in the paintings, Charlotte was impressed with not only his knowledge but how quickly he understood what she had in mind.

The Inn had an old-fashioned look with furniture that, while in excellent condition, seemed outdated. With a few pieces reupholstered or replaced, mixing classic with contemporary looks, the interior living areas would be given a fresh look.

Dylan, with his art training, agreed.

She made notes on the changes for the dining room, including changing the wall color from a pale yellow to a crisp white to offset the artwork and the deep turquoise carpet that was too new to replace. Besides the rug's color was perfect, reminding guests of the Gulf waters outside. A wall of windows lined the dining room, giving guests a view of a palm-shaded side garden where small events were sometimes held, lending a tropical feel to the interior. The room worked well with the ability to change from a relaxed atmosphere at breakfast to something more upscale for dinner and other events.

The gathering room was more difficult. As an interior space, it needed both warmth and coziness in a tropical setting. The walls were painted a soft green that both Charlotte and Dylan agreed was suitable. But the furnishings were dark.

"Paint or replace some pieces in the room with white," Dylan suggested.

Charlotte gave him a thoughtful look. "I like that idea. The couches are fine as they are, but the bookshelves, cupboards, and sideboard would look better white. I bet we can get Amby to paint them for us." She gave Dylan a high-five. "Thanks for all your ideas."

"No problem. Each room is like canvas, you know?" he said quietly.

"You're brilliant," said Charlotte, impulsively throwing her arms around him. "C'mon, let's go find the others."

They walked over to Gran's house and into the kitchen.

Livy grinned and held up a blender full of margaritas. "We've been waiting for you."

"What have the two of you cooked up?" Brooke said, smiling at them.

"Lots of interesting ideas," said Charlotte. "Let's grab our drinks and go out to the porch. Dylan has been terrific about helping us."

Livy poured the drinks, and they carried them out to the porch. An onshore breeze cooled the air and carried with it the smell of saltwater and the sound of the waves hitting the shore.

They pulled chairs into a circle, and after taking a sip of her drink, Charlotte began to talk, checking her notes from time to time.

"Fantastic" said Livy.

"And not too expensive," Brooke added.

"I know," Charlotte said proudly. She smiled at him. "As Dylan says, each room is like a canvas."

"First of all, the Inn is beautiful and well designed. That makes it easy," said Dylan. "But like Charlie says, changing things up a bit will make a big difference."

"Once the paintings get mounted on the walls, we can coordinate dining room linens with some of them," said Charlotte. "I've already made a deal with the supplier."

"What about the meeting room?" Brooke asked. "Any major changes there?"

Charlotte shook her head.

"Will it do for small private dinners?" asked Livy. "I don't want to give up on that idea. I checked. We have plenty of folding tables and dining chairs in storage if we decide to go ahead with it."

Charlotte turned to Dylan. "The meeting room can easily be used for private dining, don't you think?"

"I do," he said agreeably. "It's set up to be flexible." He checked his watch. "I've got to go. I'm meeting Adam for dinner. We're headed into Clearwater. Thanks for the drink. See you tomorrow, Charlie. I'll pick you up at ten."

"I'll be ready," said Charlotte ignoring the curious stares of her cousin.

Dylan left, crossing the lawn toward the other end of the cove where he and Adam were staying.

"What?" Charlotte finally said, holding in laughter at the curious looks her cousins were giving her.

"You and Dylan?" Livy said.

"I think it's nice," said Brooke, smiling at her.

Charlotte wasn't sure how it felt. She just knew Dylan was a nice man who got the "new" her.

CHAPTER THIRTY-SEVEN

CHARLOTTE

At ten the next morning, Charlotte stood ready by the door, waiting for Dylan to pick her up. She'd always loved art, had dabbled in watercolors but was drawn to big, bold statements in other media.

Dylan was a fun person to be around, which is why he, no doubt, was a bit amused by her obvious attempt to change. That made her feel comfortable with him. She hadn't put on one of Gran's T-shirts today. She'd pulled her long hair back into a ponytail. The only makeup she wore was a soft-pink lipstick. She wore a short skirt, a tank top, and sandals on her feet.

He pulled up into Gran's driveway in his car, and Charlotte hurried out to greet him.

Once she had settled in the passenger seat, Dylan took off, handling the wheel of his red Toyota truck with ease. "Should be an interesting day. The museum is fantastic."

"It was built a long time ago, right?" said Charlotte.

"Yes, in 1982, but the new building opened in early 2011. Wait until you see it. It's a simple rectangle that has a large, free-form glass bubble known as the 'Enigma' bursting out of it. You're going to love it."

"It seems silly that I haven't been before. At least not in years," Charlotte said, reacting to Dylan's enthusiasm. His blue eyes lit with excitement as he glanced at her and back at the road. "What else should I know about the museum?"

"The Enigma pays homage to the dome that adorns Dali's

museum in Spain. Inside there's a circular staircase. Dali was obsessed with spirals and the shape of the DNA molecule."

"You certainly know your stuff," said Charlotte, giving him a bright smile.

He grinned. "He's one of my heroes. But I promise you I won't make you stay long enough to see everything. There are over 2,400 of his works on display."

She laughed. "I'd die of starvation."

He joined her laughter and then said, "How are things going with the three of you women in Gran's house?"

"Surprisingly well. We're different enough to make it work. And we've been more or less doing things on our own, so we're not in each other's way. Being here for the summer is good for all of us."

"Yes, I'm finding it that way too," said Dylan. "I miss the mountains, of course, but I see things from a different angle, if you know what I mean."

"There's only one angle in Florida. A 180-degree one. Pretty flat."

He grinned. "I like you, Charlie. I'm hoping to get to know you a lot better."

"Thanks, me too," Charlotte said. It had been such fun to work together on ideas for the upgrades of the Inn.

As Charlotte approached the museum, she couldn't stop staring at the light-colored building with the blue glass bubble appearing to burst out of it, as Dylan had described.

"It's stunning. I've seen pictures of it, but they don't do it justice," she said.

"I think Dali himself would love it," Dylan said.

For the next three hours, Charlotte was consumed by the paintings, photos, prints, and other works of Dali. Seeing them made her wish she could talk to him. She saw cards with a few of his quotes. *"I don't do drugs. I am drugs." "Have no fear of perfection - you'll never reach it." "Intelligence without ambition is a bird without wings."*

"Fascinating, isn't he?" Dylan said, coming up behind her. "Are you ready to grab something to eat?"

Charlotte clasped her stomach as it emitted a distinctive growl.

"Guess you are," said Dylan, taking her arm. "Let's go somewhere else. We can return here afterward or come back another time."

"I'd like to come back another day. My brain is whirling with information and sights. I want time to absorb it all."

"I agree," Dylan said, leading her through the crowd.

Later, finishing her Chicken Pineapple Salad, Charlotte let out a sigh of pleasure. "This has been a wonderful day. Thank you for thinking of it, Dylan."

He reached across the table and clasped her hand. "I've been thinking of doing something like this with you for a long time. Maybe tomorrow or Friday we can plan something."

"That would be lovely, but we'd have to make it another time. I'll be with Shane in Miami. I promised Granny Liz that I'd drive him there and back."

He studied her. "Is there something going on between the two of you? Shane can't keep his eyes off you."

"What? No, we're just both accommodating Granny Liz and her need to have Shane close by while he's healing." Charlotte didn't know how else to react. Shane wasn't about to get serious about her or anyone else. Not when he was dealing with his personal issues.

"How does it feel to have saved his life?" Dylan asked. "I

heard all about it. Eric was pretty upset about the whole thing."

"It was scary. I thought for a moment he was gone." A shiver crossed her shoulders. She closed her eyes. "Thank God, Gran had all of us in the family take lifesaving courses. I hope I never have to use that training again."

"I can imagine," Dylan said. He looked up as their waitress returned.

"Anything else?" the waitress asked.

Dylan gave Charlotte a questioning look.

She shook her head. "No, thanks. I'm full."

"Okay, then, just the check," Dylan told the waitress.

On the drive back to the cove, Charlotte and Dylan talked easily about some of the art they'd seen.

"Each was different. How could one man produce so many paintings?" Charlotte said.

"Such talent," said Dylan with a note of envy.

She reached over and patted his shoulder. "You have talent, too. Think of the success you've had."

"I've been lucky," he agreed. "But when I see talent like his, it sure puts it all in perspective."

They were quiet, and Charlotte took that time to gaze out at the passing landscape. She loved palm trees. Their swaying fronds seem to whisper stories of their own. She'd liked things about New York but was beginning to believe this was a better place for her.

Dylan pulled up behind Gran's house. "Thanks for a nice day, Charlie," he said, leaning over and giving her a quick kiss.

She responded and pulled away. "It was a lot of fun. Thanks."

"I'll call to set up something else with you," Dylan said.

"Okay. That would be nice," she said, realizing she meant it. Dylan was a special man.

###

The next morning Charlotte once again met Shane next door to drive him to Miami. She was pleased to have the time alone with him. Others had seen his interest in her, yet he acted as if he didn't care. She understood to a certain degree, but it was driving her crazy. She couldn't deny her attraction to him, but she wasn't going to do anything about it. She knew enough about him to know if he made up his mind to step away, he would.

Granny Liz smiled as Charlotte joined her, Shane, Austin, and Grandpa Sam in the kitchen. "There's our chauffeur. Charlie, come have something to eat before you take off."

"No, thanks. I had a big breakfast at home."

Shane got to his feet. "I'm through. We can be on our way."

"I could've taken you," said Austin.

Granny Liz waved away his offer. "The arrangements have already been made. Besides, aren't you going to see what Livy is up to today?"

"I guess. She said something about my helping Amby move some furniture around."

"See? There you go. That's settled." Granny Liz turned to Charlotte. "Okay, you're all set. Have a safe trip to Miami. See you sometime tomorrow."

Charlotte exchanged amused glances with Austin. He knew as well as she that Granny Liz was trying to do a little matchmaking. And, for once, it was all right with her.

On the trip to Miami, Shane read through some papers he took from his briefcase, and then he turned to her. "I saw Dylan last night. He said you had a great time going to the Dali Museum."

"It was an extraordinary day. I'm still thinking about some

of Dali's work."

"He tells me you're going out again." Shane gave her a questioning look.

"Dylan said he'd arrange another day for us. He's fun to be with."

"Oh," said Shane turning his attention back to his papers.

"What's your meeting about today?" she asked.

"A family wants to adopt the foster child they've been caring for. I'm helping them go through the steps and meeting with the guardian ad litem volunteer about the case. Then I'm checking on Elijah. He has a summer job at the school, tutoring kids in math. What are you going to do while I'm busy?"

"I thought I'd do some shopping. Maybe have lunch."

"I'd like to take you to lunch," he said. "I should be through by then."

"Okay. Nothing fancy, though. I'm not dressed for it."

He chuckled. "I like the shirt." She was wearing a denim skirt, and her pink T-shirt said: "*Nope, Not Today*."

"You're fine," he said. "No worries." His cell phone rang. Frowning, he clicked on the call. "Hello, Mother. Today? I'm not sure ... I understand ..." He let out a long sigh. "Okay, but I'm bringing a guest with me. No one you know."

When he ended the call, he turned to her. "I need to ask a big favor of you."

"Your mother?"

He nodded and let out another sigh. "I've been commanded to go to her house for a late lunch. It would be a big help if you went with me."

"Okay. I'll go," said Charlotte, aware of his distress. Just who was this person who made her son so unhappy. "I'll drop you off wherever you want and go shopping. I'm not meeting your mother like this."

"I understand," said Shane, confirming her suspicion that her appearance would matter. Curious about his mother, she wanted to make a first good impression.

Later, as she changed into a new sleeveless sundress that was both fun with bright tropical colors and business-like in style, she was pleased she'd found something suitable and more like her new image. She added a funky, multi-colored bead necklace she'd found on sale but left her diamond studs in place on her ear lobes. She'd received the earrings for an earlier birthday and wore them all the time because that's what she'd been wearing when she'd decided to do as Gran asked and come to Florida. She thought of them as her good-luck pieces.

Shane called to say he was taking a cab to his condo and would meet her there. Then he'd drive them to Star Island, where his mother's house was located.

Charlotte understood the nervousness in his voice. Star Island was impressive. A manmade island in Biscayne Bay, it was filled with huge waterfront homes that a few celebrities owned or used to own.

When Shane walked into his condo and saw Charlotte, he whistled. "You look great. Beautiful."

She returned his smile, pleased.

"Okay, let's go. One is never late for one of Mother's commands," he said wryly. "That always starts off any visit badly."

"I know this isn't easy for you, especially when you're trying to deal with the past. Are you sure you want to do this?"

Shane nodded firmly. "It's one of the things I have to get over. She's my mother, and even though I don't like her and never will, I respect that. After the divorce, she made sure Austin and I had a safe life. She didn't love Ricardo Perez, but she was good to him, and he saw to it that she was well taken care of. A win-win situation for them both."

"He's deceased?" Charlotte asked.

"Yes. He's been gone now for a couple of years. He lived a long life. A bit of a loner, actually, after building and then retiring from his import and shipping business. He regretted having no children of his own and was nice to Austin and me. My car was a gift from him and my mother a few years ago. He wanted me to have it."

As they drove onto the island, Charlotte told herself to relax. It was only one lunch with a woman who was sure to be difficult, but she'd do this for Shane.

Shane pulled into the driveway behind a mammoth, two-story white stucco house with a red tile roof. She got out of the car just as Shane hurried around the car to hold the door for her.

A woman of medium height and with some girth, who had graying dark hair pulled away from her face, stepped outside in a simple black skirt and white blouse. "Shane!" she cried, holding her arms out for him.

He stepped into them and hugged her tight. "Sofia! It's always wonderful to see you. This is Charlotte Bradford." He turned to Charlotte. "Make no mistake about it, Sofia Morales runs this household."

Charlotte shook Sofia's hand and smiled into the kindness in her eyes. She liked the way Sophia's lips curved pleasantly in her plump face. She knew that whatever dysfunction Shane had experienced early in his life must have been softened by this woman who obviously cared for him.

"I've known this young man since he was ten, and I was hired as Ms. Diana's social secretary, among other things. Didn't he turn out well?"

Charlotte saw Shane's discomfort at the compliment but said, "Yes, he did."

"Now come inside," Sofia told him. "Your mother is waiting for you, and you don't want to keep her waiting."

Sofia led them into a massive, two-story entrance, through a wide hallway, and into an open entry facing the water. "You'll be dining out on the patio today. A nice little breeze has come up, making it a pleasant place to be."

They stepped out onto a covered patio that led to a beautiful, full-length pool. Beyond it, a green lawn sloped down to a dock that sat empty in the water. On either side of the property, large homes had sizeable yachts moored at their docks. The sense of exclusivity was overwhelming.

A tall blonde sat in a chair, her light-blue eyes assessing Charlotte before turning them to her son. "You're here at last, Shane, after avoiding me for far too long. You know how much I miss seeing you when we don't meet for a time." She held out her hand, and he took it.

"It has been a while," he conceded politely.

She faced Charlotte. "And who do we have here?" Her glance swept over Charlotte with a tinge of disapproval, making Charlotte feel uneasy.

"Mother, I'd like you to meet Charlotte Bradford, a special friend of mine," said Shane smiling at Charlotte. "This is my mother, Diana Perez."

"How do you do, Mrs. Perez," Charlotte said politely, shaking hands with her, finding his mother's fingers as cold as she appeared to be.

"Sofia, will you please see that Starr is ready with lunch?" said Diana. "You know how I hate making people wait."

"No worries," said Shane. "We have some time, though Charlotte and I can't stay long after lunch. I have a business appointment."

He helped Charlotte into a chair and sat next to her.

Shane's mother studied him, her erect posture making her

seem even more unapproachable. "Shane, don't tell me you're still committed to family law. It's such a waste. Ricardo made sure you met his lawyer so you'd have a place in his law firm. It's what we both wanted for you. Someone with your background shouldn't be doing such menial work with families who can't even pay you properly."

Charlotte held in a gasp.

Shane clenched his jaw and then spoke. "I'm committed to my work, Mother. I'm not about to stop doing it because I could make more money elsewhere."

His mother clucked her tongue. "You've made a foolish choice considering the opportunities you have for other work." She shook her head. "But then, you've always been impossible to deal with. Just like your father. If things don't work out, don't come crying to me for financial help."

"I wouldn't count on you for that or anything else," said Shane with an unmistakable edge to his voice.

Charlotte glanced at him, wondering how to ease the situation.

Seeing her look of concern, Shane settled back in his chair.

Shane's mother turned to her. "And what do you do, dear?"

"At the moment, I'm helping my grandmother with The Sanderling Cove Inn and also working for Shane's non-profit," said Charlotte, stopping when Shane's mother stiffened.

"That dreadful cove. So many bad memories there." Diana closed her eyes and shook her head. When she opened her eyes, she studied Charlotte thoughtfully. "Now that I think of it, I believe I met your mother there one time. A beautiful woman with red hair so like yours. There was a tragedy. A little boy who drowned, I recall. You must be the younger sister."

"Yes," said Charlotte numbly as a torrent of old feelings washed over her. She glanced at Shane.

He noticed her distress and turned to his Mother. "What social events are you attending this summer?"

"Oh, the usual. I have friends to see on Nantucket, and a trip to France is planned. Anything to get away from this heat and humidity. Ricardo never could understand why I detest it so," his mother said. She dabbed at her forehead with a lace-edged handkerchief.

"Would you like to go inside?" Shane asked.

"No, I like it here," his mother responded. "Something about watching the water is so peaceful."

A young Asian woman wearing a white chef's jacket and black pants emerged from the house carrying a tray of food. She set it down on a stand next to a round, glass-topped table.

Sophia appeared. "If everyone will come, you will be served."

Charlotte followed Shane's mother to the table at the far end of the patio. Shane gave Charlotte's hand a quick squeeze and then helped to seat his mother.

Hibiscus-pink placemats and napkins, matching the hibiscus flowers floating in a glass bowl in the center of the table were placed at each setting.

"I'm serving a Vietnamese noodle and smoked chicken salad," said the young chef, looking anxiously at Shane's mother.

Charlotte studied the noodles, carrots, red chilis, beansprouts, and what looked like mint leaves and felt her mouth water. "This looks delicious. Thank you."

The chef stood aside, and at a nod from Shane's mother, she lifted the empty tray and walked away.

Sophia served them iced tea. "Anyone want anything more?" When no answer came, she, too, walked away.

It was silent as they all began to eat, and then Shane's mother said, "Charlotte, dear, please don't think ill of me, but

I must warn you that Shane has had many girlfriends in the past. I hope you don't think anything serious would come of this. I would hate to see a beautiful woman like you get hurt."

Charlotte choked on the sip of iced tea she'd just swallowed.

Shane's face turned beet-red. He clenched his fists and threw down his napkin. "Why do you do this, Mother? Make any nice moment a mess?"

"I'm just making a fair observation," his mother protested.

"No, you're not. You're punishing me for avoiding you. I know you very well. It's nothing new. I've remembered a lot from my childhood. None of it good."

Shane's mother shook a finger at him. "We're not going back to that, remember? We're both moving forward. I'm just trying to do something nice for Charlotte. A fair warning."

Charlotte steadied her breath and turned to Shane's mother. "There's no need for a warning. As Shane said, we're friends. Very special friends who don't need the judgment of others."

"Well, I never ..."

"No, you never think about anything but yourself and the images you want to portray," said Shane. "The problem is your true self comes through from time to time. You may blind others, but I see you for the person you are." He stood. "Let's go, Charlotte."

She rose and came to his side.

"For the record, Mother, I tried, I tried to have a pleasant visit with you. But once again, you make it impossible."

As they started to walk away, Shane's mother bent her head and began sobbing.

Charlotte pulled Shane to a stop. "Settle this now."

Shane turned back to his mother. "I'm getting help to resolve some of these issues. But, I don't know why we can't have decent conversations, why you can't be considerate of me and my feelings."

His mother lifted her face. "You don't? You're just like your father. That's why."

Shane fingered trails through his blond hair. "But it's been over between you and Dad for years. Can't you get past that?"

"Don't you see? I loved him more than I can ever love anyone else again." She gazed up at him, her face a mask of pain, made wet by her tears.

"Mom, it's over. All of it. You said we have to leave it behind and move forward. That's what I intend to do. Until you agree to get help, I won't be coming here again."

His mother's face lost color and grew slack. "You called me Mom. Maybe that's a beginning."

"Perhaps," said Shane. "Let me know how you're doing." He turned, took hold of Charlotte's hand, and they headed into the house, away from the patio and the horrible woman who was Shane's mother.

Charlotte studied the lines of pain on Shane's face and gave his hand a squeeze, deeply saddened by what she'd seen and heard.

CHAPTER THIRTY-EIGHT

CHARLOTTE

As they prepared to get into Shane's car, Sophia rushed out of the house. "Oh, Shane, I'm so sorry." She stood before him. "Your mother has good days and bad days. Unfortunately, this wasn't one of the good ones."

Shane faced her. "The bad ones are only worse. You've seen it over and over again. She has this urge to hurt others. She needs help."

Sophia wrung her hands. "I've tried to talk to her about it. Since Mr. Ricardo has been gone, she's been at loose ends. He thought she was beautiful and caring. Now she has no one."

"No one to fawn over her." Shane shook his head sadly. "She needs professional treatment, Sophia. Please try to convince her to get it."

Sophia threw her arms around him. "Again, I'm so sorry."

"Me, too," said Shane with such pain in his voice that Charlotte blinked back tears.

Shane assisted Charlotte into his car and then settled himself behind the wheel.

"Are you okay to drive?" Charlotte asked him.

He nodded, took a deep breath, and instead of roaring away like she thought he might, he slowly pulled out of the driveway.

Charlotte drew a deep breath, still stunned by what had happened. She might have felt alone in her family, but she'd never experienced such cruelty as Shane's mother had shown him.

"There you have it," said Shane, flexing his jaw. "Now, you know why I can never seem to make a long-term commitment to anyone. The thought of a relationship becoming like my parents' makes me sick."

"Does your father act that way toward you?"

"No, he's a kind man. When he and my mother were together, she constantly belittled him, making him furious. I understand that now. Dad has a nice family, a loving wife, two kids. A boy and a girl. He's very good to them. He's Granny Liz's son, after all."

"What about Austin? How does he deal with your mother?"

Shane wove his way through traffic silently for a few minutes and then spoke. "She adores him. But as an adult, he sees how unhealthy that is when compared to her treatment of me. He doesn't resemble my dad like I do."

"Does Austin see her often?"

"No. She can turn on him too." He let out a long sigh. "I'm sorry you had to witness how fucked up my family is."

Charlotte reached over and patted his arm. "You're not your mother. You're a very special and wonderful man, Granny Liz's grandson. Don't let your mother ruin how you think of yourself. She's a sick woman."

He glanced at her and let out another long breath. "You're right. Thanks."

When they returned to the condo, they got out of the car.

"Didn't you say you have another appointment this afternoon?" Charlotte asked him.

He shook his head. "I just mentioned it so I could keep my options open." He let out a soft sound of disgust. "I learned to do that early on. Except I forgot how that can lead to her rant about my work."

She took his arm. "Let's go inside and take a rest. I think we both need one."

He held back and studied her. "Thank you, Charlie, for not freaking out on me. I appreciate it."

She gazed up into his face. "We promised to be honest with one another, so I'm telling you now, I'll always be here for you, Shane."

Shane blinked rapidly.

She noticed the wetness at the corners of his eye and wrapped her arms around him, wanting more than anything to take his pain away.

With a muffled sob, he pulled her close.

They hugged each other silently, though Charlotte felt the tremor that went through him.

When he stepped back, he cupped her face in his broad hands. "You'll never know how much you mean to me. Why don't you go on inside? I need some time to think."

He unlocked the door to his condo and stood aside to let her in.

"Where will you go?" she asked him, worried.

"I'm going to walk around for a bit. Don't worry. I'm okay." He waved at her and left her standing there.

With a sigh, Charlotte went inside, grateful for some time alone. She hadn't wanted to let Shane know how shaken she was by his mother's behavior that she suspected was made worse by drugs of some kind. There'd been a glassy look to his mother's eyes when she'd taken off her sunglasses to dine.

Charlotte changed into shorts and a T-shirt. Then, realizing how exhausted she felt, she stretched out on the couch. When Shane came back, they'd decide whether to stay in Miami or return to the cove.

Thinking about what Shane had experienced in his life was too much to handle. Her limbs grew heavy. She rolled on her side and let her mind empty of the memory of such a horrible scene.

Soft whispers buzzed in her ear. Groaning, Charlotte shifted her position. Then she felt a hand on her shoulder. Her eye shot open. "Wha..."

"Charlie, it's me. We've gotta talk." Shane, kneeling by the couch, looked at her with concern.

She sat up and stretched. "Give me time to wake up. I'll be right back."

After splashing cold water on her face, she patted it dry and drew deep breaths. She'd been sleeping hard and knew whatever Shane had to say wouldn't be easy.

When she returned to the living room, he was standing by the sliding glass doors looking out at his small patio.

She came up beside him. "What is it, Shane?"

He faced her. "I'm sorry. I can't do this anymore."

"Do what?" she asked. Her heart pounded with dismay.

"Us, this, friendship," he said. "Aw, hell, I'm blowing it. Look, we promised we'd be honest friends. I'm being honest now. I can't be friends with you any longer."

Charlotte felt her knees weaken. "Why? I like you? I thought you felt the same."

"See? That's why. You *like* me, but I *love* you. I felt it when I first saw you on the beach with your cousins. It was instantaneous. The feeling has grown each time I've been with you. But I'd made a promise to you, and now ..."

Charlotte's heart began beating so fast she thought she might faint. "Wait! You *love* me?"

"Yes, but our promise ..."

Charlotte reached up on her toes, hugged him tightly, and kissed him. "Stop talking," she said between covering his face with kisses and then meeting his lips.

When he finally pulled away, she said, "I've been playing along with the friends idea because I thought it was best not to want more, that you'd walk away."

He gave her a steady look. "I'm not going to walk away, Charlie, but I can't promise you anything but my love right now. You know I have things to work through before I can make any other commitment to you."

She lifted his hand and kissed it. "This is just the beginning. I know it. I love you, too, Shane."

He swept her up into his arms and held on tight. "You're the best thing that's ever happened to me," he whispered in her ear. "I promise to be faithful to you while we see if it will work between us."

She listened to his words and felt her heart fill with joy. He loved her. In the days ahead, they'd sort things out. It was what they both wanted.

That night, after they'd shared some pizza Shane had ordered delivered to his condo, they sat sipping beer and talking. Shane did most of the talking. Now that they'd come to a decision to see where their relationship might go, it was as if the words blocked inside him couldn't come out fast enough. Charlotte was relieved to hear him talk about good memories with Granny Liz and Grandpa Sam and some made with his father and his new family. "Dad wanted me to join his law firm in Atlanta, but I didn't want to work with corporate law."

"And Ricardo made some introductions for you," Charlotte prompted.

"Yes, but I didn't want to tie myself to him or my mother. As I mentioned, he was a generous man, brought out the best in my mother when she was with him, but you know what she's really like."

"I admire your choice of family law," she said. "I'm not sure what I'm going to do in the future, but it has to be something that makes me happy. I'm enjoying working on PR for the Family First, and I'm glad to be helping Gran with the Inn, but I don't like the day-to-day stuff there as much as Livy and Brooke do."

"All I know is I want to make this thing work between us," said Shane. "I want to make you happy."

"You already have, Shane. Just knowing you want us together makes me happier than I've been in a long time." Charlotte accepted the hand he offered her.

"Come with me," he said. "I can't wait any longer to show you how I feel."

She took his hand, and they walked into the bedroom together.

Later, Charlotte lay beside Shane, filled with a new sense of peace. She'd been with a man before, but not like this. Their lovemaking was as spiritual as well as physical, an awe-inspiring blend of giving and receiving.

Shane rolled over and faced her. "Your beautiful, you know," he murmured, kissing her.

Charlotte smiled. She knew it was because he made her feel that way.

When Shane pulled his car into Granny Liz's driveway the next day, she emerged from her house, followed by Austin.

"Hey, everything all right between the two of you?"

Charlotte and Shane exchanged glances.

"Yes, why are you asking?" Shane said, looking from his grandmother to his brother.

"Mom called me in one of her rants," Austin said. "It wasn't pleasant."

Shane's lips thinned. He put his arm around Charlotte. "Things are better than ever. Charlie and I have decided to date."

"Exclusively," said Charlotte, her eyes bright as she smiled at Shane.

"Hallelujah," cried Granny Liz. "That's fantastic news."

"Congrats, bro," said Austin. "Wait until your cousins hear, Charlie."

Charlotte grinned. "I called them earlier." They turned as Brooke and Livy raced toward them.

Austin grinned and stepped back as Charlotte and her cousins did a group hug.

CHAPTER THIRTY-NINE

ELLIE

Ellie sat in the business room at the inn where she and John were staying in Ireland. It had been a while since Liz had written her, and she was anxious to read the email that had just come in.

Her eyes absorbed every word. It was as if Liz was talking to her.

> "Fantastic news, Ellie! I think one plan of ours is working. Shane and Charlie have announced that they're dating exclusively. Shane has confided in me that he's working on a few personal issues, and nothing more serious can take place until he's sure of himself and this commitment. But if you saw the way they look at each other, touch one another, you'd know they're goners. Let's keep our fingers crossed.
>
> "As for the others, it's like herding cats, trying to keep track of all of them. Livy did tell me the other day she's having fun going out with any of the men who ask her. Brooke and Adam have decided to be careful of what they say or do in front of Skye, so nothing's happening there. Morgan has gone home to help with her sister's wedding. And Jake told me the other day that he's going to ask Brooke out. We'll see where that goes.
>
> "Eric, Dylan, and Austin are still question marks. I'll write you later. I'm busy seeing what other things we

can accomplish. Sam tells me to butt out, but you and I know that's not going to happen. I promised you. Right?"

Ellie closed the lid of her laptop and smiled. Shane and Charlie were perfect together. She'd always known they would be.

CHAPTER FORTY

BROOKE

Brooke and Livy walked across the lawn to the middle of the cove's shoreline. They were to meet Eric there. He'd row them in his dinghy out to the sailboat moored offshore.

"You're sure Eric didn't mind my coming along with you?" said Brooke.

Livy gave Brooke a pat on the back. "I think he was happy about it. The last time he asked you to go sailing with him, you couldn't go."

"I was sick, and Charlie took my place. That's when Shane almost drowned," Brooke retorted.

"What do you think of Charlie and Shane becoming exclusive? She was pretty quiet about it, but I know how pleased she is," said Livy.

"It happened fast, but when you see them together, you know it's right. Good for Charlie. How about you, Livy? Have any surprise announcements for us?"

Livy laughed, "None planned. I'm having fun not worrying about anything more than having a nice time here in the cove."

"What about Shane's partner, Jed? He's pretty hot, and I know he likes you," teased Brooke.

Livy stopped and shook her head. "I don't know about him. He's nice, but when it comes time to choose someone, I want fireworks, you know?"

Brooke sighed. "Me too."

Eric waved at them as they approached. "Looks like a good

day for a sail. C'mon, I'll row you out there."

Brooke noticed the name of the dinghy: *Little Grin*. "Eric, how adorable. *Little Grin* to go with *Destiny's Smile*. That's perfect!"

Eric chuckled, looking pleased. "I thought it was pretty clever considering my specialty operating on mouths."

"I love it," said Livy. "We brought some treats and cold drinks." She handed Eric a canvas bag.

"Cookies?" Eric asked.

"Yes, I brought cookies along with other goodies."

Brooke and Eric exchanged amused glances. Livy might not want to be known only for her cookies, but she managed to keep a supply on hand.

"Okay, one of you sit in the bow of the boat and the other in the stern seat. "I'll take us out there." He held onto the boat at the water's edge. "Whoever's in the stern will have to push us off."

"I'll do that," said Livy.

Brooke climbed into the boat and held the canvas bag Eric handed her.

Eric settled in the middle seat, his hands on the oars. "Okay, Livy, give the boat a shove and hop in."

As soon as she did, Eric began rowing the short distance out to the boat.

Brooke's spirits lifted. It felt satisfying to be doing something different. She'd been working hard in the office and doing random trips to stores and secondhand shops, looking for bargains.

As they approached the boat, a man stood at the rail and waved. "Ahoy, there!"

Brooke was surprised but pleased to see Jake. He hadn't called or come in lately.

When Eric brought the dinghy alongside the boat, Brooke

handed Jake the bag and then accepted his offer for help climbing into the boat.

Livy came next. Then Eric stowed the oars under the seat and handed Jake the dinghy's painter.

While Jake held onto the dinghy, Eric climbed into the boat and then walked around to the stern and tied the dinghy to a cleat.

Brooke went below and gazed around, impressed by the tidiness of the boat and how everything seemed to have its own special space and function.

"Pretty nice, huh?" Jake came into the galley area and placed the cold drinks they'd brought into a cooler sitting in the sink.

"It *is* nice," she said. "I haven't done that much sailing, but you seem comfortable with it."

"I don't have my own boat, but I'm happy to help a friend sail his. A numbers guy like me likes the idea of OPB."

"OPB?"

Jake grinned. "Other People's Boats. Saves me a lot of money."

Brooke laughed. "You really are a numbers guy. I like it."

"Speaking of that, the end of the month is coming up. I'll be coming into the office to meet with you. Thought we could go over the financials together."

Livy peeked down into the galley. "Hey, you two. No talking business. We're here for fun. Jake, how about handing up a couple of cold waters? It's hot up here."

Jake handed her the water, and after offering one to Brooke and taking one for himself, he climbed up the stairs and into the cockpit.

Livy stood with Eric behind the wheel as he started up the engine. "I'm taking the wheel when you men raise the sails," she said proudly.

"I'll stay out of the way," said Brooke taking a seat in the cockpit.

"Please, everyone, be mindful of the boom," Eric said seriously. "We don't want anyone getting hit in the head and falling overboard again. Pretty scary stuff."

"And I'm not as strong a swimmer as Charlie," said Livy.

Brooke laughed along with the others but couldn't stop thinking of the haunted look on Charlie's face when she'd told them about the accident and how she'd thought Shane had died.

As soon as he and Jake had hoisted the mainsail and jib, Eric took the helm, fell off onto starboard tack, and cut the engine. As the wind filled the sails, the boat heeled to one side, and the hull cut through the water with a hissing sound. Brooke lifted her arms, loving the feel of the wind moving them forward.

Livy took over at the helm while Eric trimmed the sails, working to keep them taut in the wind.

Jake sat down beside Brooke, stretching his tanned legs across the cockpit, securing his feet against the seat opposite them.

Brooke didn't mind the boat heeling, its port rail close to the surface of the water, and neither did Jake. He turned to her with a smile. "Nice breeze today."

"Feels delightful," she said, happy to see him. There was nothing to suggest a numbers whiz when he took off his T-shirt, exposing his well-trimmed torso. That, and the way he looked in swimming trunks sent a tingly sensation through her.

A shift in the wind brought her closer to him. He put an arm around her shoulder, and awareness of him so close to her caught her breath. She felt eyes on her and turned to see Livy smiling at her.

Brooke shook her head. Jake was Gran's accountant, seemingly happy on his own. She wasn't about to be burned by him or any other man who appealed to her. Neither Livy nor Charlie realized how appealing it felt not to be tied to anyone else and the demands they might make of her. Her only commitment to any person outside her family was to Skye Atkins, Adam's daughter. She'd promised Skye's grandmother she'd help keep Skye occupied to give Adam a break.

CHAPTER FORTY-ONE

LIVY

Livy took a break from behind the wheel of *Destiny's Smile* and sat in the cockpit, giving Jake a chance to have a turn at the helm.

"You looked at ease," said Brooke, giving her a smile. "Like a real pro."

Livy grinned. "I'd forgotten what it felt like to be out on the water like this. One of the students at culinary school had a sailboat, and a few of us used to go out with him."

"A cook and a sailor too? Perfect," teased Brooke.

Livy nudged Brooke. "You sound like my mother, trying to make every man seem interesting. Honestly, I can't tell you how much fun I'm having this summer without any of those thoughts coming from her. She knows I'm here to work, so she's laid off on any romance plans for me. It feels so freeing."

"You get along well with everyone," said Brooke.

Livy glanced at the men talking to one another. "It's a nice group of people here at the cove. That makes it easy." She grinned. "Eric told me he has a surprise for us."

"Wonder what it is," said Brooke, getting up and going over to him. When she returned, she wore a big smile. "Guess what? We're going snorkeling."

Livy grinned and gave Eric a thumbs-up sign. She'd snorkeled before, on family vacations in the Caribbean, but it had been a few years. Still, she remembered the thrill of seeing fish swim around her.

###

Later, Eric dropped anchor offshore between Anna Maria Island and Holmes Beach. “This is a suggested area to try,” he said. “All kinds of wildlife too.” A tour boat wasn’t too far away.

Livy pulled on a white T-shirt she’d brought to help prevent sunburn on her fair skin.

After trying various facemasks, she found one that fit. The flippers she was wearing were a little short but would work. The snorkel tube had been sprayed with a sanitizing liquid, and she was ready to go.

Brooke looked adorable in a bikini she and Charlie had helped her pick out. Jake seemed to think so too, from the way he kept glancing at her. Both he and Eric were appealing, as well.

“Okay, let’s stick fairly close together,” said Eric. “You all slip into the water, and I’ll follow. We don’t want to get too far away from the boat.”

Rather than jump, Jake hung his legs over the swim platform at the stern of the boat and slid into the water, gasping a bit from the cold. He treaded water and waited for Brooke, then Livy to join him.

Eric was the last one in and spent a moment adjusting his mask before he gave the “ready” signal, and they took off swimming along the surface of the clear water.

As Livy swam along, awash in memories of past vacations snorkeling in the Caribbean, she thought of Brooke and realized how generous her parents had been to her and her brothers, giving them vacations and other privileges. Now, as an adult on her own, she was determined to enjoy every day of what seemed like a magical summer.

She felt a tug on her arm and turned to see Eric facing her, pointing at something below them. She gave him a thumbs-up sign, and studied the colorful fish swimming in a small group. Then, a bottlenose dolphin playfully swam around them, and Livy's pulse raced with excitement. This was such a treat.

Too soon, Jake indicated it was time to go back. Livy treaded water and realized that what they'd seen wasn't that far from the boat. She swam to it and waited while Jake went aboard and helped Brooke. Eric signaled it was her turn, and she climbed aboard with Jake's helping hand.

When Eric came aboard, he took off his mask, turned, and grinned at her. "That was spectacular."

Impulsively, Livy threw her arms around him. "The best." She turned to the others. "I'm starving. Let's have lunch."

Too late, she realized from the silly grin on Eric's face how much he'd enjoyed that hug.

CHAPTER FORTY-TWO

CHARLOTTE

Charlotte worked the morning shift with a feeling of contentment she'd never known. Though Shane had only proposed dating exclusively, she knew enough about him to realize the greater commitment behind it. She'd decided not to rush anything and see how their relationship played out.

She liked that Shane was both strong and vulnerable. It gave her the courage to share her demons, allowing their relationship to grow much deeper, much faster than most.

She greeted two newcomers to the breakfast table, made introductions to the others, and went into the kitchen to give Billy Bob their orders. He no longer scared her as he had initially. She respected his role at the Inn and treated him accordingly.

After Billy Bob had grumbled about all the women trying to boss him around, she and her cousins had developed a friendly working relationship with him. Beryl already treated them like family and was a joy to work with. In New York, people weren't as quick to form a connection with others. It brought out a different side of her and Charlotte liked the idea.

One of the guests, a single older woman who'd brought a sulky teenage girl with her, wondered where they could shop for souvenirs. Charlotte directed them to St. John's Pass.

"You'll find all kinds of stores and restaurants there. You can even sign up for fishing trips or excursions there, too," said Charlotte, trying to bring a smile to the teenager's face.

She and the grandmother exchanged hopeless looks when the teenager didn't respond.

After they left, Charlotte carried the last of the breakfast dishes into the kitchen, then went into the office to do some research on teen-oriented activities to add to the website.

Thinking of the meal that had just been served, she decided to add a special section on the food available for guests. She'd list nearby restaurants, of course, but she wanted each guest to be assured of the high-quality of food at the Inn. When they took pictures of the dining room after its renovation was finished, she'd be sure to include displays of food on the table.

She was about to call Dylan when he walked into the office. "I'm available to work on the interior if you're interested. I've got some time this morning."

"That would be great," she said. "The dining room is ready with new white paint on the walls. Amby and his nephew did a fantastic job of it."

"I saw," he took a seat in a chair by the desk. "Heard you and Shane are exclusive now."

"Yes," Charlotte said. "But I can't thank you enough for the trip to the Dali Museum. It was a wonderful day."

He gave her a look of resignation. "If you and Shane ever change your minds, let me know. I really like you, Charlie."

"Thanks. That means a lot," she said, surprised. "It doesn't mean we can't be friends."

"I know. Let's get to work," said Dylan.

They were hanging paintings in the meeting room when Austin joined them.

"Hey, what are you doing?" he asked, leaning against the door jamb watching them.

"Rearranging some paintings," said Dylan, tape measure in his hand.

"You still up for drinks tonight, Dylan?" asked Austin. "A

couple of friends of mine want to meet us at the Pink Pelican."

"Sure. I'm available."

"Okay, I'm going to have lunch with a friend, and I'll meet up with you later." Austin signaled to Charlotte to follow him. "I need your assistant for a few minutes," he told Dylan.

Charlotte left the meeting room and went into the office with Austin.

"What's up?"

He shuffled his feet. "Shane told me how awkward lunch was with my mother, and I wanted to apologize for her. She loves to strike out at Shane. It's painful to see. On the other hand, I'm glad you and Shane have come together. I've never seen him this happy."

"Thanks. That means a lot to me." She sighed and then blurted, "Your mother is very cruel. Oh, it's all spoken in a soft voice, but that makes it even worse. Is she on drugs? I noticed her eyes looked glassy."

Austin shook his head. "She has what she calls 'nerve pills' for when she gets overly excited or depressed. But she's done that for years. Sophia keeps a close eye on that situation."

"Just so you know, the next time I see your mother, I'm going to speak up. The idea of hurting Shane because he looks like his father is so wrong that I don't even know where to begin."

"I know. Believe me, it isn't any easier to be the son she says she likes," said Austin. His nostrils flared. "Granny Liz can't stand how my mother has treated both Shane and me. Pretty sick."

"Yes, Shane is concerned about her mental health and wants her to get professional help. But then I guess that's nothing new."

Austin released a long sigh. "No. She has to learn that she can't treat Shane that way."

Charlotte gave him a steady look. “Absolutely not.”

Austin gave her a quick hug. “Glad you’re on the team.”

She hugged him back. “Me, too.”

Later, after Charlotte and Dylan had switched paintings around and completed the last of the wall repair patching, they went into the kitchen for a cold drink.

They were sipping beers when Shane came in. “That looks refreshing. Have an extra?”

Charlotte smiled at him. “For you, yes. They’re in the refrigerator. Help yourself.”

He gave her a quick kiss. “Thanks.”

“Hey, man,” said Dylan. “Congrats on you and Charlie being together.”

Shane grinned and gave her a look that made her want to grab his hand and find an empty guestroom to use. “Yeah, we’re happy about it.” He gave Dylan a playful punch on his shoulder. “What have you got cooked up for this evening? Austin said you guys were going out.”

“He’s got some friends he wants me to meet,” said Dylan.

Charlotte smiled at him. “Have fun.”

After Dylan left, Charlotte said to Shane, “I have to make some notes in the office. Want to come?”

“Sure. Do you have some time before you need to help with cocktail hour?” Shane asked with a hint of a leer on his face.

“Yes, what did you have in mind?”

“Well, I know your cousins are out on the boat with Eric and Jake. That leaves an empty house ...” his voice trailed off.

She put her hands on her hips playfully. “And what do you have in mind? Are you suggesting that we, you know...?”

He grinned and wiggled his eyebrows. “Hmmm...That’s not a bad idea. I go back to the office on Monday and won’t be seeing that much of you."

"Well ...I'll have to think about it," she murmured as he swept her into his arms.

She rested her head against his chest, hearing the rapid beat of his heart. This was a new side to Shane, and she liked it.

Much later, she was taking a shower when Livy and Brooke returned to Gran's house. Charlotte sighed with relief. Shane had left moments before, and though they'd chosen to be dating exclusively, Charlotte didn't want anyone to think that their relationship was only sexual. It was much deeper than that.

She got out of the shower, dressed, and went to see what they were up to.

In the kitchen, Brooke and Livy, looking hot from the sun, were talking and laughing.

"Oh, Charlie, you should have been there. We went snorkeling, and a dolphin came close. It was fabulous," said Brooke.

"That isn't the only thing Brooke liked," said Livy. "I have a feeling our financials are going to be very much in balance by the time Brooke and Jake go over them together."

"What about you and Eric?" retorted Brooke. "You two seemed close."

Livy laughed. "The boat isn't that big, and well, Eric is pretty hot." She held up her hand. "But don't get any wrong ideas. Remember, I'm not interested in dating anyone. No strings. No problems."

Charlotte and Brooke simply shook their heads.

"What about you, Charlie? What's going on? Looks like you're dressed for the cocktail hour," said Livy.

"I am. Shane and I are going to have a late dinner after the cocktail hour is over."

"That'll be nice," said Brooke.

"While you were gone, Dylan and I took care of the artwork. Amby will need to touch up the walls in places, but it looks much better. We had a nice crowd for breakfast, and with the new arrivals this afternoon, cocktail hour should be busy. One of Beryl's workers is on board to serve as a waitress as we all discussed earlier. I'll make sure she knows what to do, show her about clean-up, and then go over to Granny Liz's house. Shane is grilling fish for dinner."

"That sounds so 'homey,'" said Brooke. "I'm happy for you, Charlie. It seems so right for you two to be together."

"I know it might seem sudden, but it doesn't feel that way to me. I'm closer to Shane than I've ever been to any man. He says he felt something when he saw me our first day together on the beach."

'Hmmm," said Livy. "I do remember how he kept staring at you that day." She laughed. "I kept staring at him because he's so handsome."

"And kind," said Charlotte, remembering how he'd treated her when she'd broken down.

"Granny Liz is ecstatic," said Brooke. "I overheard her talking to Dylan's grandmother."

"First things first," said Charlotte. "We're only dating. It's not like we're getting married tomorrow."

"Bet it'll happen sooner rather than later. That man knows what he wants," said Livy. "Anyone seen Austin around?"

"He's having lunch with a friend, and then he and Dylan are meeting up with some of Dylan's friends," Charlotte said and noticed a look of disappointment cross Livy's face.

"Jake and I are spending tomorrow together in the office," said Brooke. "As a treat, he's taking me out tonight."

"Guess I'll be the one stuck at home tonight," said Livy with a sigh.

Cocktail hour at the Inn was a pleasant affair. Guests who'd been there for a few days loved to share their information with others. New arrivals liked to learn about things to do and where the best places to eat and shop were.

Charlotte meandered through the crowd, greeting as many by name as she could. She, too, enjoyed exchanging pleasant conversation. Through the years, Gran had talked about making friends with some of her guests, enticing them to return year after year. Charlotte understood this and delighted in speaking to them, aware her grandmother would be pleased.

Holly Willis, the young waitress offering hors d'oeuvres, seemed to be enjoying the job. At eighteen, she'd worked in restaurants before and knew the terminology for food items and drinks. Though the offerings at the Inn were limited, it helped that she was knowledgeable. In addition, she was a quiet, pleasant presence. As business grew, they'd need more than one helper.

Later, satisfied that the cocktail hour was closed down properly and things were in order, Charlotte headed for Granny Liz's house. The arrangement of her house was like Gran's, with a master bedroom on the first floor and four bedrooms upstairs. The interior was decorated more formally with family antiques mixed with more contemporary things. Grandpa Sam had taken over what would've been a library for his "man cave." Charlotte had seen it and knew his cave consisted of a lot of books, a television, a couch, and a big lounge chair. Most days, she suspected, he was in his lounge chair taking an afternoon nap.

Granny Liz greeted her at the front door. "There you are. Let's have a glass of wine before dinner. You and I can sit on the porch and talk."

Charlotte smiled, knowing Granny Liz wouldn't rest until she had more details about the relationship she and Shane had formed.

Granny Liz and Charlotte sat in rocking chairs next to one another on the front porch with a glass of chilled pinot gris. She'd always liked Shane's grandmother. But, though she knew Granny Liz was happy about Shane and her, she also knew that she wouldn't get overly involved.

Granny Liz faced her. "Charlotte, I want to talk to you about Shane's parents. It's a convenient time with Sam and Shane chatting out back. I understand you've met Shane's mother."

"Yes," said Charlotte. "Shane and I went for lunch. She's not a nice woman."

"No, she isn't," said Granny Liz firmly. "We were appalled when Henry brought Diana home to meet us. I knew right away that it wouldn't work. She's one of the most selfish, needy people I've ever met. Her background was pretty rough, so some of her self-centeredness is perhaps survival mode from the past. We tried to talk to Henry, but he was smitten and unable to see how easily she manipulated him, changing back and forth from being selfish to declaring her love for him."

"Shane told me there was a lot of screaming and arguing."

Granny Liz sighed and shook her head. "Diana and Henry brought out the worst in one another. I shudder to think what happened between them to make my Henry so upset. He was never argumentative as a child. But Diana was never satisfied with what he did for her and would belittle him in front of other people. God knows what she said to him in private. Trying to 'deal' with her is like riding a roller coaster."

"What could you do about it?" Charlotte asked, sympathetic to Granny Liz.

"Nothing. And then, right after Austin was born, things got better between them. Diana adored that little boy as much as she resented Shane. Diana's a terrible mother." Granny Liz sat back and took a sip of the white wine. "For Henry's sake and the sake of the boys, I've tried to be civil to her to keep the peace. But she knows after some of her actions that I'll never be able to fully trust her again."

"After lashing out at Shane in her particular way, Diana told us that she does that because Shane is so much like his father, and she could never love anyone as much as Henry," said Charlotte. "How can that be after all the fighting?"

"Diana might have the money and position in society she wanted, but she didn't find real love with Ricardo or anyone else. No one will ever suit her, not even Henry. Thank goodness, he's happily married to such a pleasant, gracious woman. They and their two kids are coming next week. That's why I wanted you to know the story behind Henry and Diana before Henry's visit."

"Thanks. I appreciate it."

Granny Liz's eyes grew watery. She lifted Charlotte's hand and squeezed it. "You and Shane have made us ... me ... so happy. You're perfect together, and I've never seen him happier."

"Us?" Charlotte said, her suspicions aroused.

"Oh, okay," said Granny Liz. "Ellie and me. It's no secret that we hoped this summer would bring you two together."

Charlotte shook her head. *Was anything worse than*

meddling grandmothers?

Granny Liz raised a finger to her lips. "Don't mention it to anyone else. OK?"

Charlotte chuckled. "I won't. But your plans might not work, you know."

"I do," said Granny Liz seriously. "But there's time for more surprises in the future."

Shane walked out onto the porch. Charlotte's heart filled with love for him. No matter what their grandmothers thought, she was glad they'd found each other.

After dinner, Shane said, "Want to walk on the beach? It's cooling off, and there's plenty of moonlight."

"That would be lovely," she said. "I'm full from dinner, and a walk will be good for me."

They said thanks to Granny Liz and Grandpa Sam and headed out to the beach hand in hand.

Shane turned to her with a smile. "Just so you know, Grandpa Sam thinks you're the best. He even told me I'd be a fool to let you go."

"Oh? Have you thought about it?" Charlotte asked him.

He pulled her to him. "Never."

They were standing in the water's edge, gazing up at the moon, when they heard someone jogging toward them.

Charlotte turned around. "Hey, Austin, what's up?"

"Dylan and I just got back from the Pink Pelican. Shane, I talked to our mother earlier."

"Yeah? How was she?"

"Not good. Now she's complaining that because you came to visit with Charlie, she's never going to see you again." Austin turned to her. "She knows you don't like her, Charlie. I tried to explain that you were just protecting Shane."

"What? She's blaming me for something between her and Shane?" Charlotte glanced at Shane. "Is this the beginning of another battle between you?"

Shane shook his head. "God knows. It's one thing or another. I'm sorry I even introduced you. But I'm glad you were there so you'd know what she's like."

"Me, too," said Charlotte, more than a little worried about Diana.

CHAPTER FORTY-THREE

CHARLOTTE

The next morning when Charlotte awoke, she lay in bed thinking of the day ahead. She'd postponed calling her mother but knew she couldn't put it off any longer. She checked her bedside clock. 8 AM. Her mother would, no doubt, be sitting in the kitchen with her tea.

She reluctantly got out of bed, and after taking care of her morning rituals, went downstairs for a cup of coffee. She'd need it.

Thankfully, the kitchen was empty when she entered it. She poured herself a cup of coffee and took a seat at the table, telling herself not to be nervous. She and her mother didn't always get along, but after seeing what Shane went through with his mother, it gave her a different outlook.

She punched in the number and waited.

"Hi, Charlotte. How are you? Enjoying yourself down there?"

"Yes, I am. It's been a big change for me in many ways. I'm learning about running an inn, and I'm officially dating Shane Ensley, Henry's son." Then unable to help herself, she blurted, "I love him so much!"

There was silence, and then her mother said, "Why, Charlotte, I've never heard you speak like this before. Of course, I remember Henry."

"I'm going to meet his father this week when he and his family come to visit."

"Henry's a nice man, but his first wife, Shane's mother, was a mess as I remember. I met Diana only once, but she was very controlling, very needy. Liz and Sam were unhappy about that marriage. Gran told me about some of it. I think it was pretty bad."

"All of that is true," said Charlotte. "Granny Liz and I discussed the situation. After meeting her, Diana is saying I'm going to ruin her relationship with Shane, that she knows I don't like her, and she's upset about us. She was nasty to Shane. I defended him, but I wasn't rude to her."

"Charlotte, listen to me. You might be headstrong and outspoken, but you're not rude. I've brought you up better than that." Her mother sniffed. "That woman is nothing but trouble."

"Thanks for saying that. I don't want anything to come between Shane and me. This is the first time I've ever felt this way about a man. He hasn't asked me to marry him, but if and when he does, I'm going to say yes."

"Isn't this rather sudden?" her mother asked.

"Yes and no," Charlotte replied. "Didn't you tell me once that you and Dad fell in love in a hurry?"

"But that was different," said her mother. "And then we had that tragedy ..."

"But when you married him, you loved him. Right?" persisted Charlotte.

"Yes, I did," her mother said. "But, now, I love Walter and have from the first time I met him."

"That's how I feel about Shane," said Charlotte. I can't wait for you to meet him."

"Bring him to New York as soon as you can." Her mother paused. "I'm thrilled for you, Charlotte. Mothers want their children to be happy and loved, and if your growing relationship with Shane is the right one for you, I hope it will all work out."

Tears stung Charlotte's eyes. She hadn't realized how much she wanted her mother's approval. "Thanks, Mom."

After Charlotte hung up, she felt like dancing. The worry about Diana's blame eased, and a surge of love for Shane sent her to her feet.

She was waltzing around the kitchen when Brooke walked in.

"What's going on?" Brooke asked.

"I just had an important conversation with my mother. She wants to meet Shane. After all the fuss with Jeremy, this makes me so happy."

Brooke gave her a quick hug. "We're all happy for you, Charlie. You two are superb together." She frowned. "Guess I should call my mother today. We've agreed not to talk too often, but I think it's my turn."

"Give Aunt Jo my best. I'd better get over to the Inn," said Charlotte. "The soft goods are being delivered today."

Charlotte felt as giddy as a five-year-old when the delivery truck backed up to the receiving area behind the Inn. She hoped with the new soft goods, and adding and switching around decorative accents, the rooms would look fresh and new. Like the Inn itself, the layout and paint on the walls, baseboards, and ceiling moldings were in satisfactory shape, along with the neutral carpeting in each room. The bright but subtle tropical patterns on the spreads would give the rooms a rich, colorful dimension they needed. In addition, Brooke found pillows that matched some of the colors in the spreads and would be attractive additions to the comfortable look they hoped to achieve. The upgraded wi-fi network had already been completed by Austin, providing better service that several guests had commented about favorably.

Amby and his nephew, Rocco, stood by, ready to unload the items wrapped in plastic. The linen company had delivered towels and sheets earlier, and what the staff hadn't already pulled for use in the rooms was stacked on shelves in the laundry storage room.

Beryl had doubled her crew for the day and had put her staff to work as discreetly as possible around the occupied rooms.

Livy, still wearing an apron from cooking in the kitchen, joined her at the loading dock. "Oh, these spreads are going to be beautiful."

Charlotte grinned at her. "Prettier seeing them together in different colors, huh?"

Beryl and one other staff member directed Amby and Rocco to where they should take several of the spreads. Most of the rooms in the main house were occupied, but several rooms in the wing were empty. New sheets had already been washed and placed on the beds, and they were ready to receive the spreads.

Charlotte followed along to make sure that the styles were not grouped together but were spread apart.

The minute the first spread was put on the king-size bed, Charlotte knew her choices would work.

Brooke rolled a cart into the room holding several different pillows. They easily chose the three they wanted to place on top of the bed, put two on the love seat, and stood back to admire their selection.

"Pretty," said Beryl. "So different."

Livy raced into the room. "How does it look? Oh, yes, perfect!"

Charlotte gave each of her cousins a high-five. "It works."

They all spent the rest of the morning helping to place bedspreads on beds after housekeeping had placed new sheets on them. The lightweight blankets had been purchased last year and were in excellent condition.

Beryl raced around to make sure the staff did everything to her satisfaction.

Taking advantage of rooms checking out in the afternoon, the crew quickly cleaned the room, added new sheets and towels, and placed new bedspreads on the beds.

Brooke worked with Amby replacing bathroom items, some of which Amby had to mount on walls and tiles.

By the end of the afternoon, all but eight rooms were completed, but those rooms were occupied.

As the three of them and the hotel staff who'd worked with them stood together in the last room, Livy said, "We've got to celebrate. Follow me to the kitchen. I'll make a batch of margaritas. Then, some of us better get ready for cocktail hour."

Downstairs in the kitchen, happy chatter filled the room. Charlotte loved that the staff was as eager to make each room nice as she. Gran had told her cousins and her how valuable the staff was to the operation of the hotel. Charlotte understood better how special they were. Outsiders could claim that some of the jobs were menial, but she knew better. Each staff person was essential to the operation.

She lifted her glass. "Here's to all of us for a job well done. Glad you're part of the family."

Beryl gave her a small nod of approval and lifted her glass.

Amby clicked it and smiled at Beryl in a way that made Charlotte think of Shane. She could hardly wait to spend time with him. He'd gone back to work in Miami. Charlotte was driving there tomorrow on her day off and would spend the night.

The next morning, after making sure both Livy and Brooke were comfortable with her leaving for a day, Charlotte got into her car and headed out to Miami. She'd told Granny Liz about her conversation with her mother, and they both agreed it was a good sign.

"All in time," Granny Liz said. "A lot has been going on, and there's no need to rush."

Charlotte nodded, but now that she and Shane had taken this big step, she hoped everyone understood that for the two of them, their coming together was a commitment to much more. Shane might have dated before, but she knew he'd never led on any woman, using her for his own selfish reasons. He was much too sensitive to do that.

As she drove into Miami, Charlotte couldn't help thinking of Shane's parents. She hadn't liked his mother and was anxious about meeting his father. Her mother's words about Henry had been positive, and that meant a lot. And he was the son Granny Liz adored.

Charlotte arrived in Miami early afternoon and let herself into his condo. She liked the area and wondered if this is where she might live one day. She unpacked in the guest room, unsure if this is what he wanted, and decided it didn't matter. That choice would be made later.

She called him and suggested she put together some dinner for them.

"That would be great," he said. "I'm busy catching up on things. Amazing what can happen in such a short time."

"I'll be here waiting," she said. "I'm going out now but will be back before you get home. I brought my computer to show you what I've done with the website for Family First."

"We have a meeting with Jed tomorrow morning, right?"

"Yes. No sneak peeking. You'll see it when he does," said Charlotte.

Shane laughed. "That good, huh?"

"I hope so. I'd like to get that up and going for you. Then we can do the pamphlets and other PR materials." Charlotte once again realized she was more excited about this project and the one for the Inn than she'd ever been for the company she'd worked at for years.

After ending the call with Shane, Charlotte decided to walk over to the stores and do a little browsing. She thought it might be time to change up her sleepwear from shorts and a tank top to something more worthy of her new relationship with Shane.

She munched on a granola bar as she entered the outdoor area of shops and restaurants. After living in New York, where she knew the best places to shop for bargains and specialty items, she found it fun to discover new places.

A store called "The New You" sold a line of lingerie that went from tasteful and subdued to wild and sexy at the back of the store. Amused by the designations, Charlotte headed to the back. If she was going to do this, she wanted to do it right.

Thirty minutes later, she left carrying a silver paper bag adorned with lacy pink ribbon. Pink satin bottoms and a pink short lacy top with spaghetti straps lay inside. Charlie was excited about the evening ahead. Time alone together was what she and Shane needed.

When Charlotte returned to the condo with fresh lettuce, a cooked chicken, fruit, and other groceries, she began making a cold chicken salad. She'd looked up an easy recipe for one, adding grapes, fresh pineapple, and slivered almonds to it. That, sliced Florida tomatoes with fresh basil leaves in a simple oil and vinegar dressing, and French bread would complete the meal. She'd even bought some fresh summer flowers in a jar and was using that for a centerpiece.

She'd just set the table when Shane arrived home.

He looked at her and the table, and a broad grin spread across his handsome face. He approached and swept her up in his arms. "M-m-m, is this what I can look forward to one day? Coming home to this?"

She grinned at him. "You haven't seen everything yet."

"More to come?" he said, wiggling his eyebrows.

She laughed. "Later. For now, let's enjoy a nice glass of wine before dinner. How was your day?"

"Busy, as you know, but interesting. Elijah had been accepted into an Advanced Program and will be working on college courses as well as high school ones which will be a big help when applying to colleges and universities."

"What about working the Family First program when he's gone?"

"That's something we have to decide, depending on where he ends up. Of course, there's the option of online classes, too."

"I'm pleased you're doing this, Shane," said Charlotte. "Coming from your background where finances weren't a worry, it must make you happy to help Elijah and his family."

"Elijah's mother is a terrific woman and mother. I'm happy to assist." He held up the blazer he'd carried in. "Hold on. I'll change my clothes and join you."

When Shane returned, he was wearing shorts, a T-shirt, and flip-flops.

"That's more like it," said Charlotte, placing a plate of cheese and crackers on the coffee table in the living room. "It's hot. I thought we'd stay inside."

"Okay," said Shane. "Want me to open the bottle of wine?"

"Thanks. It's in the refrigerator. A pinot grigio."

Charlotte took a seat on the sofa and studied the room. It

was attractive but lacked the warmth of a woman's touch. What would happen if she ended up moving in here? Would Shane allow her to make changes?

Shane carried their wine over to her, handed her a glass, took a seat on the couch next to her, and lifted his wine in a toast.

"Thank you, Charlotte, for being here, making things nice. I love you."

Her heart filled with joy. She gazed at him through eyes blurred with happy tears. She lifted her glass. "I love you too."

After they'd each had a sip of wine, Shane leaned over and kissed her on the lips. "Is this the kind of treatment I can expect in the future?"

"Maybe not," she said honestly. "Until things are more settled, I won't know. Remember when you suggested I could set up my own consulting business in Florida? I've been thinking about it. I want to help Gran, but I also want to keep my independence. I think I could do both by having my own business."

"Interesting," said Shane. "But you wouldn't necessarily have to set up your business on the Gulf Coast, would you?"

"No," she took a sip of wine, feeling she'd said as much as she wanted. "Things are still up in the air. A lot will depend on what Livy and Brooke decide to do and if Gran and John decide to sell."

"There's a lot to think of," Shane said, setting down his glass and cupping her cheek with his strong hand. "But there's one thing I'm sure of. I want you in my life. I know we need to take time to let things unwind. There's been a lot going on. But I mean it when I say I want you with me."

His lips met hers in a tender kiss that quickly heated.

She responded. His kiss carried Charlotte to a place in her mind where she felt safe and loved, even cherished.

When they pulled apart, Shane smiled at her with such tenderness her breath caught.

"Charlie, it was such a lucky day when I saw you on the beach with your cousins."

She couldn't resist teasing. "Even luckier when I saved you." Her eyes filled with tears, catching her off guard. "I was so scared when I saw you floating face down in the water."

He pulled her to him. "Do you believe that things happen for a reason?"

"I do." She studied him. "I think we're meant to be together, and that's why things are happening fast."

"That could be," said Shane. "I just know it feels right." He kissed her again, this time with a need she recognized.

As their wine warmed on the table, they stretched out on the couch, getting to know each other better. And later, when they emerged from the bedroom, Charlotte didn't care that she'd never had the chance to show Shane her new purchases.

CHAPTER FORTY-FOUR

CHARLOTTE

Charlotte awoke, startled to discover where she was, and then smiling, she reached over and touched Shane. He turned to her and pulled her closer.

" 'Morning, mermaid," he said softly. "You know, I really did dream of you as a mermaid when I was knocked unconscious."

She nestled against him, liking the idea of being his special sea creature.

"After the meeting with Jed, you're going back to the Inn?" he asked.

"Yes. With your father and his family coming to the Inn, I want to make sure everything is in order. We're still doing some renovations."

"I understand. Granny Liz is disappointed they're not staying with her, but as long as Austin and I are there, there isn't enough room for them in her house." He clasped her face in his hands and studied her. "Do you know how much I'm going to miss you?"

His lips met hers, and for several moments Charlotte allowed herself to pretend this is how it would be every morning if they were married.

When they pulled apart, Shane said, "C'mon, shower time. I don't want to be late for the meeting with Jed. I have a full day scheduled."

Later, Shane, Jed, and Charlotte sat in the conference room in Shane's office going over the website designs she'd set up for them to study. She had a clear favorite in her mind, but she'd learned that clients sometimes had different ideas, and she had to respect their choices.

"Which one do you like best?" Jed asked her.

She brought up the simpler one with kids of all sizes, shapes, and backgrounds. "To me, this is the easiest to navigate. We just need to be sure that all these lines of communication remain open. With fraudulent sites out there, ours must never be confused with them. Also, this simple arrangement makes it easy for you to see what is working and what isn't."

"It could be fancier, but I see your point," Jed said.

"But it's easier for people who don't know English that well," Shane added.

"Okay, now let's talk about brochures and other methods to reach those who might need you," said Charlotte. She'd drawn up a list of suggestions to make it easier to discuss.

It was almost noon when they were nearing the completion of their meeting. Instead of going out for lunch, Sarita ordered food brought in for them.

As soon as Shane finished his sandwich, he got to his feet. "Sorry to rush out of here, but I have another meeting. See you in a couple of days, Charlie. See you later, Jed."

He leaned down and kissed Charlotte. "Love you," he whispered. "Have a safe drive home."

She smiled up at him. "Thanks. Love you, too."

After Shane left, Jed let out a slow, soft whistle. "You two are so hot together."

"I know." Charlotte's chuckle was almost a girlish giggle.

Jed studied her. "I'm pleased for Shane that you're in his life."

"Once we could finally admit how we felt, it all came together quickly," said Charlotte.

"And now you've met his mother," Jed said. "How did that go? Was she her bitchy self?"

Charlotte frowned. "She's not a nice person. She takes pleasure in putting down others. I suspect the "nerve pills" Austin told me she takes are more than that."

"Yeah, me too," said Jed.

"What's Shane's father like?" Charlotte asked, nervous at the thought of their upcoming meeting with him.

"His dad is really nice," said Jed. "You'll like him. His wife too. Shane and I almost set up an office in Atlanta but decided we liked Florida living better."

"His dad and family are arriving at the cove in a couple of days. I'll meet them all then," said Charlotte. "Are you coming over this weekend?"

"Shane asked me to come for the weekend to meet up with his dad, who's been sort of like a father to me." He grinned. "Livy and I are going out on Saturday."

"I'm sure you'll have a great time." Livy was always fun to be with.

Charlotte stood and prepared to leave. As she'd told Shane, she wanted to make sure the Inn was in excellent shape when his father arrived. In many ways, he'd be the perfect test for all the new things they'd put into place both in the Inn's interior and in new management.

Back at the cove, she unpacked and went downstairs and over to the Inn to see what had happened in the short time she was gone.

A new second dishwasher had been installed in the kitchen, and a couple of new cutting boards sat atop the stainless-steel kitchen counters. At the entrance to the dining room, she stopped and studied the effect of the new white-painted walls and gave a nod of satisfaction. The room seemed brighter, bigger even, offsetting the contemporary paintings that they had added. The rich wood tones of the tables and chairs looked better too against the stark white.

The gathering room had taken on a more modern look with new and newly painted white furniture mixed in with the rich woods of the older furnishings. Livy and Brooke had added a few touches with new lamps, pillows, and a white leather love seat they'd placed along the back wall of the room, facing the television.

Charlotte went into the office and discovered Brooke there. "Hi. What are you doing?" she asked.

"I didn't know you were back. I'm working on our renovation budget. Did you notice the new things in the gathering room? I want to make sure we're keeping within the budget. The most expensive items coming up have to do with publicity. You're working on the website. We're going to print up some new pamphlets, and while you were gone, Livy and I took a look at the roadside sign for the Inn. It needs repainting, but we thought maybe it was time to come up with a logo to be used on the website and pamphlets too."

Charlotte smiled and held up the computer she had in her hand. "Funny you should mention that. I've drawn up several samples of logos while waiting for Shane to come home last night."

"How did your visit go?' said Brooke, giving her a teasing grin. "Any signs of a ring yet?"

"Brooke, we just started dating," said Charlotte, laughing.

Brooke shook her head. "We all know that's what you're calling it, but it's obvious it's much more than that. It's like you're engaged already. Don't tell me you haven't thought about it."

Charlotte sighed and sat in a chair facing her. "Of course, I have. I didn't expect to find something this intense, this perfect, so quickly. It seems a little surreal."

"It's like a fairy tale—your saving Shane and his falling in love with you," said Brooke. "Like a mermaid story or something."

"Now, you're sounding crazy," said Charlotte laughing. No way would she mention that Shane called her his special mermaid after making love with him. "What about you? Did you go out last night?"

Brooke beamed at her. "Jake and I worked late and decided to go out to supper. Nothing fancy, but nice. He makes me feel comfortable around him."

"What about Adam? Any chance of dating him?" Charlotte asked.

"No, that's not going to happen. In fact, he's leaving in a couple of days to go back and check on his business. Skye is going to stay here. Her grandmother and I will see that she's busy."

"You're awfully nice to Skye," said Charlotte.

"I try to be," said Brooke. "She reminds me a lot of myself at that age."

"How about Livy? Is she going to join us for our meeting?" said Charlotte.

"Livy said she would. I expect her any minute," said Brooke.

Just then, Livy entered the office carrying a blender full of margaritas and three glasses. "Hi, you two. Thought we'd have a little refreshment while we meet. Charlotte, did you see the new dishwasher and the new furniture in the gathering room?"

Charlotte nodded and smiled. "It looks nice. The finishing

touches too. A lot can happen around here in just two days."

"Don't you know it," said Livy. "Dylan and I are going to scout out Grace's restaurant to see just how I can fit in some baking for her. Who knows? After Gran and John come back, I may stay here in Florida and set up my own business."

Charlotte accepted the glass Livy handed her. "I've had some similar thoughts. Maybe setting up a consulting business. It's too early to make any definite decisions, though."

She took a sip of the tart, tangy drink and let out a sigh. There was a lot to think about.

Brooke studied Charlotte and Livy. "I'm not sure what I want to do. I do like running the Inn. We'll see."

"This summer is turning into one of discovery for all of us," said Charlotte.

"A pivotal time," Livy said, looking as happy as Charlotte had ever seen her.

"A new beginning," said Brooke. "I have no intention of going back home."

The three of them lifted their glasses.

"Here's to all of us," said Livy.

"Amen," said Brooke.

Smiling with satisfaction, Charlotte clicked her glass against theirs.

The next morning, Charlotte worked on the two logo ideas she and her cousins had liked the best. She'd already talked to Amby about switching out the hanging wooden sign on the signpost next to the road. Instead of a square sign, they wanted a sign curved slightly at the top, giving it a more distinctive look. The lettering would be black against the white background and would have an outline of a sanderling painted in the center. Instead of a side view of the bird, they wanted something a little different. Charlotte had found a drawing of a sanderling bending over to reach for something in the sand and decided to modify it a bit and make an outline of it. Once a design was approved, she'd set to work on the promo materials.

In the meantime, she'd begun to research material for the Family First program. That program already had a logo, though she'd received approval from Jed and Shane to change it slightly.

Charlotte loved working on her own and had been serious when she'd told her cousins that she might open her own business. She thought of Shane and how everyone thought their relationship would lead to marriage. On a whim, she decided to go see Granny Liz. She wanted her perspective on Shane. He'd talked in general about a future with her, but it was too soon for either of them to make a commitment for more. Wasn't it?

Also, with Shane's father and family arriving soon, Charlotte wanted a better sense of how his family would react to any news of her relationship with him, and, frankly, how he and his father interacted. It would tell her much more about how Shane would behave having a family of his own one day.

Granny Liz opened the door and beamed at her. "Hi, Charlie, I'm delighted to see you. Please come in."

Charlotte stepped inside, happy for the air-conditioning that swirled around her.

"How about a glass of iced tea or lemonade?" asked Granny Liz.

"Lemonade would be lovely," Charlotte said. "I'm not interrupting anything, am I?'

Granny Liz clasped her hand and squeezed it. "Heavens no. Nothing that can't wait. You're brightening my day, dear."

Relaxing, Charlotte followed Granny Liz into the kitchen and took a seat at one end of the large oval table. As a kid, she'd had plenty of meals here. Memories like this were what made the relationship between Shane and her special. Granny Liz handed her a glass of lemonade and sat at the table beside her. "What brings you here?"

Charlotte let out a sigh and hesitated before speaking. "Everyone is sure that Shane and I have made a bigger commitment than just dating exclusively. Everything's happening so fast, I guess I need a little reassurance."

"Ahh," Granny Liz said. "You're a little unsure about things?"

"About Shane? Absolutely, not," Charlotte said with a firmness she felt from the tips of her toes to the top of her head. "Still, I don't want to get hurt for being such a romantic."

Granny Liz studied her with blue eyes like Shane's. "If you're asking me if I think Shane is rushing into things or if he's going to change his mind about how he's feeling about you, I promise you, he's not. He told me how you handled Diana and that meant a lot to him. He knows he can trust you with his deepest secrets." A smile softened her face. "Shane has a lot of love to give. Love and loyalty and generosity. I think you know that already. The fact that he's chosen to give it to you is special because we all love you, Charlotte. We have since you were a little girl."

The tears that had stung Charlotte's eyes rolled down her cheeks. She remembered how she could never measure up to her dead brother, how lonely she'd felt as a child. Memories of happy times here at the cove had soothed her. Shane had always been there for her. The oldest of all the grandchildren, Shane had been the one who'd seen that everyone was included.

Granny Liz gave her a gentle smile. "My advice to you is to

let things unroll naturally. Don't let the idea of something being too good to be true or thinking it happened so suddenly take away from the miracle of finding someone you love unselfishly. I know you both very well. If I didn't, I'd have different thoughts on this."

"Thank you," said Charlotte. "I know his father and family are due to arrive, and I needed to know that what's happening between Shane and me isn't crazy thinking. I know he isn't like Shane's mother, but ..."

"Oh, honey," said Granny Liz. "Henry is a wonderful man. You'll like him, and I know he'll like you. He and your mother used to be friends back in time."

"Mom said Shane's father was a nice man, but she hadn't liked Diana," Charlotte said.

"Henry was oblivious to Diana's true nature," said Granny Liz with a sigh. "He found out any sweetness was fake. She wanted his money."

"She has even more now," said Charlotte, "but in reality, she has nothing."

"True," said Granny Liz.

CHAPTER FORTY-FIVE

CHARLOTTE

Charlotte paced the office, waiting for Shane's father and his family to show up. They'd called from the road a half-hour ago to say they'd be there shortly. Charlotte knew Beryl would go from amused to angry if she checked on their rooms one more time. The connecting rooms were in perfect order, with a vase of fresh flowers in each one, along with the usual bottles of water and a welcome letter.

When at last she heard a commotion, she raced out of the office to greet them in the reception area. She stopped in surprise. Shane's father looked remarkably like him with blond hair and blue eyes in a handsome, rugged face. No wonder Diana had mentioned their similarity.

Beside Henry stood a short woman with a cute figure, dark hair, and brown eyes. She smiled at Charlotte in a sweet way that made Charlotte's lips curve in response.

She walked over to them, her hand outstretched. "Hello, I'm Charlotte Bradford. Welcome to The Sanderling Cove Inn. We're excited to have you stay with us while you're visiting family."

"I'm Savannah Ensley," the woman said, shaking Charlotte's hand. "Our two kids are outside. They'll be here in a minute."

Henry clasped Charlotte's hand and studied her. "Hello, Charlie. I'm Henry. You certainly are Vanessa's daughter. You look just like her."

"Thank you. I'll take that as a compliment," said Charlotte, turning as two teenagers entered the room. The boy was tall with dark straight hair and brown eyes, like his mother. The girl had blond hair and hazel eyes. Both had a combination of their parents' features.

"Meet two of my children," said Henry. "Brent and Emma." He turned to them. "This is Charlotte Bradford, Shane's friend."

"Where's Shane? And Austin?" Brent asked him. "I want to meet up with them."

"Wait until we get checked in, and then you'll be free to find them," said Henry. He faced Charlotte. "Is Shane still in Miami?"

"Yes. He had a late meeting and won't return here until dinnertime," she said. "He wanted me to tell you both that he's looking forward to your being here."

"I can't wait to see him again. It's been a few months now," said Savannah. "He and Austin make our family complete."

Henry put an arm around Savannah. "Savannah is the heart of our family."

"Yeah, Mom," said Brent affectionately, while Emma moved closer to her parents.

After seeing that they were settled in their rooms, Charlotte went downstairs to help Livy and Brooke prepare for cocktail hour. Twenty couples were "in the house," a hotel phrase Charlotte had picked up. Brooke and Holly would act as hostesses for the party.

"How are they?" Livy asked when she walked into the kitchen.

"I suppose you mean Shane's family," said Charlotte, chuckling. "From what I can tell, they're fabulous. No wonder Shane and Austin have been excited about their visit."

"That's important," said Brooke.

"Yeah, that means a lot," Livy said. "I'm glad they could

come. Like you two, I don't remember them from earlier visits."

"What are we serving tonight?" Charlotte asked Livy.

"Stuffed mushrooms, a roasted nut mixture, and toast points with an olive tapenade," said Livy. "And we've invited all the cove people as you suggested."

"Thank you. Granny Liz was thrilled with the idea when I spoke to her about it." Being with Shane's family was a nice way for Charlotte to be comfortable with them. Her cell phone rang. *Shane*.

"Hey, there. Are you on your way? Yes, yes, they're very nice, and your brother and sister are adorable. Okay. Talk to you later. Drive safely. Yes, me too."

Brooke and Livy turned to her when she clicked off the call.

"Meeting the family is an important step," said Livy with a teasing grin.

"It would be for you too if you were still mooning over Austin," said Brooke.

"Yeah, Livy, what's going on with all that? I thought you still had a crush on him," said Charlotte, happy to give rather than receive some teasing for a change.

Livy's face fell for seconds, and then she brightened. "I'm exploring my options. I'm not ready for anything serious."

"Fair enough," said Charlotte, aware of Livy's discomfort.

When they'd finished with the food preparation, Charlotte said, "I'm going to change my clothes. I'll be back later." On her evenings off from hosting the cocktail hour, Charlotte didn't always attend. But tonight, she wanted to be part of it.

On her way to Gran's house, Austin trotted up to her. "Have you met the parents?"

"Yes, I checked them in this afternoon. They seem very pleasant."

Austin grinned. "I'm glad you like them. After meeting my

mother, you need to know she's not like the rest of the family."

"Yes, sadly, that's true. Did your brother, Brent, find you?"

Austin grinned. "We've already played several computer games. Smart kid. Emma, too."

Guests easily mingled with the few residents of Sanderling Cove, adding a buzz of excitement to the event. Charlotte watched Granny Liz and Savannah chatting and was pleased that they got along. She couldn't imagine Granny Liz and Diana together.

Henry walked over to her. "I'm glad for us to have the chance to speak privately. My mother has told me how you saved Shane's life. I can never thank you enough."

"Honestly, I just happened to be there at the time."

His gaze settled on her. "Do you really believe that? My mother said it's all part of why you and Shane are meant to be a couple."

Charlotte returned his steady look. "It certainly brought us together," Charlotte began. She turned as Shane entered the room. He gazed at her, and she felt a smile fill her face.

Henry chuckled. "You don't have to say more."

Shane walked over to them, gave Charlotte a quick kiss, and gave his dad a man hug. "Great to see you, Dad. Glad you two are getting to know one another." He put his arm around Charlotte, drawing her close. "I think Savannah and Charlotte are going to get along just fine."

"Me, too," said Henry, grinning when Savannah walked toward him. "Sorry about the luncheon with your mother."

"She's a mess," said Shane, his voice full of disgust. His face brightened when he caught sight of his stepmother. "Hi, Savannah."

She hurried into his embrace. "Shane, it's been way too

long. You know we don't get to spend enough time with you." She indicated Charlotte with a smile and a nod of her head. "But I see you have a meaningful reason to stay here."

Shane grinned, stepped back from Savannah, and wrapped his arm around Charlotte. "A *very* good reason."

Austin joined them. "What's everyone smiling about?"

"Shane and Charlotte," said Savannah, taking hold of Austin's hand and giving him a loving hug.

Henry said, "Thought we'd go fishing tomorrow, You two, Brent and me. How does that sound?"

"Excellent. I haven't been fishing in a long time. Too busy," said Shane.

"I want to hear what's happening with your charity project," said Savannah.

"It's doing well. Charlotte is helping us with a new publicity campaign," said Shane. "Charlotte used to work for a big PR company in New York, and she has lots of excellent ideas."

"I'm also working on something for the Inn," said Charlotte. "My cousins, Livy and Brooke, and I are handling the management of the Inn while Gran and John are gone on their summer trip."

"I understand they're married now," said Savannah. "How sweet."

"My mother and her sisters are happy they've finally made it official. Gran said the only reason they did it was to handle legal and health issues." Charlotte chuckled. "She's such a free spirit."

"It's nice that she's that way, but I hope when the time comes, I'll be present for my children's weddings," said Savannah. "I want to see them all happily married and settled one day."

Charlotte avoided looking at Shane and waited for him to respond.

"I'm learning to let go of some memories and move forward," he said quietly.

"Your mother and I were not healthy examples," said Henry. "But you certainly see one now between Savannah and me."

"Yes," said Shane. "Savannah, as Granny Liz says, you're a peach!"

"A Georgia peach," added Austin.

The four of them laughed.

"It's a family joke," said Henry, kissing his wife on the cheek.

Brent joined them. "What am I missing?"

"Your brother just called Savannah a peach. She's one fine Georgia peach," said Henry.

"We all love her," said Austin, and turned to his Dad. "Can we talk?"

Savannah and Brent left them.

"What's going on?" asked Henry.

"Diana has been terrible lately," said Austin. "Shane and I are worried about her."

"She needs help," said Shane.

"I didn't want to mention it in front of Savannah, but Diana has been calling me, asking me to get back together with her," said Henry. "I may try to go see her, but not without one or both of you boys." His expression was grim. "Like you, I think Diana is having serious mental issues."

"I'll go with you," said Shane. "You'll need a witness."

"I'll be there, too," Austin said. "We'll be a united front."

"Okay," said Henry. "Let's put that visit idea aside and enjoy what time we can together. Right now, Granny Liz is signaling it's time for us to leave for dinner. Shall we go?"

Charlotte accompanied Shane, Austin, and their father over to Granny Liz's house. Granny Liz loved to entertain, and

Charlotte knew it would be a delicious spread of food. More importantly, there would be pleasant company. Sam liked to keep the conversation going at the dinner table.

Later, after a delicious meal and a last sip of coffee, Charlotte stood to help Granny Liz clear the dishes.

"Absolutely not," said Granny Liz. "I've hired one of your staff to clean up. She wants to earn as much money as she can, and this is a big help to me."

"Then, let's go for a walk," said Shane. "I need to move around after all the steak I ate."

"Brent has challenged me to another computer game," said Austin. "I'm going to beat him this time."

"I'll come with you," Emma said to Austin.

"Ah, this will be an excellent chance for Sam and me to talk with you Atlanta folks," said Granny Liz, indicating Henry and Savannah with a smile.

Shane and Charlotte left and walked onto the beach. The temperature had cooled a bit, and the breeze off the Gulf was refreshing as Charlotte stood facing the water. Moonlight created a shimmering golden pathway across the moving water, making it seem as if she was being beckoned to a new adventure.

She gazed at Shane beside her. After meeting Henry and Savannah, Charlotte was much more at ease with the idea of becoming part of his family if or when the time came.

Shane wrapped his arms around her. "Everyone loves you, Charlotte. Outside, standing by the grill, Dad and Sam took me aside and told me not to screw up, that you were the best thing to ever happen to me."

"Heavens," said Charlotte. "What did you say?"

He laughed. "I told them I knew it." He turned her around

to face him. “You *are* the best thing that ever has happened to me, Charlie.”

His lips pressed down on hers, capturing the feeling of the moment. She couldn’t stop a soft moan from escaping. She’d never felt as welcomed, as loved as she did now.

CHAPTER FORTY-SIX

BROOKE

Seeing the way Charlotte lit up around Shane, Brooke felt a stab of jealousy. Her main goal for the summer in Florida was to rethink her life and settle the issue of her mother's dependence on her. But with all these young men sharing the cove with her cousins and her, she couldn't help but think about finding someone special. Jake, Eric, and Adam were all appealing, but none had seemed especially interested in her. Livy told her to relax and simply enjoy the summer without worrying about any of that.

Brooke moved through the cocktail crowd smiling and speaking to their guests, enjoying the interaction. She'd gone from being quite shy to liking the opportunity to welcome everyone to the Inn. It almost felt as if the Inn was hers.

When she went to speak to Shane's father, she noticed him studying her. "Hello," she said. "I'm Brooke Weatherby. We're all happy that you and your family are staying here at the Inn while you visit."

"Thank you," he said politely, giving her another long look. "You're Jo's daughter, right?"

Brooke smiled at him. "Yes. By the way, she said to say hi to you. She's still living in Ellenton, New York, but she told me she remembers you from past visits to the cove."

"I remember her, too. She was easy to get along with," Henry said. "It's nice that your grandmother and my mother arranged to have all of you grandkids here together. It's a very special group and will bring about fond memories later in life,

I'm sure."

"Yes, I think so too. How are you enjoying the Inn? Is there anything we can do to make your stay more comfortable?"

"Everything's fine," he said. "The Inn looks better than ever. The service seems a little better too."

"That's what we're hoping for," said Brooke. "I'll talk to you later."

She moved on to the next cluster of people standing and talking, filled with a new sense of accomplishment.

She looked up in time to see Jake enter the room and quickly went to greet him.

CHAPTER FORTY-SEVEN

LIVY

Livy wandered through the group attending cocktail hour, pleased to see everyone enjoying the food Holly and Brooke were passing around. She and Dylan were going to visit Grace's restaurant to see how her baking could fit in. The visit might help her answer some questions about her future. The truth was, she didn't know what she wanted to do next. Owning a bakery had been a tremendous burden. Satisfying in many ways, but too confining. That's one reason she was determined to keep having as much fun as possible.

She approached Austin's stepmother. "Hello. I'm Olivia Winters, one of the cousins helping our grandparents out with the Inn. Welcome."

"I'm Savannah Ensley. Nice to meet you. I love the idea of the three of you young women stepping in to help your grandparents. I understand they're on an exciting summer trip abroad."

"Yes, a honeymoon of sorts," said Livy, smiling at the thought.

"I also understand you're a cook and baker," said Savannah. "Have you thought of doing cooking lessons here? Emma is interested in that kind of thing."

"We haven't thought of it, but I like that idea," said Livy. "Thanks."

"Austin has mentioned you," said Savannah. "He says you make delicious cookies."

Livy pasted a smile on her face. "He likes my cookies, for

sure." The thought that he couldn't see she was more than the cookies she baked hurt.

Eric headed her way.

Livy said goodbye to Savannah and met him halfway.

CHAPTER FORTY-EIGHT

CHARLOTTE

Early the next morning, Charlotte stood with Savannah and Emma wishing the men a nice day as they left to go on their fishing trip.

After the car pulled away with the four of them inside, Savannah turned to Charlotte and Emma. "Let's make a special day of it ourselves. Emma and I are going shopping and out to lunch. Care to join us, Charlie?"

"I'd love to join you for lunch, but I can't do more than that. I have work to do here. I hope you understand," said Charlotte. She already felt guilty about Livy and Brooke covering for her for the next few days.

"Not a problem. I think it's wonderful that you and your cousins are managing the Inn so your grandparents can have such a marvelous trip," said Savannah. She took hold of Charlotte's hand. "I'm pleased that Shane is serious about you. For the past couple of years, well, probably always, he's struggled with his mother. You're like a ray of sunshine in his life."

"That makes me happy. From the first moment we met this summer, we connected in a way I've never felt."

"So, when are you going to get married?" asked Emma, smiling shyly at her.

Charlotte laughed. "I haven't even been asked."

"Why did you say that to Charlie?" said Savannah, smiling at her daughter.

Emma shrugged. "I just know it's going to happen."

Savannah drew Emma close, hugged her, and smiled at Charlotte. "We have a romantic on our hands."

Charlotte returned the smile. "I like romance as much as anybody else. But right now, I have to do some unromantic work like greeting guests for breakfast. Please let me know when and where to meet you for lunch, and I'll be there. Thanks for asking me."

Charlotte headed inside the Inn. Breakfast was about to begin.

Greeting guests and talking with them about the upcoming day, Charlotte felt more at ease, better able to remember names and stories. It was something Gran did well, and she didn't want to fall behind in performing that important task.

Fortunately, everyone came at different intervals giving Livy and Billy Bob time to prepare orders. She and Brooke helped serve. Decisions about adding permanent staff would have to be made after Gran returned. In the meantime, they'd use who they had as much as possible.

After the last breakfast had been served, Charlotte went into the office to work with the new logo for the Inn and add it to samples of brochures she was developing. She gazed out the window. On a beautiful day like this, it would be a perfect time to take photos of the Inn for the website,

Charlotte called Dylan. "Ready to work with me on photos of the rooms and exterior of the Inn?"

"Okay. Give me time to clean up the studio, and I'll head right over," said Dylan. "I'll bring my camera."

"Thanks." Charlotte loved how everyone at the cove was willing to help one another.

Dylan arrived, and Charlotte showed him the list of photos she wanted to use in brochures and on the website. More important than showing pictures of the interior, Charlotte wanted to capture the flavor of the Inn as being exceptional for its facilities and location. The Inn offered a large pool, a large spa, and private access to the beach. Guests were able to use the large cove dock and were even able to attend neighborhood beach parties. The gazebo and side garden were often used for weddings.

For the next few hours, Dylan and Charlotte worked together, focusing on photo shoots outdoors before moving inside. Livy and Brooke joined them, as excited as she about the improvements they'd made to the interior.

Charlotte was shocked to discover the time. "Sorry, everyone, but I have to leave. I'm having lunch with Savannah and Emma."

"Go," said Brooke smiling. "We'll take care of things here."

Charlotte arrived at Gracie's and almost didn't find a parking space. Gracie's had become a favorite in this part of the Gulf coast and with good reason. Their food was delicious.

Worried about not being on time, Charlotte bypassed the carved wooden statue of a sea captain by the entranceway and rushed inside.

Savannah caught her eye and waved.

Charlotte hurried over to Savannah's table and greeted both her and Emma with an apology. "I'm sorry I'm a few minutes late. Busy morning at the Inn taking photos of it."

"No problem," said Savannah. "Emma and I are about shopped out in this warm weather. We'll go again another day. This afternoon, I'm staying right on the beach under an umbrella and with a book."

"What did you get?" Charlotte asked Emma. She was a pretty girl who seemed content to spend time with her mother.

Emma glanced at her mother and turned back to Charlotte

with a happy grin. "A bikini that Mom thought was too daring, a sundress, and a cool pair of sandals."

Savannah shook her head. "I sometimes forget my daughter is growing up."

"It's nice you can shop together," said Charlotte. That had never worked well for her with her mother. Her mother wasn't one to make compromises.

"It's a way to have time together without the men," said Savannah.

"Very sweet," said Charlotte. "We women have to stick together."

"Oh, yes," said Savannah, smiling at the waitress who approached them.

After they each had placed their orders, Savannah said, "I understand you might set up your own PR consulting company here in Florida one day."

Surprised, Charlotte realized Shane must have told her that. "I'm thinking of it. For sure, I don't want to go back to New York. A lot depends on how the summer goes. Then my cousins and I will have to decide what happens after that."

"You're such an interesting trio," Savannah said. "Austin has mentioned each of you. He seems at loose ends, but I'm sure he'll figure out what he's doing next. He's a talented young man."

"And a great guy," said Charlotte. "He helped us with an upgrade to our wi-fi network at the Inn. Even paid for some of the new computer programs he installed."

"I like all you kids working together to make it a productive summer. The Sanderling Cove is such a special place," said Savannah.

"Dad said he's going to rent a boat so Brent and I can do some things on the water," said Emma.

"There's a boat the cove families own together. Maybe you

can use that," said Charlotte.

"We'll go with something smaller," said Savannah pleasantly.

Curious about her, Charlotte said, "What do you do with your time outside of all the mom things?"

Savannah laughed. "Now that Brent is driving, my schedule is a little easier. But I still have carpool duties and swim meets to go to for Emma and sports for Brent. But I'm a teaching assistant to a kindergarten teacher three mornings a week. I have a degree in early education. It's important to get children off to a good start in every facet of their young lives. I love that age."

"Have you met Skye?" Charlotte asked.

"No, but Liz told me about her. She's staying with her grandmother while her father is away for a couple of weeks."

"You'll love her. She's adorable," said Charlotte.

"Are you interested in becoming a mother someday?" Savannah asked.

Charlotte couldn't prevent a blush from creeping up her cheeks at the thought of Shane and her making a baby. "When the time is right, I'd love to start a family with at least two children. Shane and I discussed it briefly, and he knows I had a lonely childhood."

"Henry's quite a bit older than I, but we both agreed to it. I'm happy we did."

"I understand Shane spent time divided between your household and Diana's but spent summers at the cove with Granny Liz."

"Yes, before Henry and I were married. After that, summers were pretty evenly divided between Granny Liz and us because Diana had him during the school year."

Emma left to go to the ladies' room.

"Diana is such a difficult person," said Charlotte.

Savannah gave her a steady look. "You've no idea. That woman has caused so much pain. Henry has told me how toxic he and Diana were together. He told me she's like a chameleon, changing from tender and caring to ugly and angry within seconds. He never saw that until after they were married, and they had Shane. She's not a maternal person. That's for sure."

"Shane is talking with a therapist again. I encouraged him to do so."

Savannah reached over and gave her a hand a squeeze. "I hope he knows how lucky he is to have met you."

"After not seeing each other for years, it's amazing how things have worked out."

Emma returned to the table as their food was being served, and the conversation turned to more pleasant things.

That night, in honor of Henry and his family, the women of the cove put together a beach party. Barbequed chicken, hot dogs, hamburgers, and steaks were available on the grill. Potato salad, pasta salad, a couple of green salads, and deviled eggs were followed with brownies and cake and watermelon. A few curious guests from the Inn were asked to join them.

Seeing everyone together, knowing three generations had enjoyed good times here at the cove, Charlotte knew she didn't want to go far. Somehow, when the summer ended and Gran and John returned, she'd make a business of her own succeed.

Shane came up beside her and put his arm around her. "Nice evening, huh?"

"Yes," she said. "It's so special to have your family here, Shane. They're fantastic."

He grinned. "That's what they're saying about you." He bent down and whispered in her ear, "I love you."

CHAPTER FORTY-NINE

ELLIE

Ellie sat in her hotel room and eagerly opened her laptop, hoping for another chatty message from Liz. Until now, Liz had followed through on her promise to keep Ellie updated on any news.

She and John were having the time of their lives, taking in sights, enjoying food wherever they wanted. The South of France, where they were now staying, was a dream come true for both of them. That bread, wine, and cheese—tasty.

A message from Liz popped up.

> "Dear Ellie, I think you're going to be very pleased with your granddaughter, Charlie. She and Shane have become a close twosome almost overnight. Henry and his family are visiting, and you know how thrilled that makes all of us, especially Shane and Austin. Henry's darling Savannah has a sweet way of pulling that family together with abundant love. For me, seeing Henry happy brings me almost to tears.
>
> "In the past you've been worried about Charlie feeling she wasn't truly loved for herself. We had a big cove beach party last night. If you could've seen Charlie surrounded by Shane and his family, you would have had as many stinging tears as I did observing how happy she was.
>
> "As for the rest of our plans, Karen, Sarah, Pat, and I

are all doing our best to see that everyone has more than one opportunity to get together. Adam is away for a couple of weeks. The others are here. Our chances are pretty good something else will turn out the way we want, but I'm afraid patience will be required.

"We all love you and miss you. Hope you're having a fabulous time.

"Your co-conspirator. Liz"

CHAPTER FIFTY

CHARLOTTE

Charlotte awoke the next morning and lay in bed revisiting the past two days since Henry and Savannah had arrived with Brent and Emma. Being with Shane and his family made her feel included in a way she'd never experienced, as if, whimsically, it was part of a plan that had been put in place a long time ago.

Savannah had confided to her that Shane had never brought another woman to one of the cove picnics. It made Charlotte more certain that she and Shane shared something special. Last night, before he said goodnight to her, he told her that he wanted time alone with her after his family left. They planned a getaway to Key West.

Charlotte checked the time and got out of bed. She was becoming used to being up early in the morning to help get things organized for the day at the Inn. Though Livy and Brooke were helping her in the afternoons by managing the hotel while Shane's family was here, she'd agreed to keep to her morning schedule. Livy worked in the kitchen most days, but when she was off, she usually slept in. This morning wasn't one of those days.

After getting dressed for the day, Charlotte hurried over to the Inn. Billy Bob was in the kitchen. She greeted him and went into the dining room. She needed to put out fresh coffee, hot water for tea, and muffins for guests wanting a little something before breakfast.

After getting that ready, she went into the kitchen. Livy was there mixing up fresh biscuits. Billy Bob was cooking bacon strips. Though he was a quiet man, he seemed to be getting along with Livy, who was humming a song to the music on her phone.

"I'll be in the office if you need me," said Charlotte. "I want to check the website and the phone for messages."

Livy looked up from the dough she was working on and nodded.

Inside the office, Charlotte sat down at the desk and pulled up the website on the computer. Looking at it, she could hardly wait to complete the upgrade. Compared to what she was creating, this one was bland.

On the website, someone requested information and dates for the fall. Charlotte made a note of it. She was to meet with the printers on an updated brochure as soon as she and her cousins approved all changes. Now that they had a number of new photographs and the new logo to add, she was eager to get it going.

She checked for messages on the phone. One of their guests was requesting extra towels in their room this morning. She made a note for Beryl and called the room. No one answered, so Charlotte left a message that a housekeeper would leave extra towels for them.

When Henry and Savannah came in for breakfast, Charlotte eagerly greeted them. "It's going to be another beautiful day. Do you have plans?"

"Henry and I are going to visit friends in Sarasota," Savannah said. "We haven't seen them in a while, and it'll be a treat to catch up."

Henry's cell rang. He stepped away and took the call. When he returned, he was visibly upset. "That was Sophia Morales. I can't believe it." Henry took a breath and slowly released it.

"What?' asked Savannah.

"Diana's dead." He shook his head as if he couldn't believe it. "Sophia found Diana dead."

"Oh, honey, I'm sorry," said Savannah, wrapping her arms around him. "Was it drugs? Did she kill herself as she'd threatened so many times?"

When he nodded, Charlotte's heart dropped. As angry as Shane had been with his mother, he would be upset to learn this news.

He stared into space. "Sophia asked me to tell Shane and Austin. She wants the three of us to come there right away." He scrubbed his palm over his face. "This is a mess. They both have had terrible arguments with Diana recently, and I don't want them to think any of this was their fault."

"What can I do to help?" asked Charlotte.

"I don't know." Henry turned to her. "I'll call Shane and Austin. As soon as they're ready, we'll eat a quick breakfast and be on our way. Sophia needs us. She's hysterical. She called 911, and the police are there now."

Charlotte hurried into the kitchen to tell Livy what had happened. "I'm going to go to Granny Liz's to check on Shane."

"Oh, yes. By all means, go," said Livy. "I'll call Brooke and ask her to come in."

Charlotte flew out the door and raced across the lawn to Granny Liz's house. Like their father, she was worried about how Shane and his brother would react to the news.

Granny Liz was on the front porch and got to her feet as Charlotte approached. "What's going on?"

Charlotte filled her in. "Henry has called them. He's taking them to Diana's house right away. Sophia needs them."

"That's awful. I'm sorry it's come to this," said Granny Liz shaking her head.

"Henry doesn't want Shane and Austin to feel responsible

in any way."

"Yes, that's important," said Granny Liz. "Their relationship with their mother has always been difficult, unsteady."

Charlotte stepped inside the house. Shane was coming down the stairs; his hair was still wet from a shower. When he saw Charlotte, he rushed over to her and swept her into his arms, hugging her tightly. "What a damn mess."

"I'm sorry, Shane," she murmured. "Such a tragic thing."

Austin descended the stairs and came over to them. Charlotte put her arms around him. "I'm sorry about your mother."

Shane and Austin exchanged looks, their expressions sad.

Shane's face flushed red. "It's so like my mother to do something like this."

Austin's eyes filled. "I talked to her a day ago and told her I couldn't come to see her because Dad was here. Maybe ..."

"We don't have all the facts," said Charlotte cutting him off. She wondered if Diana tried to do something for attention, and it got out of control. They'd never know for certain.

"C'mon," said Shane to Austin. "God knows what's waiting for us at Mom's house."

"Nothing good, I'm sure," Austin grumbled.

Charlotte walked with them to the Inn.

Henry met them as they entered the dining room and gave each of his sons a hug. "As soon as you're ready, we'll head out."

"Are you sure you want to get mixed up in this?" Shane asked him.

"If I can be of help, I'm willing to go with you," Henry answered. "Sophia asked me to come."

"Thanks, Dad," said Austin. "We appreciate it."

After Henry left with Shane and Austin, Savannah turned to Charlotte. “I think I could use a second cup of coffee. How about you?”

Charlotte emitted a tremulous sigh. “A strong one.”

“Diana had a way of manipulating people, and Henry doesn’t want this event to be tied to Shane and Austin in any blameful way.” Savannah lowered herself into a chair at one of the small tables in the dining room and let out a long sigh.

Charlotte handed her the coffee and sat down opposite her with a cup of coffee of her own. “I feel bad it’s happened like this. Especially with Diana knowing you and Henry and the kids were here.”

Savannah’s lips thinned. “I’m certain that played a part. Do you know she’s been calling Henry and asking if they can meet up? She apparently has an idea that Henry and I aren’t happy. Wishful thinking on her part.”

Charlotte patted her hand. “Anyone can see that you are.” She took a sip of coffee. “What is going to happen to Diana’s house? I can’t believe either Shane or Austin would be interested. It certainly doesn’t hold pleasant memories for them.”

“I imagine they’ll sell it,” said Savannah. “All that remains to be seen.” She shook her head. “I’m sure the estate will be handled professionally. Ricardo would have seen to that.”

“I’m glad Henry will be there to help Sophia,” said Charlotte. “She seemed dedicated to taking care of Diana. No wonder she’s so upset.”

Brent and Emma came into the dining room. “Where’s Dad?” Brent asked. “I want to see if we can rent a boat today.”

“I’m sorry. Dad is with Shane and Austin. Their mother has died, and Dad is taking care of some issues. But we’ll plan something fun to do instead.”

“I heard Eric is coming to the cove today,” said Charlotte.

"He owns that beautiful sailboat. He might be interested in taking you out on it. Would you like me to ask?"

Brent's eyes widened. "Really? That would be awesome."

"It might not work out, but I'll check with him." Charlotte got to her feet and headed into the office, hoping Eric would be open to the suggestion. He loved the opportunity to use his boat.

When she got hold of him on the phone, Charlotte explained the situation. Eric said he'd be glad to take all three if they wanted. Brooke had already agreed to go out with him, but the more, the merrier.

Brooke came into the office. "What's up? I heard that Shane and Austin and their father left here in a hurry this morning."

Charlotte explained and then told her about the invitation for Savannah and the kids to join her on Eric's boat.

"Okay. Brent can help handle the lines," Brooke said. "And I wanted the chance to get to know Emma and Savannah better. They seem nice."

"They are."

"I'm sorry about Diana, but from what you've said, she was very troubled," said Brooke.

"Yes." Charlotte pushed away her gloom and gave Brooke a sly smile. "So, you and Eric? Anything special?"

Brooke shook her head. "I'm going to be like Livy and just have fun."

"Fair enough," said Charlotte. "I'll stop teasing you."

"It doesn't mean if the right one comes along, I'll ignore him," said Brooke.

Charlotte raised her eyebrows. Seems Brooke's had a change of heart.

###

Late that afternoon, Shane called Charlotte from the car as they were nearing the cove to tell her they'd be there soon. She got in touch with Savannah, who'd elected not to go on the sailboat. Together, they went to the Inn to wait for them.

When the car pulled up to the front of the Inn, Charlotte and Savannah moved toward it in tandem.

Shane climbed out of the front passenger seat and went into Charlotte's waiting arms.

Savannah hugged both Henry and Austin. "How was it?" she asked softly.

"Surprisingly well organized," said Henry. "Sophia called Diana's lawyer, and he appeared. He said there was no problem in our knowing about the will and that he would handle the estate as requested. Sophia is to receive a large sum of money, which she certainly deserves. Other funds will go to charities that Ricardo favored, and the boys will receive some funds along with the house and all its belongings."

"We're going to sell it and most everything in it," said Shane with determination.

"I talked to a realtor who'll handle the sale when the estate is settled. In the meantime, Sophia has agreed to continue living there," said Austin.

"The poor woman feels responsible for Diana's death because she'd left Diana alone to visit family," said Henry.

"Such a shame, the whole thing," said Savannah. She went to Shane and Austin and gave them each a hug. "It's okay to be sad, you know. Diana was your mother."

Austin nodded, too emotional to talk.

Shane's eyes filled, but he said nothing. Charlotte was certain a whole lot was going on inside him and took hold of his hand.

"I suggest we all relax," said Henry.

"Livy and Holly are handling the cocktail hour," said

Charlotte. "How about coming to Gran's house? I've made some extra hors d'oeuvres, and there are plenty of refreshments."

"Thanks," said Austin. "I'm going to change my clothes first."

"Me too," said Shane. "I'll be back soon."

Charlotte turned to Henry and Savannah. "I hope you'll come too."

"We will," said Savannah. "Thank you. We need this family time together. Brent and Emma are sailing on Eric's boat. They should be fine. I'll text them both while you change and get comfortable."

Charlotte was pleased she'd had plenty of experience hosting small groups in New York. She slid into the role, wanting to make sure everyone was comfortable and well taken care of.

Savannah seemed to sense her nervousness and made sure to compliment her. Even so, it was a somber group. Diana had affected them all.

"Sophia said your mother had often talked about her death, wanted to be cremated, and didn't want a big service, just a few friends and family," Henry said to Shane and Austin. "I suggest you delay any decisions on a memorial service until things have settled down."

"Sophia told me that Mom wanted you at the service," said Shane.

"Savannah and I will attend together," Henry said, looking to Savannah for approval.

She patted his knee. "Yes, the two of us together. I agree that any service should wait. People might need to be notified."

"Or not," said Austin glumly.

"Even though the lawyer made the process seem simple, these things take time. I remember how it was when my parents died," said Savannah to him. "Regardless of what has gone on, it's a sad occasion. Give yourself time to grieve, Austin. You too, Shane."

Sitting next to her on the couch, Shane squeezed Charlotte's hand. "I will. I'll take phone calls and texts regarding the estate, but I don't want to go back to Star Island unless I have to. Ricardo made it bearable when he was alive, but it wasn't a pleasant place for me."

"Are we agreed we'll deal with this as necessary but will continue with our normal lives?" said Henry.

"Yes," said Shane and Austin together.

"I'm sorry you two have such mixed feelings about the situation," said Henry. "Your mother had her problems."

Shane glanced at Austin and shrugged. "The problem was we never knew what we were going to get—the nice mother or the other one."

"I wish things had been different," Henry said grimly, and Charlotte couldn't help wondering what his marriage to Diana was like. She glanced at Savannah. Such a sweet, loving woman. Charlotte was glad Henry had found her.

When Henry and Savannah got up to leave, Austin rose too. "I'm going to take off. See you later. Thanks, Charlie, for having me here. I'm going to talk to Granny Liz."

After the three of them left, Shane turned to her. "Want to take a walk on the beach?"

"Sure, that usually makes me feel better."

Out on the sand, Charlotte faced the water and drew in deep breaths. Her own emotions were in a whirl. She hadn't liked Diana, had been furious over her treatment of Shane, but still hated the thought that Diana had died alone and, most likely, on purpose.

She glanced at Shane, knowing he must have some of the same feelings. It was all so senseless.

They walked side by side, stopping every few steps to pick up a shell. Skye was saving seashells, and they were now all contributing to her cache.

CHAPTER FIFTY-ONE

CHARLOTTE

Over the next few days, they all tried to make the vacation time pleasant for Brent and Emma and their parents. Granny Liz especially enjoyed having Henry and his family at the cove and worked hard to put together family meals, including Charlotte as often as possible.

Amby finished painting the new sign for the Inn, and Charlotte was as thrilled as her cousins about the new look. It symbolized all the things they'd done to refresh the Inn.

Charlotte kept busy redesigning the Inn's website. When she wasn't doing that, she worked on information for Family First. She loved being in total control over her projects and setting her own timeline for completion. The more she thought about it, the more she liked the idea of setting up her own company.

Shane left to go back to Miami to take care of business with the promise that he'd return the next day. Though she missed him, she thought it was wise for him to focus on something besides the emotions surrounding his mother's death.

Henry and Savannah left for a day trip to visit their friends in Sarasota, and Brent and Emma went sailing once more with Eric. This time Livy went with them, and Brooke stayed behind to work at the Inn.

The next day, Charlotte was surprised when Henry requested to extend their stay an extra two days.

"Not a problem. We'll take care of it," Charlotte said, pleased. She loved having him around. He was a calming influence.

When Shane called later that day, he said, "I'm done with my meeting. I'm on my way."

"I'm glad. We're having dinner at Mimi's house tonight." Mimi was Dylan and Grace's grandmother and a terrific cook.

"All right. I'll see you when I get there."

Charlotte decided to ask Livy to trim her hair. Then she and her cousins spent rare time alone doing their nails, chatting and laughing like old times. Charlotte realized how she'd come to count on them to fill her life with their friendship. Their mothers might not be close, but she and her cousins more than made up for it. When Shane returned, Charlotte was ready to greet him with a shorter hairstyle, freshly painted nails, and a new sundress.

"You look terrific," said Shane when he came to Gran's house to escort her to Mimi's. He swept her into his arms.

She relaxed against him. It felt so right to be with him.

He held out his elbow. "C'mon, I'll walk you across the lawn. We don't want to be late for one of Mimi's meals."

Dinner at Mimi's was as delicious as expected. She served cold poached salmon with a creamy dill sauce, crisp, cold snow peas, a green salad, and blueberry pie with vanilla ice cream. Dylan was out of town at an art show, but Grace and her wife, Belinda, showed up at their grandmother's. Charlotte was happy to spend time with them catching up. And, as always, she enjoyed Shane's family. Mimi and Henry talked about old times when he was a kid spending time at the cove. Brent and Emma listened to all the stories with interest, occasionally teasing their father.

"I'd like to come and stay at Granny Liz's next summer," Brent announced. "Eric thinks I can get a job at one of the nearby marinas."

"Seems promising, but we'll have to wait and see," said Savannah. "You might want to do an internship in Shane's office or help Austin with a computer project. I think there will be lots of opportunities for that."

"We can talk about it," said Shane. "You might be a big help with Family First."

"Knowing Brent, he's going to change his mind a million times before deciding," said Emma. "Me? I know I want to be a nurse."

"You'll make an excellent one," Savannah said, winking at her. "Think of all the help you've given to your dolls over the years."

Everyone laughed, and Charlotte was struck once again by how easily the family got along. She'd been guided from an early age to understand her place was in New York in a productive work environment until a man came along to maintain the rich lifestyle her mother thought she should have.

After dessert, the family disbanded. Henry, Savannah and the kids wanted to take a swim in the pool at the Inn, and Austin had plans. Charlotte thanked Mimi for a delicious dinner and accepted Shane's offer for a walk on the beach.

It was one of those Florida nights Charlotte had come to

love. An onshore breeze swept away the heat of the day, the moon added a golden glow to their surroundings, and the water continued to caress the shore and move away in a comforting rhythm as old as time.

Shane took her hand as they walked along the water's frothy edge resembling a white lace fringe against the dark water.

She looked up at the sky. Stars twinkled against the black backdrop, and she wished she could stretch on her toes, reach up to gather them, and hug their brightness to her.

Shane was silent as they walked.

Charlotte studied him. "Are you alright?" she asked softly.

He turned to her. "Just wondering what to say."

She stopped and frowned at him. "About what?"

He cupped her face in his broad hands. "About how much I love you and want you to be by my side. Now and forever. I've loved you from that first moment on the beach. And then, with that vision of you as a mermaid, what I thought was love grew into something much more meaningful, deep. I never want to let go of you or that feeling." He knelt in front of her. "Charlotte Bradford, will you marry me?"

Charlotte's breath left her. This moment, this setting, this man was perfect. She stared at the face she'd grown to love sincerely, her heart filling with happiness. "Yes, Shane Ensley, I will marry you."

He held up a velvet box he'd pulled from his pants pocket and opened it. Inside lay a sparkling emerald-cut diamond surrounded by tiny baguettes.

"It's beautiful," gushed Charlotte.

"Not as beautiful as you are," said Shane sliding it onto her finger. It fit perfectly.

He stood and hugged her. "I know it's happened fast, and the timing may be strange to some, but in a way, the tragedy made me realize how important it is to live well every day. And with you in my life, it can happen."

She gazed into his eyes and saw the moisture there, proving to her how moved he was by this moment. "Oh, Shane, I want so much to be part of your life and to share mine with you. For the first time in my life, I know what it's like to truly love someone. I'd save you over and over again."

"You do that each day you're with me," he said and pressed his lips to hers.

She responded, letting him know how much he meant to her. If they were lucky enough to live a long life together, she'd prove that to him every day.

He took her hand and led her over to the Inn. "We have to tell my family."

Trying and failing not to stare at her ring as she walked beside him, Charlotte allowed Shane to guide her. When they entered the Inn, she discovered a group of family and friends had collected in the gathering room. Granny Liz and Grandpa Sam were there, along with the other grandmothers in the cove. Brooke and Livy stood in a crowd of the younger cove people and waved to her with broad smiles.

"You did it," said Henry coming forward to shake Shane's hand.

Charlotte held out her fingers. "Isn't it beautiful? And it was so romantic."

Austin walked into the room. "Guess a bump on the head woke you up, Shane. Congratulations, Bro. You and Charlie deserve happiness. It's not every day someone is saved by a mermaid." He kissed Charlotte and hugged his brother, patting him on the back.

"Wait! You all knew this was going to happen tonight?" said Charlotte staring out at the crowd.

"That's why Shane wanted us to stay a couple of extra

days," said Savannah, coming over to her and giving her a hug. "Welcome to the family."

Charlotte's emotions got the best of her, forcing the tears welling in her eyes to trickle down her face. She did her best to dab at them with the tissue Granny Liz handed her. All her life, she wondered if she'd ever measure up to anyone's expectations. But, here, tonight, with Shane, his family, and her cove family, she knew she'd found the place she'd longed for her entire life.

"We all love you, Charlie," Shane whispered in her ear. "Me, most of all."

Too touched to say anything, she reached up and kissed him, laughing with joy as everyone around them applauded

CHAPTER FIFTY-TWO

ELLIE

Ellie's cell phone rang and, startled, she reached for it sitting on the bedside table. She checked Caller ID and sat up.

"Hi, Liz. Is everything all right?"

"More than all right," Liz said. "Shane just asked Charlie to marry him. After all that mess with Diana, I wondered if he'd decide to wait a while. But, no, he asked Henry and Savannah to stay an extra two days so they could all celebrate together. I wish you could've been there to see how happy everyone was. I'll send you the pictures after we hang up. I just couldn't wait to tell you."

Ellie's eyes filled. "That's such wonderful news. I'm ecstatic that it's happened, just like we hoped."

"When you come home, you're going to be pleased with all that's going on at the Inn," said Liz. "I miss you like crazy, you know."

"I do," Ellie said, grateful for their friendship. "But as we planned, I can't come home quite yet. I have to wait until the end of summer to give Brooke and Livy a chance to make some major decisions of their own. Hopefully, by then, they and the other cove kids will have similar stories to tell."

"Love stories you mean," prodded Liz.

"Yes, that too," said Ellie. "How is everyone else?"

"If you mean the other grandmothers, they're fine. Anxious as you and I are to see what love connections we can help along the way. But as I've said before, we might have to be patient. Can't tell who'll fall next."

Ellie couldn't help the giggle that escaped her. If the young people knew the plotting going on behind their backs, they'd be surprised. But then, Sanderling Cove was a special place with beloved people, and they all deserved happiness.

Beside her, John stirred. "Who's that you're talking to? Is everything all right?"

"Liz, and it's better than all right. Shane and Charlie are engaged, which means they'll stay in the area."

"Nice," he murmured and rolled over.

Ellie shook her head. He just didn't get it. If she and the other grandmothers didn't help things along, it might never have happened. She wondered who would be next.

# # #

Thank you for reading *Waves of Hope.* If you enjoyed this book, please help other readers discover it by leaving a review on your favorite site. It's such a nice thing to do.

To stay in touch and to keep up with the latest news, here's a link to sign up for my periodic newsletter!
http://bit.ly/2OQsb7s

Enjoy an excerpt from my book, *Sandy Wishes,* Book 2 in The Sanderling Cove Inn Series, which will be released in 2023:

PROLOGUE

Eleanor "Ellie" Weatherby, now Ellie Rizzo, sat on the patio of the small inn in Provence, France, thinking about her latest message from her friend and co-conspirator, Liz Ensley. Liz and the other three women who lived in Sanderling Cove on the Gulf Coast of Florida, grandmothers all, had decided to make it a special summer for their beloved grandbabies by bringing them all together. With only three great-grands in the bunch, it was time for action, and who better for their grandchildren to marry than other cove kids?

They were trying to be discreet about their matchmaking, of course, but the grandmothers all had reasons to ask their grandchildren to spend time at the cove. For Ellie, it was truly important. She'd married her long-time business partner and lover after years of living and working together so that each could provide guidance on health decisions going forward. In her seventies, Ellie had decided it was time to choose between selling the Sanderling Cove Inn or finding someone in the family willing to keep it going.

Her granddaughters—Charlotte, Brooke, and Olivia—were a marvelous trio of smart, capable young women. Her hope was that somehow one or the three of them together would be willing to keep the Inn in the family. After spending the summer managing the Inn while she and John enjoyed a long-awaited auto trip and honeymoon through Europe, the three young women should be able to give her an answer.

As for the other business at hand, Charlie had already found the love of her life in Liz's grandson, Shane. She wished them all the loving luck in the world. Brooke and Livy? More time would tell if they'd be as lucky.

CHAPTER ONE

BROOKE

Brooke Weatherby sat on the beach in the early morning light in a complete funk. She was tired of being the dependable one, the boring one out of everyone at Sanderling Cove. She'd agreed to come to the cove unaware her two cousins, Charlotte "Charlie" Bradford and Olivia "Livy" Winters, would be there. All three had been invited to help Gran and John with The Sanderling Cove Inn over the summer while Gran and John went on a long road trip in Europe. She loved her cousins and was happy to have the summer with them. But being with them sometimes made her own failing all too apparent.

She wiggled her toes in the sand, wishing she was different, that she'd find the freedom she needed to be herself. She was filled with determination. They might seem like only sandy wishes to others, but she was going to make them come true.

Gran had especially wanted Brooke to be able to spend the time away from her mother. Though sweet, her mother, Jo Weatherby, suffered from fibromyalgia and depression and depended on Brooke to be her caretaker at times and her friend at other times. It was an exhausting situation that had cost Brooke a relationship in the past. She didn't want that to happen again.

"Time to kick up your heels and have fun," Gran had told her. "You deserve it." She'd gone on to say that the co-dependent relationship with her mother wasn't healthy for either of them.

Later, leaving their small town in upstate New York and arriving in Florida had felt to Brooke as if she'd been given wings. But it would take more than a stay on the Gulf Coast of Florida to change things permanently. Brooke had to decide just who she wanted to become away from the past. She wanted to add some much-needed freedom to her life.

Brooke studied the waves washing into shore for a quick kiss before pulling away again. The ageless pattern was soothing to her. Sandpipers and sanderlings hurry past on tiny feet, leaving their marks behind in the sand. That was one thing she wanted for herself—to leave her mark behind. Something stronger than that of caring for a sick mother.

She looked up as Livy joined her and sat on the sand beside her.

"What are you doing up this early?" Livy asked. "You're not on duty today."

On the short side with curly, strawberry-blond hair and blue eyes full of mischief, Livy was everyone's favorite. The fact that she was a fabulous baker was another reason some of the men in the cove gravitated toward her. That, and the fact that Livy was always up for a fun-filled adventure. But she was a hard worker too. She handled the kitchen duties for breakfast, along with Billy Bob, an ex-con who'd worked alongside John for years.

"I was restless and needed some time by the water to collect my thoughts," said Brooke.

Livy frowned, concern etching her brow. "Is everything all right?"

"I guess." Brooke shrugged. "I'm contemplating the future and trying to decide what I want out of life. A lot of deep thinking for sure." She brightened. "On a different, more edgy note, I'm thinking of getting a tattoo. Something to prove that I'm not still caught in a rut."

“A tattoo?” A smile spread across Livy’s face. “You know what? You, Charlie, and I should each get one. Something to always remember this summer. What design would you choose?”

“I’m not sure. What about you? A cupcake? Or cookies?”

Lily laughed. “I like the idea of a small cupcake. You could choose something like a seashell because you and Skye spend so much time looking for them.”

Brooke cheered up. She and Adam Atkins’ four-year-old daughter Skye had become shell-seeking buddies. Adam was a wonderful, single father who intrigued her, but they were simply friends. If Skye wasn’t adorable and hadn’t attached herself to Brooke, Brooke might not spend much time with them. But when Skye ran to her for a hug, Brooke would never turn her away.

Livy checked her watch and rose. “I’d better get to the kitchen. It’s a slow morning, but I can’t let Billy Bob think I’m not serious about my job.” With Gran and John gone for the summer, Livy’s task was to oversee the kitchen staff for the breakfasts for which the Inn was well known.

Billy Bob was a giant of a man, an ex-con who was frightening until you got to know him. The scowls on his face softened only slightly around other people. Tic Tacs seemed to be the only things that made him happy enough to smile. That, or one of Livy’s chocolate chip cookies.

After a while, Brooke decided to go to the Inn herself. She wanted to work on the upgrade to the guest registration program Austin Ensley had set up for them. All information from there flowed to their financial reports. She’d been observing the process for a while, and she wanted to make some changes to the new system. Having worked for years in an accounting office, Brooke’s role was to help with the financials for the Inn alongside Jake McDonnell, the Inn’s accountant and financial advisor.

She and Jake had hit it off from the beginning. A self-made man who'd been raised by a friend of Gran's after his mother died of an overdose, Jake was a kind, ambitious, handsome man who'd never forgotten his roots. Brooke admired him for more than his looks.

When she entered the Inn, Charlotte was in the dining room chatting with a couple who'd risen early and were getting their own coffee from the sideboard in the dining room before breakfast was served. Tall and slim, with auburn hair tied back in a low ponytail, Charlotte was a striking young woman. She, like Livy and Brooke, was in her late twenties. Recently, Charlotte had become engaged to Shane Ensley. Their relationship had bloomed early and grown quickly into a deep love. Everyone in the cove, including her, thought they were perfect together.

Charlotte greeted her with a wave and walked over to her. "What's this about tattoos? Livy says we're all getting one together and mine has to be of a mermaid."

"Mermaid? That's perfect for you," said Brooke. "Yes, let's do it. I'll do some research and set something up."

Charlotte grinned. "Okay, but mine is going to be small. Nothing that could show in a wedding dress."

"That's cool. Mine will be small too, but I don't care. It's something different. I'm in such a rut." She emitted a long sigh.

Charlotte's expression grew serious. "Are you all right?"

Brooke nodded. "Just full of wishes, I guess."

"Anything I can help you with?" Charlie asked.

"No, but thanks. It's something I have to decide for myself." Feeling better, Brooke headed to the office with a cup of coffee. There, numbers were easy to work with. They were either right or wrong.

###

Brooke was still working on numbers sometime later when her cell rang. She checked caller ID. *Jo Weatherby*.

"Hi, Mom," said Brooke. She hadn't talked to her mother in days, and though they'd agreed to limit their conversations this summer, Brooke was uncertain about her mother's response, hoping she wouldn't be sent on a guilt trip.

"Hi, Brooke. It's been so long since we've talked that I had to call. How are things going with the Inn? Are you bored to tears?"

"Bored? Anything but," she quickly replied. "Gran and John have done an amazing job of managing the Inn. Charlie, Livy, and I are all busy trying to do the same plus make some improvements."

"I keep thinking of you in that hot, humid summer climate," said Jo.

Brooke knew what her mother was doing—making it sound as if she was concerned for Brooke when actually it was a lead-in to asking her when she was coming home.

Sure enough, Jo said, "I can't wait for you to come home. The house is empty without you."

"Mom, you know I'm committed for the summer and, perhaps, beyond. Nothing is going to make me change my mind." Brooke took a deep breath. "How are you feeling?"

"I've been better, but nothing for you to worry about," her mother said. "If it gets any worse, I'll call the nursing service and have them send someone to stay with me."

Guilt, like a prickly porcupine, poked Brooke in all her sensitive places. She shook her head. She couldn't go back to past behavior, rush home to help. "I'm sure they have capable people on their staff. We've used that nursing service once before. Remember?"

"Yes. They were good. Not as great as having you here, but

acceptable."

"That's how we'll leave it, then. Sorry but I'm in the middle of working on financials here and I'd better go. Jake is due to arrive soon, and I want my work done before he gets here."

"Okay. Love you, sweetie. Talk to you later." Her mother clicked off the call, and Brooke let out a huge sigh. She and her mother had always been a twosome which made her fight for independence more difficult. Her father had died in Iraq before Brooke was born, leaving Jo to fend for herself. Rather than move closer to her family, Jo had opted to stay in the house in New York she and her fiancé had purchased together.

Brooke went back to her work, but her emotions were still churning. When Jake arrived, she was happy to see him. She had a few ideas she wanted to share.

After agreeing to the changes Brooke wanted to make to the registration process, Jake left the Inn. Brooke paced the office, her mind going over the conversation she'd had with her mother. She desperately wanted to do something to prove her independence. The tattoos would have to wait. She needed to do something now.

She drove to a hair salon nearby. She was tired of being the same person day after day, the one everyone depended on, the one who couldn't seem to relax and just enjoy life.

She entered the salon, and when the owner offered a few surprising suggestions, Brooke smiled. This was more like it.

Later, purple streaks accented her brown highlighted hair. Brooke studied her image with surprise, staring at the way the purple in her hair made her hazel eyes change hues to something browner. She knew that for some people, doing something like this was no big deal. But for her, it was a daring move. She'd been programmed always to do the right, the ladylike thing.

She left for Gran's house proud of her new bold statement.

In her bedroom, she studied her reflection in the mirror still surprised by what she'd done. Of medium height, her features were a cross between Livy's and Charlie's, both cute and classic.

Lily peered into Brooke's room. "Wow, a new 'do. I love it! Wait until Charlie sees it. She'll be as surprised as I am," said Livy. "Are we meeting downstairs like always?"

"Yes." Brooke held up the papers she'd prepared for the meeting. "I've got a few new ideas for the registration of guests. That, and a quick review of where we stand on our budget."

"Great," said Livy. "I want to talk about something too."

Brooke liked that her cousins were as sincere as she about doing an outstanding job for Gran and John. She, probably more than they, enjoyed managing the Inn enough to consider doing it in the future. It was a fascinating business.

She and Livy went downstairs to the kitchen.

When Charlotte entered the room for their meeting, she took one look at Brooke and squealed. "What did you do to your hair? Turn around. Let me get a better look."

Brooke twirled in a circle.

"I love it," said Charlotte. "With my auburn hair, it wouldn't work. But on you, it looks great."

Letting out the breath she didn't realize she'd been holding, Brooke felt more confident. Charlotte was more reserved than Livy, and if she liked Brooke's attempt to be different, it was an important sign.

Livy took fresh lemonade from the refrigerator and poured them each a glass before she took a seat at the kitchen table.

"What new things do we have to discuss?" asked Brooke. As the financial manager for the Inn for the summer, she'd been designated to oversee the renovation budget.

"I've done some mockups of brochures I need to show you and Livy for approval," said Charlotte.

"I'd like to get a new grill for the kitchen," said Livy.

"Okay, let's take a look at the budget," said Brooke. "We've completed almost everything on the list of updates. The PR budget is still pretty open. The funds for the kitchen are mostly spent. Livy, how much would the grill cost? And why do we need it?"

Sitting back, listening to Livy, Brooke liked being in charge. She knew she was a capable accountant, but at her job in New York, her work had never been given the respect it deserved. She'd hoped for a partnership one day, but now the thought was unappealing. Another reason not to go back to her old job, her old life.

Charlotte agreed that Livy could have some of her PR funds for the new grill. And when she showed them the new brochures and pamphlets she wanted to have printed, Brooke and Livy eagerly gave their approval for Charlotte to take them to a printer to be produced.

Satisfied things were running smoothly, Brooke ended the meeting.

Charlotte and Livy each had plans for the evening, so Brooke decided to take a walk on the beach. The salt air, the rhythmic sound of the waves rushing to shore and retreating, and the antics of shorebirds skittering along the sand always lifted her spirits.

As she crossed the lawn and entered the sandy beach a small figure raced toward her crying, "Brooke! Brooke!"

Brooke's lips curved. She held out her arms, and Skye rushed into them. An adorable four-year-old with blond curly hair and blue eyes that missed nothing, Adam's daughter and Brooke shared a special relationship.

Skye's arms loosened around Brooke's neck. She stared at Brooke, and then a huge smile spread across her face. "You've got purple in your hair. How did you do that? I want purple too." She patted Brooke's head gingerly, her face alight with excitement.

Brooke laughed. "I love your hair just the way it is. Like Livy's."

"But I want ..."

Before a real whining session could occur, Brooke said, "Did you find any new shells today with Mimi?"

Skye wiggled to get down and ran over to a bucket nearby, picked it up, and carried it back to her. "We found a scallop shell this morning."

Impressed, Brooke said, "You're learning the names of the shells. That's good."

"Mimi is showing me. She has a book," said Skye proudly.

Skye's great-grandmother, Mimi, walked over to them. She glanced at Brooke's hair and grinned. "Time for something new, huh?"

Brooke returned her smile. Mimi was a lovely woman, upbeat, social, easy to talk to. "Yes. I thought it was time I did something totally different for me."

"Well, I like it," said Mimi. "How are things going with your mother? Is she getting used to having you gone?"

"It's a work in progress. I talked to her earlier. She has her ups and downs."

"Ellie was especially anxious for you to spend the summer here, hoping it would change the situation for you both. I know you're working hard at the Inn, but have fun too, hear."

Brooke grinned. "That's exactly what I intend to do."

Dylan Hendrix, Adam's cousin, walked toward them. "Hey, what's up?" He stopped when he noticed Brooke's hair. "Purple?"

She grinned. "Yes."

"I like it. A shade of amethyst."

She laughed. Only Dylan, who was a well-known artist, would use that word.

"I'm thinking of going out tonight. Want to join me for dinner?" When Dylan smiled as he was doing now, his blue eyes lit.

"That would be great." She studied him. His brown hair was tied back in a man-bun, which accented the features of his face and matched his well-toned body. Dylan was a few years older than she, and his bold paintings had caught the eye of a number of famous people, sending their popularity and their prices into the stratosphere. Yet he was as humble a man as she'd ever met. She liked that about him.

Maybe like her hair, her future was about to change color, become brighter. She wished it would all come true.

About the Author

Judith Keim, a *USA Today* Best Selling author, is a hybrid author who both has a publisher and self-publishes, Ms. Keim writes heart-warming novels about women who face unexpected challenges, meet them with strength, and find love and happiness along the way. Her best-selling books are based, in part, on many of the places she's lived or visited and on the interesting people she's met, creating believable characters and realistic settings her many loyal readers love. Ms. Keim loves to hear from her readers and appreciates their enthusiasm for her stories.

Ms. Keim enjoyed her childhood and young-adult years in Elmira, New York, and now makes her home in Boise, Idaho, with her husband and their two dachshunds, Winston and Wally, and other members of her family.

While growing up, she was drawn to the idea of writing stories from a young age. Books were always present, being read, ready to go back to the library, or about to be discovered. All in her family shared information from the books in general conversation, giving them a wealth of knowledge and vivid imaginations.

"I hope you've enjoyed this book. If you have, please help other readers discover it by leaving a review on the site of your choice. And please check out my other books:

The Hartwell Women Series
The Beach House Hotel Series
The Fat Fridays Group
The Salty Key Inn Series
Seashell Cottage Books
The Chandler Hill Inn Series
The Desert Sage Inn Series
Soul Sisters at Cedar Mountain Lodge Series
The Sanderling Cove Inn Series
The Lilac Lake Inn Series

"ALL THE BOOKS ARE NOW AVAILABLE IN AUDIO on iTunes and other sites. So fun to have these characters come alive!"

Ms. Keim can be reached at **www.judithkeim.com**

And to like her author page on Facebook and keep up with the news, go to: **https://bit.ly/3acs5Qc**

To receive notices about new books, follow her on Book Bub: **http://bit.ly/2pZBDXq**

And here's a link to where you can sign up for her periodic newsletter! **http://bit.ly/2OQsb7s**

She is also on Twitter @judithkeim, LinkedIn, and Goodreads. Come say hello!

Acknowledgements

And, as always, I am eternally grateful to my team of editors, Peter Keim and Lynn Mapp, my book cover designer, Lou Harper, and my narrator, Angela Dawe. They are the people who take what I've written and help turn it into the book I proudly present to you, my readers! I also want to thank my coffee group of writers who listen and encourage me to keep on going. Thank you, Peggy, Lynn, Cate, Nikki Jean, and Megan. And to you, my fabulous readers, I thank you for your continued support and encouragement. Without you, this book would not exist. You are the wind beneath my wings.

CPSIA information can be obtained
at www.ICGtesting.com
Printed in the USA
BVHW051656180822
644933BV00004B/68

9 781954 325401